Som... ... ...

Catherine Hunt is a journalist who has spent most of her career with BBC News where she edited the flagship TV news shows, in particular the Six O' Clock News, and also edited live coverage of many major news events at home and abroad.

Before joining the BBC, she was a reporter for the Press Association and for the *Daily Mail*. She began her career working on regional newspapers, including the *Evening Argus* in Brighton.

Catherine currently runs a media consultancy business. She lives in Surrey.

Someone Out There

CATHERINE HUNT

an imprint of HarperCollins*Publishers*
www.harpercollins.co.uk

Killer Reads
An imprint of HarperCollins*Publishers*
1 London Bridge Street
London SE1 9GF

www.harpercollins.co.uk

This paperback edition 2015
1

First published in Great Britain by
HarperCollins*Publishers* 2015

A catalogue record for this book is available from the British Library

ISBN: 978-0-00-813967-4

Set in Minion by Born Group using Atomik ePublisher from Easypress

Find out more about HarperCollins and the environment at
www.harpercollins.co.uk/green

CHAPTER ONE

Laura was tired and she was late. Sarah had kept her talking in the office and then, because Sarah needed a shoulder to cry on, she'd gone with her to a wine bar to talk things through. Now it was almost nine o'clock and Laura just wanted to get home. The traffic lights stayed obstinately red. She drummed her fingers impatiently on the steering wheel. Rain lashed down on the windscreen.

A car drew up in the lane beside her. A four-wheel drive with tinted windows. Huge and dark and menacing. A monster. It loomed over her, music pumping – a heavy beat pulsing against her driver's window, drowning out the rain.

It stopped very close to her, far too close, with its bonnet stuck out aggressively in front. She didn't look across, kept her eyes straight ahead, but she had the feeling that the driver was staring at her. Another idiot, she thought, who'd seen a woman in a sports car and had decided to show her who was boss.

The lights changed and she didn't try to race it. She would just sit back and let it burn up its tyres on the wet road.

Laura waited but the monster didn't move. It sat there with the lights at green. A horn sounded from behind. It still didn't move, just stayed close beside her, and that was when the alarm bell first began ringing in her head. Not much of one, no big deal, no more than a tinkle really.

She drove off then – fast, using every bit of the 0 to 60 in six-point-five seconds that the Audi TT's engine had to offer. Off and away, leave all the trouble behind. She liked that thought; it fitted her new philosophy for life. She'd moved on, settled down with Joe, and given up the London rat race.

Out in front, she slowed down, back within the speed limit. She looked out for the four-wheel drive but it was nowhere in sight. Her mind went back to thinking about work and especially about the Pelham divorce case.

Her client, Anna Pelham, had rung that morning to say she'd had two emails threatening to kill her. She'd sent them on to Laura. They were vicious, explicit death threats and Anna was certain her husband had sent them, though they had not come from his email address. There had been other emails sent to Anna from the same address, ranting and blustering, but these were the first to threaten her life. These were in a different league altogether and it was a dangerous escalation.

Laura had reported the death threats to the police and pressed them to charge Harry Pelham with harassment. Anna was being incredibly brave. She refused to be intimidated, sticking to her guns over the divorce. In fact, the threats seemed to have made her more determined than ever to protect her interests and especially those of her eight-year-old daughter, Martha. Good for her. If Harry Pelham had hoped to beat her into submission, his plan had seriously backfired.

When Anna had first instructed Laura to act in the divorce, she had explained how jealous and controlling Harry was. His abuse and rages had got worse and worse and then he had started hitting her. She had not wanted to leave him, had tried to keep the family together, but in the end it got so bad she had no choice. On Easter Day, after he'd slapped her hard in the face and said he'd hated her for the last six years, she walked out of the family home taking Martha with her.

Laura had heard similar stories before in her career as a divorce lawyer and she thought she'd stopped being upset by them, but somehow Anna's graphic descriptions of what she had endured at the hands of Harry had got under her skin. They brought back all the old memories of her parents' marriage, memories she had tried to bury.

Driving on autopilot, thinking about what more she could do to help Anna, Laura turned off the main Brighton road and into the lanes that led to home. An empty road ahead, no speed cameras here, she touched the accelerator and the Audi surged forward. She liked to feel its power. She knew the road well; the clear straight runs where she could have fun and the two big bends where she had to take care. Her foot pressed harder on the accelerator, the woods flashed by on either side.

A wild wind was bringing down the autumn leaves. They danced across her windscreen, pinned down now and again by the rain, then whirled away by the speed of her passage.

Laura relaxed and the cares of the day dropped away. She thought of Joe waiting for her and smiled. She would soon be home.

The red tail lights of a car in front were coming up fast and she changed down a gear ready to overtake. There was plenty of time before the bend. No doubt about that. She pulled out.

Lights. Headlights. Full on and heading straight for her, fast. Where the hell—Adrenaline pushed the thought from her brain before she could finish it. Too late to fall back. She was committed. Her foot stamped down on the pedal and she'd never been so glad that she drove a sports car.

The seconds played out in slow motion. The lights dazzling, filling her head, illuminating the channels of rain running down the windscreen, illuminating her white knuckles on the wheel. The ear-splitting, never-ending blast of a horn, sowing madness in her mind. Waiting for the impact, for the smash and crash of tearing metal and flesh.

Then she was past. Intact. Back on the right side of the road. Wide, terrified eyes looking in the mirror. The car she'd overtaken was far behind, dwindling at an alarming rate. It had slowed right down, maybe stopped. But where was the other? The one that had almost killed her. No sign of it at all and that was a scary thing, because the road was straight and it had to be there.

Not as scary as the other thing though. The thing that had the alarm bell in her head ringing out loud this time. She had recognized that car. It was the four-wheel drive again. The monster. And now it had disappeared.

Suddenly the big bend in the road was upon her. In her fear she had forgotten it and she hit it far too fast. Braked too hard, wrenched the wheel too far, the car went out of control. It skidded across the wet road and up onto the bank on the far side. For a moment it teetered, poised to turn over, a toss-up which way gravity would take it. Tails you win, heads you lose. The wheels came back down to earth.

It was the bank that saved her, saved her from the trees she would have ploughed into if the land had been flat. It slowed the car enough for her to wrench back control. Thank God there had been no one coming the other way.

Laura stopped the car, pulling off the road at the entrance to a wide track leading into the woods. Her arms and legs were jelly. She opened the door, swung trembling legs to the ground, and sat, eyes tight shut, sucking in great breaths of the cold, wet air.

The sound of a car made her open her eyes nervously and she watched with a jolt of panic as a drop of something more solid and sticky than rain fell on her skirt. There was another … and another. She touched it; put the finger to her lips. Tasted blood. The mirror showed a bloody gash, above and through her left eyebrow.

Another car passed. She could see the faces of the occupants, a young couple looking out at her, curiously, as they went by. Immediately she felt terribly vulnerable. What was she doing sitting alone and injured by the side of the road in a dark wood? She must get out of here. Suppose someone stopped, suppose the four-wheel drive came back?

4

She was cross with herself. She didn't scare easily, she shouldn't let herself get in a state. She'd had a near miss, that was all; a nasty near miss but it was over now. As for the 4x4, she thought she'd recognized it but how could she be sure? There were dozens of them, all the same, hard to tell one from another. But hadn't she heard that same music again as it tore past her? That heavy beat pulsing in her skull.

She shook her head to clear it and blood spattered on the dashboard. She was a bit dizzy; she wasn't sure she should drive.

Call Joe. That was the best idea. Get him to come out and collect her. They could leave her car and pick it up the next day. But she didn't much like the idea of it being left there overnight. She hesitated.

More cars coming, that decided it. She would call him. She reached for her bag on the passenger seat but it wasn't there. Saw it, fallen on the floor, and stretched down to pick it up and take out her mobile. The movement made her feel faint. She stopped with her head bent down and waited.

She listened to the noise of an approaching car. There was something wrong with it. It was different but she couldn't work out why. She left the bag, pulled herself upright and as her eyes came level with the passenger window she saw it. In the wood, lights blazing.

That was why the noise had sounded wrong, she realized. It was coming from the wrong direction, it was charging up the track towards her. It was the 4x4.

There was a locked barrier across the track, about thirty feet into the wood from where she was parked. It stopped access for the general public but allowed in forestry vehicles whose drivers had the key. Surely it would stop the monster.

Something told her not to bet on it. Not to wait and see. She knew she had to move. But she sat for vital seconds, fascinated, unable to drag her eyes away from the oncoming lights. No wonder, she thought, that rabbits froze, transfixed in the road, waiting to be run down. With an effort she slammed shut the driver's door, yanked on the seat belt and started the engine.

It was perilously close to her now but still she hesitated. Vaguely her mind registered that this must be how it had appeared and disappeared so suddenly – by using the woodland tracks. It came to a slight rise in the ground, and as Laura watched, appeared to rear up before her, a huge, malevolent metal beast, eyes piercing and engine roaring. She jammed in first gear and fled, tyres shrieking. Behind her, the barrier disintegrated.

The feeling of faintness had gone, swept away by fear. Her head was clear of everything except the need to get away. She was only seconds ahead, had moved only just in time. She looked in the mirror, saw her pursuer turning out of the wood and on to the road.

There was no doubt anymore that it was pursuing her. Who was the driver and what did they want? A small part of her brain told her to observe. Read the licence plate, identify the make of car, pin down the details. Gather the clues to the who and the why. Vital for later, but worthless now. The rest of her brain cared only for safety. It told her to run and run, find sanctuary, nothing else mattered. The chase was on – she was the wildebeest, injured and fleeing for its life.

Sanctuary. Where was sanctuary? On a dark night, an empty road, still eight miles from home.

It was gaining on her. She knew these roads, she was driving a fast car, but it was gaining on her, for God's sake. Headlights – on full beam, blinding her – filling the car, filling her head. Drive faster, panic yelled in her head, but she took no notice. She knew that if she did, she was going to crash, she was a dead woman.

Sanctuary was other people. She had to reach them. They would make her safe. It could not pursue her then. But she daren't try to find her mobile; it was in the bag on the floor and she needed all her concentration for the road. In any case, no one could get to her in time.

There was no time. It was right behind, pushing, intimidating, inches from the rear bumper. She heard the music blasting, saw the monster looming over her. Jesus, it was going to hit her!

She tensed for the blow, but it didn't fall. A car was coming in the opposite direction. The 4x4 backed off a fraction. She started pumping the horn, flashing her lights, hoping for help. It did no good. The car came and went, its driver probably delighted to give them both a wide berth.

The monster surged back and she felt a sudden dread. Oh yes, she thought, I know what you're going to do. You're going to overtake, jam on your brakes and force me to stop.

Faster. Go faster. Panic was shouting to her again, screaming at her to run. The Audi could beat off the 4x4 with no trouble. Race away, top speed, before it's too late, but self-preservation stopped her. She wasn't ready to die yet.

There was a turn-off not far ahead, she remembered. A narrow road; little more than a lane. She might be safer there, less room for her pursuer to manoeuvre, more chance for her to persuade an oncoming car to stop. Or maybe not. Maybe a narrow lane would be a trap. Should she take it? She couldn't decide. Her brain felt hot and choked.

The lights behind moved and the engine revved. It was coming out, it was overtaking. Her decision was made.

It was level with her now and she forced herself to look. Observe. Log the evidence. She was a lawyer and lawyers were supposed to be good at that. But there was nothing to see. Desperately, she stared into the night but there was just the rain on the tinted windows and darkness beyond. Impenetrable.

It stayed put. Not passing by, just staying level getting closer and closer to her. Dear God, she thought, it's going to run me off the road!

Where was the turning? She should have reached it by now. Please let it be there, she prayed. And then she was on it, almost missing it. She wrenched the wheel violently to the left, so sharply that for a moment she didn't think she would make it. She felt the back of the car skid on the wet tarmac, collide with the side of the four-wheel drive before peeling off alone into the lane. She changed down into second, brought the car under control, and slammed her foot to the floor.

Nothing in the rear-view mirror. Her pursuer was gone. A wave of euphoria buzzed through her, ridiculous, of course, because it couldn't be long before it was back. But for the moment that didn't matter. She had shaken it off, if only briefly, and that was just great. Tears of relief filled her eyes. Hell, she thought, now I can't even see where I'm going. She wiped away the tears and felt the side of her face sticky with blood.

No sign of it. She couldn't believe it. Kept looking in the mirror but it stayed clear. She thought that time was playing tricks – that what seemed to her, in her terror, like an eternity, when the 4x4 could have turned round and caught up with her three times over, was in reality just a few seconds and it might only now be turning into the lane after her. She stared at the clock on the dashboard and when another whole minute had gone by, she really started to hope. Another turning in the road. She took it. Took every turning she came to, kept driving fast, with no idea or care about where she was going, but each one making her feel a little bit safer, twisting and turning away from danger.

She must have driven round in circles several times, her heart stopped by every passing car, her eyes strained for lights in the woods as she imagined it chasing her cross country, her brain punch-drunk, unable to focus on finding the route home. It was almost ten minutes later that she made it out of the lanes on to a main road she recognized, and joined a welcome convoy of traffic.

Reaction set in seriously then. Her arms were shaking, her teeth were chattering and it was with tremendous relief that she saw the service station. She pulled in, parked by the café and tottered inside.

The man behind the counter looked worried and when she caught sight of her bleeding, tear-streaked face in the mirror, she could understand why. He wanted to call an ambulance but she told him she hadn't been physically assaulted and she wasn't drunk or drugged and he settled for her phoning her husband and handed over what she needed most – a strong black coffee.

She sat huddled over it, trying to remember. But there was nothing, nothing she could recall but the dark and the fear and the noise. No make, no model, no part of a licence plate that could be dredged from her subconscious. No clue as to who the driver had been. Not a single fact to tell the police. And she knew the police – without facts and details and evidence, she was wasting her time.

The door opened and she looked up. Joe. How fast he'd arrived, a white knight charging to her rescue in record time. Her battered heart gave a thump of joy. Tall and solid and hugely comforting. Things would be all right now, she thought.

CHAPTER TWO

It was 4 a.m. and Harry Pelham lay awake thinking about the poisonous, scheming bitch who was doing her best to hang him out to dry. He smiled bitterly to himself. No, he wasn't thinking about his wife, though she also fitted the description; he was thinking about her lawyer, Laura Maxwell.

She had been responsible for the nineteen-page divorce submission designed to crucify him. It damned him as a bully, a wife beater, and a bad father. He could remember every word of those nineteen pages. They sent him into a frenzy of rage and resentment. It was a vile, disgusting diatribe, full of lies and exaggerations. It had lodged in his brain like splinters of glass.

His wife had no doubt provided the raw material but she'd been egged on by the toxic Maxwell woman; she wouldn't have done it by herself. The weaving together of that deadly, distorted whole, calculated to tick every box against him, had been the lawyer's work. He was sure of it and he hated Laura Maxwell for it.

His own solicitor, Ronnie Seymour, usually so shrewd, had been like a lamb to the slaughter. He played through in his head the previous day's conversation with Ronnie.

'Slight problem, Harry,' Ronnie had said on the phone, 'nothing to worry about, though. Come over and we'll talk it through.'

How many times in the last few months had he heard those words 'nothing to worry about' from Ronnie Seymour. Inevitably, they meant the opposite.

Ronnie had been his good friend and trusted adviser for more than twenty years. He had sorted out, with no trouble at all, the frequent problems that Harry had run into with his property development empire. When Harry had gone too far, had bent the rules, had tried rather too aggressively to 'persuade' people who stood in his way, Ronnie had been there to smooth out the consequences. Like a few months ago, when old Charlie Rhodes refused to sell part of his back garden, a crucial piece of land that Harry needed for one of his developments.

Late one evening, Harry knocked on the old man's door with a higher offer. Charlie yelled at him to piss off, called him a piece of shit and Harry lost his temper, pinning the pensioner against the wall by his throat and telling him how much better for him it would be to take the offer. It turned out that Charlie's son was a police officer, and shortly afterwards, the police arrived at Harry's office to question him about the 'bullying and harassment' of Charlie Rhodes. It was only because of Ronnie's efforts that Harry avoided being charged.

Ronnie was a fixer and the business had flourished. Harry was rich. That was why he'd been so keen that the man should also sort out his marriage break-up. Ronnie knew his secrets and Harry didn't want a stranger nosing around in his financial affairs. But although Ronnie might be clever, and spot on when it came to property law or criminal law, he was no expert on divorce or family law. That was another thing, another thing entirely and Harry thought Ronnie wasn't up to it. Correction. Harry knew that Ronnie wasn't up to it.

'They've frozen your business bank accounts,' Ronnie told him as soon as he arrived. 'It's a nuisance but there'll be no problem getting them unfrozen.'

Harry glowered at the tall, blond-haired lawyer and gritted his teeth: 'You said there'd be no problem over money. You said the undertakings we gave the court were enough, you said—'

Ronnie held up his hands to stop the protest, his usual smooth manner just a tiny bit ruffled.

'Different judge, I'm afraid. Frankly, I'm surprised at this. It's quite unnecessary.'

'How long before I get them back?' Harry growled.

'Depends how quickly we can get it listed for a hearing. Then, when we get it overturned, the court order has to reach the bank.' He smiled reassuringly. 'Shouldn't be too much of a delay.'

'How long, Ronnie? That's what I want to know,' Harry demanded. He had learned long ago never to expect Ronnie to give a direct answer containing a specific fact for which he could be held accountable later. That was the way with all lawyers, wasn't it? You just had to keep on asking the question.

'Of course, I can't give you a date,' Ronnie said, nettled, 'but take it from me, it will be all right.'

'If you say so,' Harry said without conviction.

'There's something else. I'd like you to see a psychiatrist,' the lawyer said, successfully distracting his client from the bank accounts.

'Me? You must be joking.'

'Unfortunately not. The allegations they're making about the emails, we need to take them seriously.'

Ronnie was on home ground now – the emails had the whiff of crime about them and he was an astute criminal lawyer. He had wanted chapter and verse on everything in the divorce submission. Everything except the email allegations. He didn't want to hear about them. If Harry had broken the law, and Ronnie knew about it, he wouldn't be able to act for him in criminal proceedings if Harry chose to deny it later. Better, then, that he didn't know.

'Are you intending to say I'm mad?' Harry snarled. 'I thought you were supposed to be on my side.'

Ronnie was annoyed. He was doing his best for the man. He'd said at the beginning he didn't want to take on the divorce. He'd made it clear he was not a specialist but Harry had insisted. Ronnie understood why, but still thought his friend should hire an expert.

12

He had assured Harry that financial disclosure to another lawyer could be 'finessed'. But Harry would not budge. In the end, Ronnie had reluctantly agreed. He wasn't going to take any flak, though, now the going had got tough.

'I'm sorry if you're not satisfied with the way I'm handling things,' Ronnie's tone implied that Harry would be most welcome to go elsewhere.

'I don't want to see a shrink.'

'It's the only safe way. We need a mental health defence in place in case the allegations cause problems. Prepare the ground for saying that whatever you did, you did it when your mind was unbalanced by the stress and trauma of your marriage breakdown.'

'If you say I'm crazy I'll never get to see my daughter,' Harry said, furious.

Ronnie looked at him impatiently.

'You've got to be realistic, Harry. You'll just have to take your chances over Martha. There's a lot of very nasty stuff alleged about what sort of husband and father you are. The priority now has to be to look after yourself and your assets.'

'That fucking lawyer has twisted everything. It's lies, all of it. She needs to be taught a lesson, needs to learn she won't get away with it,' Harry spat out the words.

Lying sleepless in his bed, the desire for retribution was strong, like acid eating into his soul. He was not going to let some smart lawyer destroy him, a lawyer who had turned his wife into a vindictive, ungrateful bitch of the first order.

Harry had met Anna eleven years ago when she was twenty-two and had applied for a post as his PA at his main office in Hove. By mid-way through the interview he was craving her. Not surprisingly, she got the job. A year later they were married. He was thirty-four, his property development business had taken off, and he wanted a wife and children. He had thought her so sweet, so loyal, and so terribly in need of him. But he had been wrong, totally wrong. She had thrown his love right back in his face.

13

Now her solicitor was demanding a ludicrously large settlement. If she got it, she would close on wipe him out, though Ronnie kept telling him that some of his assets, salted away over the years in various overseas accounts, could be kept safe and undisclosed. But Ronnie's assurances were proving less than reliable.

'This Laura Maxwell your wife's using,' Ronnie said soon after the divorce began, 'the judge isn't going to like her tactics.'

What garbage that had turned out to be, Harry thought savagely. The judges barely seemed to grasp the issues involved let alone the strategies of his wife's malicious lawyer. Despite the five court hearings he had so far attended and the growing pile of paperwork associated with his case, he'd never seen the same judge twice.

Harry knew the financial damage would be bad. Most of his assets were visible, and however hard he tried, he couldn't hide the fact that he was a wealthy man. Equality was the yardstick in divorce settlements these days and didn't Laura Maxwell just know it. Equality – what a joke that was. Harry lay on his back, his body rigid with fury, sweat on his forehead though the night was cold.

He had made what he considered to be a generous offer to his wife, a very generous offer indeed, and a lot more than the greedy cow deserved, but Laura Maxwell had dismissed it out of hand. All she wanted was to confront him and crush him.

Gone 5 a.m. and still no sign of sleep. He thrashed around in the bed. Harry Pelham was good at fighting. He'd needed to be to survive in the cut-throat world of the property developer. He was forceful and physically intimidating. Six-foot-two, brawny, with a thick black moustache, above it, dark, deep-set eyes that looked you over as if he couldn't care less about you, but at the same time, he was sizing you up, calculating your strengths and weaknesses. At forty-five, he had learned to be as hard-nosed as they come.

Harry wasn't used to losing and he wasn't going to get used to it now. He'd made other plans. With that comforting thought, he finally fell asleep.

The first time they knocked they didn't wake him. The second time they would have woken the dead.

Damn postman, he thought.

He dragged himself out of bed, downstairs and opened his front door. Four men stood before him. They didn't look much like postmen.

'May we come in?' said one of them barging past into the hallway.

Harry Pelham was under arrest.

CHAPTER THREE

Laura made tea while Sarah Cole sat miserably in her office clutching the Hakimi file to her chest and picking nervously at a corner of it. Sarah's dark hair was greasy and her eyes were tired and puffy. She put the file down on her lap, took a HobNob from the packet in front of her and nibbled at it.

'Oh my God, it's such a mess!' she said.

Laura set two mugs of tea down on the desk and pulled round a chair so she could sit next to Sarah.

'Don't worry; I'm sure it can be sorted out.'

Sarah shook her head, 'There's no way. Have a look; you'll see what I mean.' She handed the file to Laura and took one of the mugs. Her lower lip trembled and she put it back on the desk.

'The thing is, it's not my fault. She should have told me,' Sarah said defiantly, screwing her mouth into a scowl.

Laura opened the file and began to read and Sarah hoped that with all her experience and all the successful cases she had under her belt, Laura just might be able to come up with a solution. She picked up the mug again, dunked the biscuit, and watched as a lump of it broke off and disappeared under the surface of the tea. That was just typical, she thought, of her luck and her life these days.

Her eyes went to the photo on Laura's desk. A summer's day somewhere on the South Downs with Laura standing beside a horse, her husband Joe next to her, his arm around her waist. Joe looked outrageously gorgeous with his bright blue eyes and the cleft in his chin. It was a picture that made her wince and hate the world for being so unfair. Sarah's long-term partner, Andrew, had left her eighteen months ago and moved in with one of her best friends.

Laura remembered the Hakimi case because Sarah had asked her about it at the beginning. It was a situation she had dealt with several times before and she'd been happy to advise how to handle it. That advice had been fine; the mistake had come later, with an awful result.

'The boy is in Tunisia!' she exclaimed in dismay before she could stop herself.

'I know. It's hopeless, isn't it? We'll never get him back from there.'

'It makes it a bit tricky but not impossible,' Laura replied with a supportive smile, and carried on reading. Sarah took another HobNob from the packet. She had put on two stone since Andrew left.

It was a wretched story. When Mary Hakimi, née Walters, had left her Tunisian husband she knew very well there was a chance he might abduct their ten-year-old son, Ahmed, and take him to Tunis. She had done all she could to prevent it, even waiting patiently in her car outside her husband's house while Ahmed was visiting his father. More than a year ago, she'd come to Morrison Kemp solicitors for help, and Sarah had got a court order stopping Mr Hakimi obtaining a passport for the boy.

Last Friday, Ahmed had met his father after school and disappeared. Mary Hakimi had been frantic and had called the police but, she thought, at least they can't have left the country. She rang Sarah who assured her that was the case and that the boy would be traced.

And then yesterday, Mrs Hakimi found out Ahmed was in Tunisia. She had rung the Passport Agency and discovered that a passport for him had been issued to her husband the previous month.

'No,' she had sobbed down the phone, 'no, no, please, that can't be right. You're not allowed to do that. You must have made a mistake.'

There had been a mistake but it wasn't the Passport Agency's, it was Sarah Cole's. When the twelve-month court order expired, Sarah had forgotten to ask for it to be renewed. The only protection Mrs Hakimi had in place against her husband's threat of abduction had disappeared.

It was the worst possible situation, Laura knew. Tunisia had not signed the Hague Convention on Child Abduction and that made getting Ahmed back extremely difficult. If he'd been taken to a country which had signed, there was a fairly straightforward process to follow because those countries were required to order his return to the place where he usually lived, in this case England, and an English court would then decide the matter.

But those rules didn't apply in Tunisia. Mary Hakimi's only option would be to start custody proceedings in the Tunisian courts under Tunisian law. It would have different priorities and traditions, she would not be on the scene, she would have to communicate with her lawyers from a distance, probably the proceedings would be lengthy and expensive with every chance of failure.

Sarah brushed biscuit crumbs from her black skirt, got up from her chair and walked over to the window. Laura's office was on the first floor and Sarah looked down on to Black Lion Street, a busy road in the heart of Brighton's Lanes – the old town full of narrow passages housing shops, restaurants, and bars. A strong wind was blowing off the sea, buffeting shoppers and office workers taking an early lunch hour. Sarah watched them, twisting her hands in agitation.

'She's coming in soon. Will you see her for me?'

'Who's coming in?' Laura glanced up from the file with a sinking heart. Sarah turned back from the window with a pleading, hunted look in her eyes.

'Mary Hakimi. I can't face her. Not today.'

Laura sighed heavily. Her head was throbbing and she felt exhausted. She hadn't slept much last night. She'd told the police

18

what little she could about the lunatic who'd tried to kill her. They'd written it down, asked a lot of questions which she couldn't answer and then got out a breathalyser. She'd been outraged, though heaven knows why – she was a solicitor after all and knew the form. Joe had made a big fuss, stomped around, but she'd still had to take the test. She was under the limit, luckily, despite the two glasses of wine she'd drunk earlier with Sarah. When they got home, Joe made her some food, cleaned her wound, cheered her up, but all night long that terrifying chase had played in her head.

'When will she be here?'

'One o'clock. I'd be soooo grateful.'

It flitted through Laura's mind to make an excuse and say she had a lunch appointment. The last thing she felt like today was getting caught up in this. But then she thought of Mrs Hakimi desperate to get her son back and Sarah unable to help and determined not to be blamed.

'All right, I'll see her,' Laura said. She closed the file, put it on the desk and wondered what on earth she could say to Mrs Hakimi. 'Sorry, we made a mistake, sorry we ruined your life,' was all that came into her mind.

Sarah blew out her cheeks in relief and flopped down again in the chair. Maybe it wouldn't be so bad after all, maybe she would get away without too much damage. If she didn't have to see Mary Hakimi face to face, there was no danger she would admit anything or dig herself a bigger hole. She reached for a biscuit, then frowned at the packet and took her hand away. If she did get away with it, she would pull herself together. There would be no more errors and no more HobNobs.

She slipped into default mode and started talking about Andrew. He wouldn't be able to stand living with Mollie for much longer and then he'd come running back to her but she'd tell him to eff off, to start with anyway. Sarah was like a broken record on the subject and Laura knew better than to point out that eighteen months had gone by with no sign of the great man's return and maybe she should move on.

'When you first got the court order, did you tell Mary Hakimi she needed to remind you when it was running out?' Laura asked without much hope.

'No.' Sarah looked at the floor then said quietly, 'no-one told me I had to.'

Laura ignored the implication that someone, Laura presumably, should have told her. She was a little hurt that Sarah should try to spread the blame but then Sarah was upset.

'What about a note on the diary to say when the court order ran out?' she asked.

It was all basic stuff drummed into trainees from Day One. If you got a court order you had to tell the client, in writing, that they were responsible for letting you know if and when it needed renewing. You needed to put everything in the diary so there was a clear reminder of what needed doing and when. It was routine procedure and part of that most sacred of legal traditions called 'covering your back.'

Sarah crossed her arms defensively and said nothing.

Laura was not surprised Sarah had forgotten. It was soon after Andrew had left her and she had been close to a total breakdown. In another job, with a more sympathetic boss, she could have taken time off sick. As it was, she had battled on, but only just.

There had been other mistakes which Laura had sorted out. She wanted to help with this one, not just because she felt sorry for Sarah, but because she liked her. They had the same sense of humour and were allies in the vicious swirl of office politics. The problem was that this mistake was much more serious than any of the others had been, and much more difficult to put right.

'What about Marcus? Does he know yet?'

'God no,' Sarah said, horrified, 'I was hoping he might not find out.'

Sarah was in a bad way if she could delude herself that an error like this would escape the attention of the firm's senior partner.

Surely the victim – Laura corrected herself – the client, would have been on to him already. If not, she certainly would be if she didn't get satisfaction from this afternoon's meeting.

Laura imagined what Marcus Morrison would say. She ought to tell him, she knew, before Mrs Hakimi arrived. She could hear the low angry hiss of his voice. He always hissed when he was annoyed or disgusted, one reason his colleagues had nicknamed him 'the snake'. The other reason was his slipperiness. He never admitted to anything, never took any blame. He would have no sympathy whatsoever. This was the sort of mistake he would never have made and would never understand.

She tried to think what Morrison would do. What slippery manoeuvre would he come up with to get out of trouble, but nothing occurred to her. Sarah had been careless and there had been a terrible consequence. That was the truth of it. The only real solution was to somehow get the boy back.

Never apologize, never explain. Rule number one. They should have it inscribed over the entrance to Morrison Kemp, Laura thought. But she had to give Mrs Hakimi some explanation. Otherwise it was what it was – negligence – and Marcus Morrison would not tolerate that.

'I suppose I may have mentioned it to her', Sarah said abruptly, 'when the order was first granted, you know, sort of in passing.'

'In passing?'

'All right. I'm sure I told her. I remember now. I said it to her quite clearly, don't forget you have to tell me if you need this renewed. OK? Is that OK, Laura?'

It wasn't OK. Not at all. Sarah was lying and Laura knew she was lying, and in any case, it had to be in writing.

Without warning, the door to the office opened and Morrison appeared. He glided across to Laura's desk and stood beside it, polished shoes neatly together. He had no intention of sitting down, it was easier to intimidate from above. He looked at them seated in front of him and frowned.

21

Morrison always made Laura uncomfortable, even at the best of times. She felt like he was constantly judging her and finding her wanting, that he thought she was rather lightweight. She tried hard to suppress the feeling because she suspected it was what he wanted her to feel and that his condescending manner was designed to get that very result. She had no reason to feel that way; she'd done a lot more in her career than Morrison ever had, but knowing that didn't seem to make any difference. Worst of all, she sometimes tried to impress him and that made her furious with herself.

Laura knew she looked younger than her thirty-four years. She had large, hazel eyes and smooth, youthful skin. To give herself gravitas, she wore her glossy black hair tied back in a utilitarian knot, and on occasion – and this was just such an occasion – she put on a pair of heavy spectacles she didn't really need. Joe teased her about it and he was right to do so because it was pathetic, really it was, and what good did it do anyway? Whenever she met Morrison she still felt like an errant schoolgirl instead of the competent, experienced solicitor that she was.

Morrison saw the Hakimi file on her desk, pulled it casually towards him and tapped it lightly with his index finger. His small, calculating eyes fixed on her like a pair of pincers.

'We have a problem,' he hissed 'why wasn't I told?'

There was something chilling about him, Laura thought. A quiet malevolence. She would have felt a whole lot happier if he'd shouted.

'You mean Mrs Hakimi?'

'I mean Mrs Hakimi. Tell me.'

His voice was almost a whisper, his eyebrows raised in inter-rogation. The little steel-grey eyes glinted behind his spectacles.

He must have known the story anyway, at least some of it, otherwise he wouldn't be here. But she guessed he wanted to hear her tell it, wanted to put her on the spot.

She began, wondering how she was going to avoid dropping Sarah in it without appearing evasive and obstructive. She knew how ruthless Morrison was and she didn't want to fall out with him. He was powerful, well connected and with a word or two, here and there, he could blight her career forever.

She came to the tricky bit. Out of the corner of her eye she caught sight of that pleading look on Sarah's face.

' … so you see the order wasn't renewed because we were never told to renew it.'

'And Mrs Hakimi knew she had to tell us, did she?'

Laura squirmed, 'I believe so,' she said, wishing immediately that she hadn't used the phrase. It was what lawyers always said when they wanted to avoid a question.

'You believe so. I think you'd better know so.'

'Yes. So do I,' she said, stupidly.

Morrison's long, angular face leaned towards her. He reminded her of a bird of prey; a hawk, maybe, or more likely, a vulture.

'You see I've had her brother on the phone and he claims that no one ever warned his sister that she had to notify us.'

Laura was silent. She hoped Sarah might help her out, but Sarah had been struck dumb.

'You won't be surprised to hear that he was extremely angry. Of course, I know we'd never be stupid enough to forget to warn her so I was able to inform him quite firmly that his sister must be mistaken,' Morrison paused then very softly said: 'I presume we have it in writing.'

Laura bit her lip and said: 'Apparently it was more a sort of verbal warning.'

For the first time, Morrison addressed Sarah.

'Would you mind leaving us for a moment.'

Sarah hesitated, torn between relief at the chance to escape Morrison's grilling and fear about what might be said about her when she'd gone. He waited, silent, glaring at her, until she got up and left the room.

'I'm sorry, Laura, you misunderstand,' he said when they were alone. 'That wasn't a question. I wasn't asking you if we had it

23

in writing, I was telling you we had it in writing. Have I made myself clear?'

She felt alarm but not much surprise. He expected her to tell Mrs Hakimi that she'd been sent a letter setting out her responsibilities at the time the court order was first granted; he expected her, if necessary, to forge a copy of such a document and he expected her to say to Mrs Hakimi that what had happened was nobody's fault but her own.

'Yes, perfectly clear.'

'Good,' he waited a moment then said carelessly, 'I want you to fire Sarah ASAP.'

This time Laura was shocked. 'I can't do that Marcus,' she protested, 'I mean why would I?'

'Come on, we both know the answer to that. She is responsible for this fiasco. You're a senior lawyer here and you know what's happened, so there we are – get rid of her. This afternoon, I suggest.'

'But that's just not fair,' she burst out, 'You must see that, after all—'

The look on his face stopped her mid-sentence. More calmly she said, 'Surely a written warning would be enough. She's been going through a difficult time in her personal life and—'

'Spare me the violins, please.' Morrison interrupted, his mouth a thin line under his hawk nose.

'It seems very harsh to fire her,' Laura persisted, 'Can't we at least wait and see if this thing can be sorted out?'

'You disappoint me, Laura. Seriously disappoint me. I thought you were ambitious, wanted to get on, wanted a partnership here. Isn't that so?'

'Yes, of course I do. Absolutely, it's just that … '

'Then fire her. It's not nice, I know, but it has to be done. She's made a bad mistake, the sort of thing that could mean a large and embarrassing negligence claim if we don't, ah, sort it out. You see that, don't you?

'Yes.'

'You'll have to toughen up a bit if you want to succeed in this firm.'

The schoolgirl had been suitably chastised. He started to move away then stopped.

'Hurt yourself, have you?' He was staring at the cut on her eyebrow. She'd hoped the thick spectacles would hide it but very little got past Morrison.

'Oh that,' she attempted a laugh, 'Just an accident.'

'I hope it's not too painful,' he hissed.

Her body tensed. For one horrible moment she thought he might reach out and put his arm around her shoulders. But he didn't. He wasn't that sort of person. She relaxed – just a little.

Ten minutes later the phone on her desk rang. Mrs Hakimi, and her brother, had arrived in reception.

CHAPTER FOUR

Harry Pelham sat glowering and silent while the policemen took his home apart. There were four of them: two from Sussex CID and two from London, from the Metropolitan Police's Specialist Crime and Operations Unit. This was no ordinary police raid. This was a high powered team tackling an outrageous crime.

'We're arresting you, Mr Pelham, on suspicion of downloading and possessing indecent images of children.'

The officer in charge, Detective Inspector David Barnes, laid it out for him. They had information that he was a paedophile. They had search warrants, for his home and his office, and they were looking for child pornography. When the searches were done, he would be taken to the police station for questioning.

He stared at the detective, his face tight with fury, 'You cannot be serious. I've got a young daughter of my own. Jesus, what sort of man do you think I am?'

Barnes stared back. It was clear from the slight curl of his mouth what the answer to that question was.

'We'll need to take your computer to check the hard drive,' he said.

'Look,' Harry took a step towards him, 'I am not a paedophile. The idea disgusts me. Understand that.'

'That's what we're going to check, sir.' Barnes's face was expressionless now but his voice oozed disbelief. He was big with broad shoulders, reeking of ambition and confidence, bordering on arrogant. Harry wanted very much to hit him.

'There's personal stuff on my computer. What right do you have to look at that?'

'We can look at whatever we want,' said Barnes and paused, watching Harry for a reaction, then added, 'But in fact we only read the things that are relevant to the investigation. We'll be scanning the photo files and doing key word searches connected to the child pornography we think has been downloaded.'

'I'm telling you there's none of that filth on my computer,' Harry snarled.

'In that case, sir, you have nothing at all to worry about.'

The urge to smash his fist into Barnes's poker face was almost uncontrollable but as well, growing stronger all the time, were feelings of fear. Barnes's assured attitude worried him.

'What evidence have you got?' he said more quietly, 'I'm sure this is all a misunderstanding that I can explain.'

'We'll go through that at the station,' said Barnes smoothly.

They started searching downstairs, clearing cupboards, tipping out drawers, shaking books and magazines to see if anything incriminating would fall out. They made it clear he wasn't allowed to go anywhere on his own, without supervision. He must stay with them, in their sight, so they could be sure he wasn't destroying evidence. When he went to the bathroom, one of them followed and waited outside.

They spent most time in the room he used as an office which was a bit of a mess. The cleaner who kept the rest of the large house in good order, didn't go in there because Harry preferred it undisturbed. They sorted through methodically, taking files from shelves and a cabinet, sifting the contents, collecting up memory sticks, CDs, his laptop and iPad, putting everything they were taking away in a pile on the floor. They fired up the main computer, checked it was working properly, then closed it down and separated the parts before taking them out to their van.

They drove it all, and Harry, to the police station at Hollingbury. The place was heaving; busy with the fallout from a drugs raid, and the only free interview room was the size of a small box with one tiny window high up in the wall. Harry paced up and down in it waiting for Ronnie Seymour to arrive and for the interview to begin. There was a tape recorder bolted to a table. The table was bolted to the floor.

Ronnie had had a not very satisfactory conversation with Barnes before coming to see Harry. The detective had been cagey, reluctant to give away too much of his case but Ronnie, whose long experience had given him a sixth sense about these things, suspected Barnes had something to justify his bullish approach. As he entered the interview room there was a frown on his round, sleek face.

'What's going on, Harry?' he said.

'I've no idea. What have they told you?'

'That they think you're involved in child pornography and they can prove it.'

'It's not true. You know that, don't you?' Harry demanded.

'I'm sure it's not true,' the lawyer was impatient, 'But why are they saying it?'

'I don't know. I wish I did.'

'All right. Let's see what they've got.'

Barnes and a detective constable called McLaren, one of the officers who'd searched his home, conducted the interview though Barnes asked almost all the questions. His bulky presence dominated the small room, and right from the start, Harry, who was a big man himself, complained that he felt cramped and claustrophobic, like there was not enough air for all four of them to breathe. McLaren inserted two separate cassettes into the tape recorder and set them running simultaneously. He stated the time and who was present and asked Harry to confirm that he had been cautioned prior to the interview. Then Barnes took over.

'Mr Pelham, what credit cards do you have?'

'Hang on a minute,' Ronnie said at once, holding up his hand, 'before my client answers anything, I think it's only fair that you tell him what grounds you have for making these very serious allegations against him.'

Barnes considered. He hadn't encountered Ronnie Seymour before, but he knew he had a reputation as a wily and effective criminal lawyer. No need to make this difficult, Barnes thought, no need for confrontation. After all, the evidence was clear.

'OK,' he shrugged and sat back, putting his hands behind his head with his elbows menacingly pointed out, looking sure of himself, 'We have information, and material, that implicates Mr Pelham in child pornography, possibly as part of a paedophile network. We have discovered that indecent images of children were downloaded from websites, paid for by a credit card registered in his name.'

'That's crap,' Harry snapped, 'I've never been near that kind of website. The whole idea is sick. Totally sick.'

'So, what credit cards do you have?' Barnes repeated.

'A few of them. Some business, some personal, but I don't use any of them to buy that muck, all right?'

'Can I see them, please.'

Ronnie shook his head. 'I am sure, Detective Inspector, that my client has no objection to showing you the cards,' he said for the benefit of the tape, 'but before he does call you please tell us the number of the card you're talking about.'

The solicitor was anxious to avoid a fishing expedition. He wanted to make sure the police had a particular number that they could reasonably believe was registered to Harry.

Barnes tore a piece of paper from his notebook, flicked through the rest of it with large, rather elegant fingers, then wrote out a 16 digit number on the paper. He handed it to Harry.

'It's a Visa card number, sir. Is it yours?'

There was a slight nod from Ronnie, and reluctantly, Harry reached into his jacket for his wallet and took out his Visa card.

The numbers matched. The small room seemed to shrink. He started to sweat badly.

'It's nothing to do with me. I am not a paedophile,' he said.

Ronnie sat forward, stroking his chin, 'As everybody knows, you don't need to actually have the card in your hand to be able to use it on the Internet. Someone else could easily have got hold of the number and used it. Credit card fraud is very widespread.'

Barnes turned dark, confident eyes on him, 'That's why we're checking Mr Pelham's computers. To see what's on the hard drives.' He managed to make it sound both polite and threatening.

'There's nothing on the fucking hard drives. How many times do I have to tell you that?' Harry leaned towards Barnes and banged down his fist hard on the table.

Barnes looked at him, 'Are you a violent man, Mr Pelham?'

'Can we keep to the point, Detective Inspector,' Ronnie intervened before Harry could react.

The policeman had brought with him a large brown envelope and now he took out of it a set of photographs, spreading them on the table in front of Harry. They were pictures of children. Hard core child pornography.

'Have you seen these before, Mr Pelham?'

'Jesus Christ.'

'Does that mean you have seen them before or you haven't seen them before, sir?'

'No, no, no. Of course I haven't seen them before.'

Harry felt nauseous and his legs were shaking. He opened his mouth to drag in air. Really, there was no oxygen left in this room, he could hardly breathe at all now. He saw Barnes watching him, and for a moment, just before he fell to the floor, was suddenly aware of his own open mouth, the nervous licking of his lips, the sweat marks left by his hands on the table. His body language was shouting out a message, a message that the detective had surely heard loud and clear, that Harry Pelham was indeed a thoroughly guilty man.

CHAPTER FIVE

'It's like the end of everything for me because Ahmed's my whole world. I'm just devastated. I think I always knew it would happen but that doesn't help, you know, when it does.'

Mary Hakimi, tears rolling slowly down her face, went on to explain to Laura what it felt like to have her son snatched away. She wasn't ranting; she was just terribly sad which made it all so much worse. She was thirty four, the same age as Laura, but her face was strained and careworn with lines of worry already carved between her eyes.

'It's been the worst two weeks of my life. I can't even face going into his bedroom. When the news came – that he was in Tunisia – I suppose I should have been relieved that he was alive, but for me it was my worst fear come true; the fact that he was there and then knowing that I won't be able to get him back.'

Laura glanced at her brother. Clive Walters listened, scowling, simmering, occasionally grunting or puffing air into his cheeks.

'I was always worried about it,' Mary Hakimi repeated, 'That's why I came to you. And I thought once I had the order from the court that a passport couldn't be issued, then Ahmed was safe. That's what I thought. It was all I had.' She sounded dazed at how stupid she'd been to rely on such fragile protection. As if she'd had a choice.

Laura nodded, tried to say some words of comfort but they sounded wholly inadequate.

'And to find out that you just forgot to renew it, well, it's beyond belief and I don't know how you can make that kind of mistake because it's people's lives you're ruining. My son should have been protected by the law and now he's been taken away.'

An angry rumble of agreement came from Clive Walters. His fleshy face, with its heavy jowls, looked increasingly belligerent.

'And don't try telling us it's not your fault,' he said, 'You won't get away with that one. I've been on to your boss and he says there's no doubt that Mary would have been sent a letter about renewing the order. That's crap and you know it. She never got sent any letter.'

Mary Hakimi seemed not to have heard what her brother had said; she was still in that dazed world of her own.

'You have to understand, it's my family that's gone. Have you got children?' she asked.

Laura shook her head.

'Then maybe you won't understand how this has torn my life apart.'

Laura picked up a piece of paper from the file in front of her. Sarah had thrust it into her hand as she was on her way to the conference room on the ground floor where Mrs Hakimi and her brother were waiting for her. It was a copy of a letter – the letter that had supposedly been sent to Mary Hakimi. Sarah had just written it.

It did the job. Most likely it would get Morrison Kemp off the hook. She could see no easy way it could be challenged. All she had to do was hand it to them. Clive Walters would be furious, would deny his sister ever received it, but he would have the devil's own job proving it.

She put the letter firmly back in the file and took a deep breath.

'Mrs Hakimi, I do understand and I want you to know that I will do absolutely everything I can to get your son back.'

There was a spark of hope in the woman's eyes but her brother was having none of it.

'Hang on a minute. Empty promises are no good to us. It's your fault he's been taken. You were negligent and we want compensation. How much is what we should be talking about.'

Laura kept focused on his sister, 'Mrs Hakimi, as you know, it's only possible to get a court order for the return of your son if he's been taken to a country that has signed the Hague Convention. Unfortunately Tunisia hasn't and so you have to rely on the courts in Tunis and start custody proceedings there.'

'You are joking I take it,' Clive Walters interrupted, 'She's got sod all chance of winning there as I'm sure you're well aware.'

'I'll get in touch with a lawyer in Tunis who deals with this sort of case,' Laura continued, 'I assure you we'll do everything we can to bring Ahmed home to you. Every possible avenue will be explored.'

It sounded better than it was, she was painfully aware there were no grounds for optimism.

'And you think we're going to be satisfied with that? No way. There's been a major cock-up and I want to know how much you propose to pay in damages.'

'Mr Walters, I'm afraid I must make it clear that Morrison Kemp in no way accepts any liability for what has happened, although, of course, we very much want to help in any way we can.'

'I know what's going through your mind,' he growled, 'you're thinking that I can't prove it. Can't prove there was no letter reminding Mary about the court order. Well let me tell you that whatever you say, I will make the most tremendous fuss. I'll go to the press, to the Law Society, whatever it takes to get justice. Your name will be mud.'

'Please, Clive,' said his sister, 'This isn't helping. All I want is to get Ahmed back.'

Tears flooded her eyes. 'Anything you can do, I'd be so grateful,' she choked out.

'You can trust us to do all we can.'

'Trust you,' burst out the brother, 'why should she trust you now when you couldn't be trusted to do the job properly in the first place?'

Good point, thought Laura. Excellent point.

'I know it won't be easy,' Mary Hakimi swallowed hard, 'but I'll try anything, anything you can think of. Please let me know.'

Clive Walters looked at her with disgust. He'd seen the chance of a big fat pay-out and he wasn't going to let it slip away. But for now he was stuck. He had no claim, he wasn't the injured party. It was up to his sister and his sister was off in cloud cuckoo land. Reluctantly he got to his feet, refused to shake Laura's hand and instead put his arm around his sister's shoulders and guided her out of the room.

The second they had gone, Sarah came through the door.

'What happened? Did you show them the letter? Did it work?' she said, slumping down in the chair just vacated by Mary Hakimi.

'I don't think that letter was … ' Laura stopped. Sarah was likely to lose her job over this; that was bad enough, there was no point in rubbing her nose in how badly she'd screwed up.

'I told them I'd talk to a lawyer in Tunis and see if he can help. Mrs Hakimi was keen to give that a try.'

'Great. With a bit of luck she won't make any more fuss to Marcus then and I should be in the clear.' Sarah gave a short nervous laugh, realizing what she'd said sounded uncaring and Laura didn't look too happy.

'I feel so sorry for Mrs Hakimi,' she added quickly, 'I'll do all I can to help get the boy back. You know I really didn't want to write that letter, but Marcus insisted, he said if I didn't produce it that minute and give it to you before you saw Mrs Hakimi, I was out of the door there and then. He was really scary, you know how he is,' she tailed off, looking at Laura for approval.

Laura knew exactly how he was. She could imagine him in another life, as the head of the secret police presiding over a reign of total terror without ever raising his voice.

She nodded and felt a stab from the headache. She pressed her palm to her forehead and held it there, trying to push the pain further back inside. Sarah thought she was safe now she had done what Morrison wanted. He, on the other hand, would be expecting Laura to sack Sarah at the first opportunity. Well she wasn't going to do it. Not yet anyway, not until she had tried to get the boy back.

'Do you think we can get away with it?' Sarah asked in a conspiratorial voice. It had occurred to her that Laura was up to her neck in it too, now that she'd handed over the forged letter to Mrs Hakimi.

Laura swallowed the urge to snap back that she wasn't trying to get away with anything. She was losing patience with Sarah who was so clearly concerned with saving her own skin. Her eyes smarted from lack of sleep and a wave of tiredness hit her.

'I need to make some calls,' she said, standing up to leave.

CHAPTER SIX

When he woke it was with the memory of fear though he couldn't immediately recall what had caused it. He was in the Royal Sussex County Hospital in a room on his own, off the main ward. He saw Ronnie sitting in a chair beside his bed, reading a newspaper, and then he remembered. So, it was not a bad dream after all.

'That was one way to stop the interview,' Ronnie said when he saw Harry was awake but neither of them laughed.

'What happened?'

'You collapsed. At the police station. You were being questioned.'

'I remember.'

'How are you feeling?' Ronnie said drily.

'How do you think?' Harry said, glancing at him. In the second before Ronnie looked away, he saw something in the man's eyes, something very like revulsion, and it sent a chill through him.

'I did not download that muck, Ronnie. You've got to believe me.'

'We will have to wait and see what they find on the computer.'

'They won't find anything because there's nothing to find. This is all complete rubbish.'

'Let's hope so.'

'For God's sake, man, how long have you known me? Twenty, twenty five years. Do you really think I would do this?' Harry demanded.

There was no immediate reply.

He doesn't believe me. He thinks it's true. Harry wondered what else Barnes had said to Ronnie.

'The police will want to finish questioning you when they think you're fit enough,' Ronnie said eventually, his eyes shifting away again,

'Then they'll release me, right? I mean they're not going to keep me in, are they?'

'I shouldn't think so. No reason why you shouldn't get bail. There may be conditions though.'

'What sort of conditions?'

'They could restrict your contact with Martha,' Ronnie said coldly, 'And there's likely to be a condition that you don't contact your wife in any way. I should tell you the police believe you've been sending her death threats and want to question you about those as well.'

'That's bollocks. Of course I haven't.'

'They say Anna has recently received emails threatening her life.'

'If she has, it's nothing to do with me.'

'Anna's solicitor is claiming they are deliberate harassment calculated to scare your wife into backing off in the divorce,' Ronnie continued as if Harry had not spoken.

'This is bullshit. Laura Maxwell bullshit. It's just the sort of thing she would invent as part of her campaign to destroy me,' Harry said furiously,

'Do you know a man called Paul Giles?' Ronnie asked.

Harry hesitated, 'Doesn't ring a bell. Should it?'

'It should do, yes. Supposedly he's an old friend of yours. He sent the death threats to your wife.'

Harry stayed silent.

'Don't lie to me, Harry. I don't like it.' Ronnie looked disgusted.

'All right, I was going to tell you before but you didn't want to know, did you? It's what those allegations in the divorce submission are all about. Paul Giles is an account set up by me.'

Ronnie grimaced. 'You set up an email account, in a fake name, with the specific purpose of threatening your wife. Is that correct?'

'No it damn well isn't. All I did was send her a couple of harmless messages.'

'If they were so harmless why did you pretend they were from somebody else?'

'Because I knew if she saw they were from me she'd just delete them, straightaway, without reading a word. I just told her to stop …' he sucked air through his teeth, 'being so fucking unreasonable.'

'And when that didn't have the desired effect you became more and more aggressive and then, still masquerading as Paul Giles, you explicitly threatened to kill her.'

'No, I did not! It's all being twisted, turned into something it isn't,' Harry's hand touched the other man's arm, 'Come on, Ronnie, it's what Laura Maxwell does.' He said the name as if it was an obscenity.

Ronnie shook off the hand and finally looked Harry in the eye. 'Let me give you some advice. If you have done what they say you've done, any of it or all of it, then it would be better to admit it now. The sentence will be lighter that way.'

'I've told you everything there is to tell,' Harry said stiffly. Fear rose inside him. So far as he could recall, in all their long acquaintance, the lawyer had never before suggested admitting anything.

'I see,' Ronnie's disbelief was obvious, 'I should let them know you're awake,' he said abruptly, getting up from his chair and saying a curt goodbye.

Harry assumed he was talking about the nurses until, as Ronnie opened the door to go, he caught sight of two of the policemen who had searched his home. They were standing outside his room and Ronnie stopped to talk to them.

He realized then that he had a police guard.

CHAPTER SEVEN

Laura swallowed two more Paracetamol, took off her glasses and tentatively touched the wound on her eyebrow. It had bled a lot at the time but the cut wasn't deep and it hadn't needed stitches. She had been lucky. A shiver went over her; she was not looking forward to the drive home tonight.

She began searching for the phone number of the lawyer in Tunis. She had met him a few years ago at an international conference on child abduction. He had been a ladies' man, a bit of a pest really, but she thought he would remember her and might be willing to help. It would be almost impossible to get Ahmed Hakimi returned through the Tunisian courts. But there was another way; something she knew had been done before in this sort of case. It was a thin chance, it depended on luck and being in the right place at the right time. You wouldn't want to pin your hopes on it, but it was worth a try.

Before she could find the number, there was a call from Monica at the front desk to let her know that Anna Pelham was in reception.

'She hasn't got an appointment but she says it's urgent. Can you see her?'

Anna often dropped in unannounced though she always apologized for it. She rang up a lot too, but it didn't bother Laura the way it sometimes did with other clients. Anna had had a rough time, was still having one, but she was determined not to be a victim any longer and to do the best she could for her daughter, Martha. Laura liked her for her guts and for never giving in to self-pity.

Anna had been putting on a brave face about Harry's death threats but Laura thought she must be badly worried by them.

'OK, no problem, I'll be down in a minute.' She picked up the Pelham file and went downstairs to the conference room where Anna was waiting for her.

'I know I should have told you I was coming in, but my mind's been all over the place. To be honest, I'm a bit scared.' Anna smiled apologetically.

As usual, Anna was underplaying her own feelings and trying not to make a fuss. She didn't often show signs that the divorce, or her husband, was getting to her, kept it all bottled up inside. For her to say she was 'a bit scared' most likely meant she was absolutely terrified. Laura guessed her self-effacing behaviour was the result of years of Harry's abuse. He had conditioned her to stay quiet about what was happening to her in the hope of avoiding more punishment. Her own feelings were unimportant; she should keep her views to herself and take what she got without complaining.

Laura remembered how her own mother had behaved the same way, worn down to timidity and obedience by her domineering father, spending her life walking on eggshells, trying not to trigger another outburst.

'I'll get on to the police again; push them hard to take some action.'

'That's what I came to tell you. The police have been to see him. One of the neighbours rang me, she said they were at the house this morning. I thought you might be able to find out what's happening.'

'Of course I will. Did she say anything else?'

Anna shook her head. 'I hardly know her. She only had my number because I once had to ask her to look after Martha for a couple of hours. She just said she thought I might want to know.'

Harry had discouraged Anna from talking to the neighbours, discouraged her from getting close to anyone or keeping up with her friends. He thought it best, Anna said, that they 'kept themselves to themselves.' It was what men like Harry did; they isolated their victim, shrank their world so they rarely talked with anyone else, so they came to think the abuse was normal.

'I'm worried what he might do next. I mean if they tell him I've complained about the threats, he'll be really mad.' Anna's voice was shaky.

'He'd be a fool to do anything with the police on his tail.'

'I don't think that will stop him. He does what he wants.'

At their first meeting, Anna had reluctantly told Laura what Harry had done to her for years. She had not wanted to give details but gradually Laura teased them out of her. Mental, sexual and physical abuse, he had ticked all the boxes. It had got worse after Martha was born.

'When was the first time he hit you?' Laura asked.

Anna's face shadowed and she stared at the floor for a while.

'Martha was three weeks old. It was a Sunday afternoon and we'd taken her out along the sea front when we ran in to one of Harry's business mates,' Anna said, haltingly, 'he made a big fuss of her, said what a cute baby she was. When we got home, after I'd put Martha down to sleep, Harry accused me of flirting with the man, smiling at him in a provocative way. I said that was ridiculous and then he punched me in the face. Just like that, no warning.'

Anna looked up from the floor, straight at Laura, suddenly worried. 'I hadn't done anything, really I hadn't. The man asked me about Martha and I had to speak to him, didn't I? I smiled at him, but it was just a normal smile, because I was happy to have such a lovely baby.'

The punch had split open both her lips. Harry had been sorry, terribly sorry. It would never happen again, he said.

By then, Anna was well aware of how sexually jealous her husband was. He was obsessed with details of her sex life before they met, made her write down all her previous sexual encounters in a small black notebook he kept locked in his desk.

Anna sat up straight on her chair, smoothed out the creases in her dress. She looked her usual immaculate self despite the stress she was under; careful make-up, manicured nails, smart clothes. She had every right to look a mess but she never did.

'He liked me to look nice,' Anna had told Laura, 'Soon after we got married, he started telling me how to dress because he thought the clothes I usually wore were too slutty.'

Harry told her how to style her hair, how to behave and who she could talk to which was hardly anyone; if she ever got it wrong, he would scream abuse at her.

'I never knew what was going to upset him. He'd be OK one minute, then go crazy the next.'

As time went by, he hit her more often.

'No matter how hard I cried in front of him, no matter how much I begged for him to stop hurting me and no matter how many times he said he was sorry and promised he'd stop, he never did,' Anna's voice was flat, desensitized.

Her words brought a vivid picture into Laura's mind; her childhood self creeping out from her bedroom and tiptoeing down the stairs, listening to her father screaming at her mother, criticising her, hearing her mother's constant, feeble protest, 'Don't say that, darling,' as she tried to placate him.

'Is there any chance of getting him locked up?' Anna asked.

'No chance, I'm afraid. It would take an actual assault before that could happen.'

'He's done it often enough.'

'The trouble is he's never been charged and found guilty by a court.'

'I should've reported it, I know that. But every time he was sorry and I thought that maybe if I could stop making so many mistakes, act better, not make him jealous, then it would stop.'

'You didn't make mistakes, Anna, he made you think you

did but you didn't. It's what wife beaters always say – she made me do it.'

Anna nodded, took a tissue from her bag and blew her nose, 'Sorry, Laura, sorry to make such a fuss. I'll be OK in a minute.'

'Let me talk to the police and find out what's going on,' Laura found the number in the file and called it while Anna waited. The officer she wanted wasn't there and she left a message.

'If we can persuade them to charge him with harassment, he'll probably get bail but with a bit of luck there'll be a condition that he can't come anywhere near you,' Laura thought for a second, 'And we'll press ahead with getting a non-molestation order from the family court to keep him away from you.'

'Sometimes I think he's watching the house.'

'Have you seen him?' Laura asked, worried.

Anna hesitated, 'Maybe. I don't know for sure. I get this creepy feeling like there's someone out there. Martha gets it too.'

'Is there anyone you could go and stay with for a few days or could come and stay with you?' Laura instantly regretted the question. She'd asked before about family and friends and Anna had told her there wasn't anybody; she was an only child and her parents were both dead. She had no close friends, Harry had seen to that.

'I'm all right,' Anna said, suddenly fierce. 'I can cope. He's not going to get away with it anymore.'

There was a look on Anna's face that Laura had seen before. A set, purposeful look and it meant that Anna had gone into fight-back mode, like a switch had flipped in her brain; the victim mentality was banished, replaced by total determination never again to let her husband bully or control her.

'Don't let up on him, Laura. I don't want to give him an inch.' Anna's eyes were bright, not with tears this time, but with a kind of crusading zeal. The traumas she had gone through seemed to have given her strength; she wasn't bowing her head now.

'We'll get there in the end. You've done fantastically well so far,' Laura encouraged.

'I couldn't get through this without you, I'd fall apart.' Anna shuddered then looked at her watch, 'I should go, I have to pick up Martha.'

'Soon as I hear from the police, I'll you know.'

Anna stood up to leave and Laura stood too, gave her a hug. 'Take care,' she said.

Anna eyes went to the cut on Laura's face, 'You take care too.'

'Oh that. It's nothing. Just me being careless.'

There was a knock on the door and Sam O'Donnell, the office manager and IT expert, stuck his head in.

'Laura, sorry to interrupt but could I have a quick word when you're free?'

'It's OK, I'm just going,' Anna said.

Sam shut the door carefully behind her. He was a big bear of a man who liked a chat and a joke but now he stood silent, fidgeting with a piece of paper he had in his hand.

'I thought you should see this. It was posted on our divorce forum.'

It was from someone with the username 'themaxwellbitch.' Laura felt her face turn scarlet.

Morrison Kemp had a divorce message board on its website where members of the public could share experiences, give opinions, or ask advice and it was part of Sam's job to keep an eye on it. The message had been added to a thread called 'Final Settlement.'

'I've removed it and blocked the sender so they can't post any more,' he told her.

Laura read it, conscious of Sam's eyes on her. She hoped he wouldn't be chatting about this.

'Do you have any idea who did it?'

'Afraid not. Whoever it is, is a bit of a joker though. The email they've used is registered as "marcus.morrison3"', Sam grinned awkwardly at her. 'I know the boss can be a bit of a shit but I don't think it's him.'

Laura couldn't raise a smile.

'Sorry, Laura,' Sam cleared his throat, 'Lousy sense of humour.'

CHAPTER EIGHT

'Laura Maxwell, you are an evil bitch. You destroy lives. You feed off men's misery – you take their daughters away from them. Understand how much I hate you. I think about it all the time, how to put a stop to you, how to settle the score. I'm not planning on settling in court. I have other plans for a final settlement. Better watch out.'

It was not the first time in her career that Laura had been called a bitch and threatened; in fact, she'd been called a lot worse and had had to grow a tough skin over the years. Really, she thought, the posting should not have rattled her as much as it did. But the last twenty four hours had left her jittery.

Laura watched Joe as he read the message; saw his expression change to one of outrage. They'd been together for five years now but she never got tired of looking at him. He was distractingly handsome; tall and muscular, without being too beefy, he had thick black hair and a broad smile that brought dimples to his cheeks. His eyes, framed with long lashes, were blue and dazzling.

'Charming. Any idea who sent it?' he said.

'I'm wondering if it could be this guy Harry Pelham. I'm representing his wife and he's been sending her deaths threats. Maybe he's lashing out at me too.'

They were sitting on the sofa after dinner, cosy in front of the TV, half watching a programme about the hotel industry. Joe had wanted to see it as it featured a hotel he knew further along the coast but he'd lost interest, complaining it was rubbish and only interested in negative, headline grabbing stuff. Laura took the chance to raise her own problems. She didn't often discuss her work with Joe but tonight, just for once, she had an urgent need to spill it all out. She'd had a night and a day from hell and it had left her feeling anxious and vulnerable. She reached for the wine bottle on the table and poured herself another glass.

'Have you talked to the police?' he asked.

'I got some info from them this afternoon. Harry Pelham was arrested this morning but now he's in hospital for some reason. He's under arrest there apparently, but I couldn't get any more out of the duty officer and can't speak to the guy in charge until tomorrow.'

Laura wished she had more contacts in the local police and could use the back channels to find out more details, but she hadn't been around long enough to get to know many of the officers. The name of the man running the Pelham investigation, Detective Inspector David Barnes, meant nothing to her.

Joe picked up the remote and turned off the sound on the TV. He put his arm around Laura's shoulders and kissed the top of her head.

'Sounds like the crazy Mr Pelham needs locking up permanently.'

'Fat chance. Best I'll get is a restraining order to keep him away from his wife.'

'If he's threatening you too now, they need to do something.'

'The trouble is Sam says it's impossible to prove who posted the message. Whoever it is has hidden their tracks well.'

'So it might not be him at all.'

'No, it could be one of my other admiring fans.' Laura forced a laugh and snuggled up against him, touching the cleft in his chin, then running her fingers down to his chest.

She told him about Mary Hakimi and how Morrison had behaved, and Joe called Morrison a pathetic old wanker and then did his impression of him which made her laugh for real. It was good to be able to talk to Joe about work for a change. He hardly ever asked about it and she knew he found it a difficult subject. She had had, was still having, a very successful career. He had not. Of course, he'd chosen the most precarious and unpredictable of jobs. He'd wanted to be an actor, and although he had the looks of a Hollywood leading man, he'd never made it. His biggest claim to fame had been playing, if that was the right word, a corpse in *Holby City*. Now he was playing second fiddle to his younger brother in the family hotel business.

Laura understood why it might bother him and never gloried in her own success. She thought it was not her success that rankled with him, he was not that petty, but his own failure, at the age of thirty-five, to have done much in the world, to have made any kind of mark. She hoped his reinvention as a businessman would change things. As a mark of faith she had invested a substantial sum of her own money in the Greene hotel chain. She loved him very much and it had been one way of showing that love.

Joe had resisted joining the business. Since his father died ten years ago, his mother had run it with the help of her younger son, Peter. Helen Greene had been an iron lady, managing the family's four hotels with tremendous energy and sound business sense accumulated over more than thirty years. But two years ago, when she was only fifty-nine, she'd had a stroke. It had paralysed her and she'd recovered only a bit. She could talk but her mental sharpness was gone and she could walk no more than a few steps. The hotels would have to soldier on without her for Helen Greene was not coming back. Now she lived in a nursing home on the South Downs, a few miles out of Brighton.

Joe had been forced to give up his job as a director with a small experimental theatre in London and become Peter's business partner. It had made up Laura's mind. She was burning herself out working for a big London legal firm and beginning to wonder why. Yes she had a big salary and a glittering CV and great prospects, but she was into her thirties now and she wanted other things in life, was keen to have a family. She had been happy to scale down, move out of the fast lane. She would aim for a partnership in the provinces and maybe become a big fish in a regional pool.

Joe had not been so happy. He loved the theatre and found it hard to knuckle down to the hotel business. He'd had a few run-ins with Peter but Laura was keeping her fingers crossed it would work out in the end.

She felt his hand massaging the back of her neck, soothing and reassuring.

'If he did post that message, maybe he also had something to do with what happened last night?' she said.

'I think that was just some scumbag who thought it would be fun to scare the life out of a woman in a sports car.'

'I guess so. Probably worrying about nothing.'

'Of course you are, hun. You've had a lousy day and it's no wonder you're stressed out.'

He was right, she thought, and felt some of the tension leave her. She sat up, pushed her hair back behind her ears and took another large swig of the white wine, draining her glass. She picked up the bottle and frowned at it. It was empty too.

'I think we might need one of the Greene specials.' Joe grinned and went to get another bottle, one of the good ones he liberated from the hotel supplies. By the time she had drunk another glass or two, the cares of the day – and the night before – had slipped from her shoulders. She leant her head on Joe's shoulder, closed her eyes, and began to giggle.

'What's the joke?' he said, laughing too.

'I was thinking. Married couples – the awful things they do to each other.'

'And that made you laugh?'

'I know. Not funny. Sad. Did I ever tell you about this guy, this husband with really, really long hair who came in wanting a divorce? They'd been having problems for a while but the thing that brought it all to a crunch was when his wife told him he couldn't have a cat. So he said, right, I shan't cut my hair until you let me have a cat. And so it went on. No cat, no haircut, until by the time I saw him he had hair down to his waist.'

'Sounds a bit of a shaggy cat story to me.'

Laura opened her eyes and looked at him, 'Love you,' she said.

CHAPTER NINE

Detective Inspector Barnes called Laura at work early the next day and told her what she had expected – that Harry Pelham would not be held in custody. He also told her what she hadn't expected – that Harry was suspected of being a paedophile. That was the main reason for the raid on his home though the emails were also being investigated. They'd seized computers from the house and from his offices in Hove which they'd raided simultaneously.

She pressed the policeman for more details, but either he didn't know any more or he wasn't going to say. He agreed to tell her when Harry was well enough to be questioned again. Doctors at the Royal Sussex had not been able to find anything obviously wrong with him, but he was being kept in for observation for the next few days. At the moment, Barnes said, officers were guarding him but he didn't have the resources to leave them there for long. It was likely Harry would be given bail later that day and the officers would be withdrawn.

Laura pushed for conditions on the bail preventing Harry from going anywhere near his wife or threatening her in any way and Barnes agreed to consider that. He told her that after they'd finished questioning Harry and looked at what was on his computers, they'd decide if there was enough evidence to charge him, either over the child pornography or the death threats. If there was, in either case he'd most likely get bail. Regarding the pornography, it would depend on the seriousness of the offence – was he part of a paedophile network, had he been distributing the material, was it for his own use, how much did he have and how long had he been doing it. But it would have to be very serious for him to be locked up; just downloading and possession of indecent material would not be enough.

It was the same story with the death threat emails. If the police could prove that Paul Giles was in fact Harry, by finding evidence on his computers, they would charge him with harassment. But it wouldn't warrant a custodial sentence – a restraining order only, would be the likely result. There was a silence on the phone. The conversation was over unless she had any more questions. She hesitated. She told Barnes about the website posting but decided against mentioning the car chase. She was afraid he might think her a little over-anxious.

Laura had slept well after the wine and a couple of Nytol and she felt a whole lot better today. The car incident didn't seem so threatening. She liked that description – the 'car incident'. It minimized the whole thing, brought it down to manageable proportions. The thought of it didn't make her heart beat as fiercely as it had.

Twenty minutes later, after talking to her friend Emma Fletcher, Laura felt better still. Emma always cheered her up, right back from when they were at school together. Laura's mum had used to call Emma 'Mrs Brightside' because she was always so positive.

Emma's life had been very different from Laura's – she had a husband and three sons and a part time job as a primary school teacher – but the two women had stayed close friends and now Laura had moved back to Sussex, they saw each other a lot.

'I agree it sounds like a random piece of bad luck,' she said, when Laura told her about the chase, 'Joe's probably right that it was some nutter who wanted to frighten a woman in a sports car. Why not go green and trade that gas guzzler in for a smart car. No-one will be chasing you then. Not even Joe.'

Laura laughed, said she'd give it some thought, and Emma suggested meeting up on Sunday to go shopping. Her husband was taking the boys to Speedway and she'd have most of the day to herself.

That suited Laura well because she wanted to chat to Emma about her father. He had been in touch again, asking to meet up, and Laura wasn't sure what to do. She hadn't seen him for nearly seven years, not since her mum's funeral, and most of her didn't want to see him now or ever again. But a part of her did, an annoying, nagging part; despite everything he had done to her mum, he was still her dad.

Michael Maxwell had never been aggressive towards his daughter, he loved his little girl and, although Laura heard his verbal attacks on her mother, she never once considered he might be hitting her. He made sure none of his bullying and abuse happened in front of Laura, not the shouting, not the humiliating, and certainly not the punching. He did it in the evening, after dark, when he thought his daughter was safely tucked up in bed. He was not the only wife beater to act that way. Anna had said the same about Harry Pelham – he only hit her when Martha was not around to witness it.

But from her bedroom, Laura could hear her father's hectoring, intimidating voice. She would get up and creep closer, listen to him rant at her mother, telling her how stupid and worthless she was, laying down the law about who she could talk to, and where she could go. It upset Laura but it also irritated her. She wished her mother would fight back, would stop letting herself be such a victim. If she would only stand up for herself, her father would back off, Laura was sure.

She felt guilt flood her, the way it always did when she remembered her young, self-righteous self. She should have done more to help her mum, she should have confronted her father. She should have understood. She had never been able to forgive herself for not realizing how serious the abuse was. She had never heard anything that sounded like violence and her mum had done her utmost to hide it, but that was no excuse. She should have known.

A memory came to her, stark and raw, of the morning a starling had fallen down the chimney and got trapped in the living room. She called out for her mum to rescue it, but when there was no response, ran upstairs to find her. Her mum was in the bathroom and nine year old Laura burst in just as she was getting out of the shower. Her buttocks, hips and breasts were covered in yellow, black and blue bruises. She saw the shock on her daughter's face and immediately related a story of how she had tripped at the top of the library steps and fallen heavily down them. She must have had the story ready always, just in case. Laura knew that now but at the time she hadn't questioned it, had all but forgotten it in the excitement of freeing the panicky bird. Laura's mum never again left the bathroom door unlocked.

It was years later that Laura had to face the truth and it left her in bits. She was living in London and in the middle of her law exams when her mother was diagnosed with breast cancer. The doctor who found it, also found serious bruising, vaginal and anal scarring and signs of old injuries. She had rung Laura, and the police, to say she suspected domestic abuse.

Jenny Maxwell left her husband but refused to give evidence against him and he was never charged. She came to live with Laura for nine months while she sorted out her life and beat off the cancer, but she would never speak about the violence however gently her daughter raised it. Just once, when Laura was going cautiously round the houses trying to approach the subject, she interrupted sharply, 'Never let yourself be a victim. Never. That's all I'll say.'

A year later, when Laura was twenty five, the cancer came back and this time Jenny Maxwell lost the battle. In an agony of guilt and regret, Laura wondered if the years of abuse had brought it on in the first place and whether, if she had realized what was going on and had spoken out, her mum would still be alive.

Laura forced the thoughts away. She picked up a dog-eared business card from her desk. It had the details for the Tunisian lawyer and she called his number.

CHAPTER TEN

The police guard made it impossible to get near Harry Pelham without explaining who he was and the reason for his visit. Ben Morgan had no intention of doing either. He'd had dealings with the police before and he didn't want to renew the experience. He had been lucky to miss them at Harry's house the day before and he had been lucky again to find out about the guard before it was too late. He arrived at the ward to find Harry nowhere in sight, so he asked a nurse for directions. She pointed to a side room and told him he'd have to ask the police officers if he could see Harry. There were two of them and one was standing outside the door to the room.

'Why are they here?' he asked.

'No idea. All I know is any visitor has to get their permission if they want to talk to him.'

'Do you think they'll be staying long?

She shrugged, then said, 'He's lucky he's not handcuffed to one of them.'

Ben laughed nervously at that and the nurse said she wasn't joking. She had heard them talking about it but, in the end, they'd decided not to.

'Are you family?' she peered at him curiously, as if he might be related to a serial killer. He was late thirties maybe, tall and skinny with a patchy beard and pale, restless eyes.

'No' he hesitated, and when she obviously wanted more, said, 'Just a friend.'

'Looks like he needs one.'

'Would you be able to give him a note for me?'

Her eyes narrowed suspiciously. She didn't reply and started walking towards the policeman.

Ben Morgan turned the other way and fled, making himself walk at a normal pace. Then he heard the nurse call to him and he ran down the stairs and out of the building, hurrying away from the hospital as fast as he could.

He jogged for fifteen minutes along the sea front until he came to a bar beside Brighton beach. He went inside and asked for an orange juice. He didn't dare risk alcohol. He ordered a sandwich but was too wound up to eat it. He sat by the window staring out to sea. It was wild today, whipped up by a strong onshore wind which had blown away the earlier rain. He could feel his high mood turning sour. He was edgy and irritable, frustrated that he hadn't been able to talk to Harry.

'I do not have to get angry over this,' he muttered, 'I am choosing not to get angry. Just chill out.'

Ben Morgan had been in Brighton for almost a month now. He had forced himself to be cautious and to check out the situation thoroughly before making his move. For once, everything he had done had been carefully planned. He was pleased with himself about that. He hadn't jumped straight in with both feet and no thought as to the consequences. He had a habit of doing that when he was feeling good, he knew, and it needed to be controlled.

The medication did control it pretty well but he wasn't always so good about taking it; it had been a bit random lately. He noticed that his right leg was bouncing up and down on the floor and with an effort he stilled it and took a few deep breaths to try to calm himself down. He recognized the signs. The anger, the desire for action, the ideas racing through his head, the total confidence in himself. He had learned to be wary of these things. Learned the hard way.

He had been watching Laura Maxwell, following her, studying her routines and gathering details about her life. When he first arrived he had stood across the road from Morrison Kemp waiting for her to come out. What a shock it had been to see her again, what nightmare feelings the sight of her had aroused, feelings he had tried to bury deep but which kept bubbling back to the surface. The experience had literally made him ill. He had scuttled away and been sick in an alleyway.

Ben Morgan felt sick now thinking about what had happened to him. And Harry's case was so similar to his own – his torture, at the hands of Laura Maxwell, so exactly what Ben had endured. When he had discovered that, he had wanted to die. It brought back, in technicolour, all the trauma of six years ago.

Well this time the result would be different, he would make sure of that. He had been there and would not stand by and let it happen again. Hatred and bitterness filled him. He was going to put a stop to it, once and for all.

Ben Morgan shook his head and tried, unsuccessfully, to get the ugly memories to go away. The Maxwell woman had made him seem like a complete danger to his young daughter, a father with a serious personality disorder. His medical notes had been taken to pieces by her, selective quotes taken from his psychology sessions, from his psychiatric assessments, from his previous medical history – he had been destroyed as a person and as a father. She had consigned him to hell.

He had sat in court listening to her make judgments about him, biased judgments designed to make him suffer, along with social workers and other so called experts who discussed his bipolar disorder, discussed his behaviour and thoughts and emotions as if he were invisible, as if they were able to understand what was going on in his head. The whole inside of his mind had been invaded by her – someone who knew nothing about him or his illness. He had been violated and degraded and he felt it again now just as keenly as he had done at the time. The taste of acid filled his mouth.

He remembered how tormented he had been over what to do about it, what action he should take. Sometimes it had been so bad it was like a physical pain. It had only got better when he had stopped thinking about possible consequences and started following his instincts. But that, of course, had not worked out well. He had stabbed a police officer, been sectioned for hospital treatment, and lost all contact rights to his daughter.

The bar was starting to fill up with the lunchtime rush. He hated crowds and noise. They stressed him out and could trigger off his illness. He wanted to run. It was one of the few strategies he had for coping with stressful situations – to run through the streets, faster and faster, until all he could think about was the burning in his lungs and his legs. He liked to think it was a positive thing, a definite plan to help himself, but in his darker moods he felt that all it amounted to was running away.

The afternoon was cold and the rain was spitting again. Ben Morgan stood for a moment gazing up uncertainly at the heavens with a tense and troubled face. Then he set off at high speed for his appointment, his tall, thin figure racing towards the café near the crumbling West Pier.

CHAPTER ELEVEN

The Tunisian lawyer, Karim Chehoudi, did remember Laura and he was happy to help. She was grateful and agreed to meet him for dinner next time he visited London. He knew much more about child abduction cases than she did and she noticed he was careful not to raise her hopes of success too much. Given that he wanted the dinner date, he was probably trying to sound as optimistic as possible, and secretly rated her chances as zero.

She gave him the details for Ahmed and his father, sent him their photographs, and he promised to pass them on to the Tunisian immigration authorities with a request to be informed if the pair left the country. If they went anywhere which had signed the Hague Convention it might be possible to intercept them there and get the boy returned to England.

Karim Chehoudi said he had good contacts among the immigration officers and assured her he knew how to get them to take his request seriously. Laura wondered if he meant money and whether she should offer to pay for any necessary expenses. But she worried he might take offence so she said nothing except how much she appreciated his help. He sounded pleased and she hoped she had done the right thing. Now she could only wait and keep her fingers crossed that the chance came up. It was all she could do for Mary Hakimi. She thought that it wasn't very much.

There was an email from Anna in her inbox asking if she could find out from the police how long Harry was going to be in hospital and how long he would be held for questioning. Anna desperately wanted reassurance that action would be taken to protect her and Martha before, as she put it, 'that vile man is on the loose again.' Laura had called her earlier to tell her the news from Barnes, and Anna had been very shocked and disgusted to hear what her husband was suspected of.

'I can't have him seeing Martha anymore, Laura, I just can't,' she sobbed down the phone. 'Really, I couldn't cope with that. It makes me wonder if ... '

Anna hadn't been able to finish the sentence but Laura knew what she was wondering. Had Harry ever abused his daughter? He had never been violent towards Martha, Anna had said, but what else might he have been doing?

Laura pulled a bundle of papers from the Pelham file, details of Harry's financial affairs. There were property developments, options for building projects, company directorships and various bank accounts, a number of them overseas. Some of these had slipped his mind when he'd listed his financial resources for the court. Anna had filled in the gaps and Laura was preparing to raise the discrepancies at the next hearing. Anna knew that Harry was concealing large amounts of money and had done her best to gather evidence to prove it.

'He's been cheating and hiding things for years,' Anna had said in one emotional outburst. 'He thinks I don't know but I do and I want the judge to know exactly how mean and deceitful he is.'

Laura warned against personal abuse or appearing too vindictive because it didn't go down well. Of course, Harry must be honest about his financial resources and if there was evidence that he was not, the court would take that very seriously. But the judge wouldn't be interested in dishing out blame or hearing vitriolic attacks by one partner on the other. The court's sole aim, after ensuring Martha's welfare, would be to achieve a fair settlement between husband and wife. It wanted compromise not retribution.

It was Laura's duty to advise Anna of these things, it was up to Anna if she took any notice. She didn't. Laura may as well have been talking a foreign language that she didn't speak a word of. Anna was haunted by the terror that if she showed the slightest weakness, the slightest sign of wavering, he would take advantage and somehow return to controlling and manipulating her.

'If I ever told him "no" he wouldn't accept it. He just insisted on what he wanted until my "no" became a feeble "yes". I didn't know how to stand up to him, but never again,' she said.

It was the reason Anna at first refused point blank to take part in mediation.

'I'm scared stiff of meeting him again, Laura, he'll just try to get power over me.'

Laura did eventually manage persuade her to give mediation a try but it had gone badly. Laura had not been there but heard about it from Anna. Harry was loud and domineering, wanting everything done his own way. Seeing his behaviour again at close quarters had triggered her intense fear of him.

She had screwed up her courage and told the mediator how she'd been forced to leave home because of his increasing violence. She hadn't known what he might do next or if Martha was safe. Harry went mental over that, Anna said, shouting that he'd never hit anyone and would never harm his daughter.

The mediator had tried to get the session back on track and to talk about important things that needed resolving, such as Martha's future, and her financial arrangements, but Harry had started accusing Anna of having an affair, calling her a slut and demanding to know how many other men she'd slept with during their marriage. Anna had surprised herself then; for a moment she'd forgotten to be frightened. She fought back, defiantly giving details of her husband's extreme, mindless jealousy.

He was obsessed with the idea that she had a lover. He'd bugged the entire house. The telephone, the toilets, every room had been wired for sound. She hadn't even been able to visit the bathroom without being recorded. There'd been a couple of cameras, one hidden in a clock, the other in a smoke alarm. He'd read her emails, monitored her mobile phone calls. He'd even tested her clothes for semen stains with something called a semen detection kit.

The mediation had come to a swift, unhappy end. Afterwards, Anna became even more determined to stand her ground.

Laura once asked Anna why she had married Harry.

Anna hesitated, then said, 'There was a boy I loved, when I was young, but it didn't work out,' she paused again, 'then Harry came along. He was strong and he said he loved me and no one had ever said that before. It made me feel happy and safe and I liked it. Of course I didn't understand then why I liked it and that I wasn't safe at all.'

She realized now that she had liked it because of her own neediness and low self-esteem. She'd never had any confidence, had been badly bullied at school; it was like she attracted abusers. She thought Harry Pelham had sniffed her out as a victim and homed in on her as someone he could dominate and control.

The phone rang. It was Morrison, abruptly summoning Laura to his office. She had been waiting for it, she'd been lucky to get away without seeing him the previous afternoon. He would have been expecting an update on Mary Hakimi. He would be annoyed that he'd had to ask.

As she arrived, Sarah was coming out. Laura said 'Hi' but Sarah brushed past with her face averted.

Morrison gestured towards a chair. He provided two sorts of chair for his visitors; which one they were offered depended on their status. Important clients, and people he was on friendly terms with, were ushered into a large, comfortable leather armchair which mirrored the one on his side of the desk. Laura had first sat in it when she came for a 'chat' – there had been nothing so crude as a job interview – about moving to Morrison Kemp from her prestigious London firm. She had occupied it on every occasion since. But today she was faced with the other one, a small, hard, functional chair that was lower than Morrison's so that anyone offered it, unless they were a giant, would find themselves having to look up into the cold grey eyes opposite.

Laura was not very tall and she realized at once how effective the chair was in making its occupant feel inferior. The familiar, uncomfortable impression was upon her that he thought she wasn't quite up to the mark, that he had expected great things from her, which she had not delivered. She shifted in the chair, trying to find a position in which she could relax, in which she didn't feel like an underperforming pupil in front of the headmaster. She was wearing her glasses but they weren't helping much.

He leaned towards her, putting his elbows on the desk and his hands underneath his chin. 'So,' he said softly, 'the Hakimi fiasco. What have you got to tell me?'

The shrewd little eyes fixed on her as if she was a specimen in a jar. She considered asking him what Sarah had told him, but decided not to – he was unlikely to tell her and would interpret the question as a sign of weakness.

'I've talked the problem through with Mary Hakimi and assured her we'll do all we can to get her son back. Obviously she's very distressed but she agreed that was the best way forward for now.'

'And how exactly do you plan to get the boy back?' He made no effort to hide the scepticism in his voice.

Laura told him. As she spoke his eyebrows rose and his lips set in a thin line.

'Snowball's chance,' he said dismissively.

'Well, yes, I know it's a long shot but there might … ' Laura stopped. It was stupid to start justifying herself; it would only further undermine her. She changed what she had been going to say. 'I felt it was really important to demonstrate that we cared and we wanted to help.'

'We always care about our clients, Laura. You'll be aware that that is one of the guiding principles at Morrison Kemp.'

'I was quite honest with her,' Laura continued, 'I told her I couldn't promise anything.'

'Of course, you were honest with her. I hope you've been honest with her at all times, Laura.' He paused, took off his glasses and put them down on the desk. He sat up straight in his chair and leaned further towards her. 'I trust she understands that this firm is not to blame in any way for what's happened?'

He was waiting for her to dig herself into a hole. She guessed Sarah had told him she had given the forged letter to Mary Hakimi because, so far as Sarah knew, that was what she'd done. She also guessed that he would deny ever telling Sarah to write the letter and was busy distancing himself from the whole thing. She wondered if he had come to some arrangement with Sarah and if that arrangement meant dumping the blame for the deception squarely on Laura. If he believed she had handed over the letter, he would realize at once that it made her vulnerable. He would be licking his lips at the sight of a scapegoat.

'Absolutely. I hope I was able to convince her of that. By the way,' Laura added, smiling sweetly at him, 'do you still want Sarah Cole fired? I met her coming out of your office just now and I was hoping you might've had second thoughts.'

He retreated across the desk, replacing his glasses on his hawkish nose. He sat back in his big chair, steepled his fingers together and frowned.

'I'm afraid she told me a very worrying thing which I don't think can be right.'

Laura waited, not asking. He wanted her to, but she wasn't going to give him the satisfaction. He'd have to tell her anyway if he was going to put the blame on her. It didn't take long.

'She says Mrs Hakimi was never sent a letter telling her to remind us about the passport order. She tells me that a copy of a letter to that effect, which you gave to Mrs Hakimi yesterday, was in fact a fake and you were well aware of that when you gave it to her.'

It was what she had expected but she still felt shocked that he could be so shameless. How did he sit there and brazenly ignore the truth of what had happened? He showed no sign of embarrassment or regret. Instinctively, she knew what his reaction would be if she reminded him of his involvement. He would give her that thin-lipped, patronising smile and she would hear him whisper, 'I think you must be mistaken, Laura, and I think I've been mistaken about you.' Then he would throw her to the wolves.

A large part of her wanted to do it, wanted to confront him, make him show his true colours and then, when he had behaved in the despicable way she knew he would, bring her rabbit out of the hat and tell him that his informant was wrong, that no letter had been handed over. It would humiliate him and he deserved it. But she knew it was a step too far. He would not forgive it and she would have made a dangerous enemy.

'Sarah must be confused. I certainly didn't give Mrs Hakimi any such letter,' she told him.

There was a flicker of puzzlement on his face but he recovered fast. He was smart as well as devious.

'Let me get this straight. Sarah brought you a letter but you didn't hand it over?'

'That is correct.' She took off the heavy spectacles and put them in her jacket pocket. Never again would she let herself be intimidated by this man. She stood up. 'Is that all,' she said. It wasn't a question.

He looked up at her from his big chair. There was something like admiration in his eyes. Worse than his contempt, she thought. It gave her the creeps.

CHAPTER TWELVE

Morrison decided to fire Sarah himself late on Friday afternoon. He told her to clear her desk and leave the building at once. She had gone, but not quietly. Most of the office heard her bitter parting words. Laura wasn't among them because she'd been busy with a development in the Pelham case, and that was just as well because many of them were aimed at her. They included 'dumped on', 'betrayed' and 'up herself.'

Barnes had called to say the police guard on Harry was being withdrawn – he'd been given bail which included a condition that he stayed away from his wife and daughter. It might be some small comfort for Anna, Laura thought.

It was Morrison who let her know what he'd done or at least his version of it. He had told Sarah that forging the letter was inexcusable. He had explained that it was dishonest and therefore he could not give her a second chance though he would, as he termed it, 'in the interests of all concerned' give her a generous pay-off and a glowing reference. Presumably he hoped this would be enough to buy her silence on the matter. He had also told her that, but for Laura's good sense, the firm would be in deeper trouble than it already was because of her original mistake. Laura winced. She could imagine what else Morrison had said. In his poisonous way he would have left Sarah in no doubt that Laura was to blame for what had happened to her.

'Good riddance,' he said in a cheerful tone, rubbing his hands together. The hiss and whisper of the morning were gone.

'Now,' he continued, 'I've been meaning to talk to you about the Law Society dinner next week. I'd like you to come. Good chance for you to get to know the people who matter in this part of the world.'

Jesus, she thought, what it was to be back in favour. She forced a smile, told him she'd be delighted to go.

But that was next week and this was Saturday morning and Saturday mornings belonged to Valentine. There he was at the stable door, looking out for her, excited and eager to be off on a ride. He was a little bit wild and mad and she loved him for that. The stables' owner, Michael Donoghue, had nicknamed him 'Crazy Horse'. Sometimes, when they were galloping over the Downs, she wasn't sure who was in charge, but he never frightened her and never let her fall.

She had agreed with Michael that others could ride him during the week but she knew he wasn't popular – a lot had tried him and never asked for him again. He took lorries, tractors, busy roads in his stride but, if he didn't like the rider, he could be difficult. He would get a wicked look in his eye and do his best to scare them half to death.

Laura had been riding since she was eight, but never before had she known a horse quite like Valentine. It was as if they were made for each other and he seemed as happy with her as she was with him. He could read her mind, she thought, could understand her. They flew across the hills together as one being.

Joe had given her Valentine as a birthday present just after they'd moved to Sussex. She had protested; said it was too much, but Joe insisted, telling her that now he was a partner in Greene's he could afford it. It was the first time in his life he'd had any money and he wanted to spoil her. Together they set off to find the perfect horse. As it happened, it hadn't taken long for Valentine was only the second horse they looked at. Laura knew the moment she met him that he was the one.

'What shall we call him?' she'd asked.

Joe had rolled his eyes at her.

'Come on, honey, you must know the answer to that one. Or am I just a hopeless romantic?'

And then she'd got it, of course. Her birthday was on Valentine's Day. His name, no doubt about it, was Valentine.

As she reached the stable, the horse moved his head towards her. The white star on his forehead – the only part of him that wasn't a deep glossy black – nuzzled against her arm, then her pockets for the peppermints he knew would be there. She gave him one and stroked his neck.

'It's been a shit week, Valentine, and I've been so looking forward to seeing you,' she told him.

It was a cold, windy morning in late October and maybe the wind was upsetting him because he seemed more restless than usual or maybe he'd had a shit week too, bored because no one wanted to ride him. The sooner she was on his back and racing across the downland, the happier they both would be and the sooner her mind could blow away the troubles of the last few days.

Laura leapt up into the saddle. She expected Valentine to be away at once but he stayed put. She had to squeeze with her legs and gently kick her heels to get him to move. It was odd; usually she never had to urge him on.

'What's wrong?' she said in his ear, bending forward and letting the reins go slack. But whatever the trouble was, he seemed to get over it and trotted through the field towards the start of the trail through the woods. She relaxed and sat back as he began to canter. He knew the way. First the woodland track leading out on to the Downs, then a fast and furious gallop across open country towards the sea.

They were reaching the end of the bridle path through the woods. The chill wind was bringing leaves tumbling from the trees. The early frost had gone and the ground had softened.

Ahead the view opened up and Valentine sniffed at the sea air and quickened his pace.

Valentine was flying now. Galloping at top speed across the side of the hill, the springy turf flashing beneath his hooves. She felt a buzz go through her, a thrill of excitement, she was carefree and untamed and on top of the world. She let out a yell of exhilaration, and the horse, who'd heard it before, went faster still.

They reached a fence that was the barrier between the downland and some rough woodland that led to the sea and Valentine gathered himself and soared across it. This was their secret. It was where they broke the rules. They were not supposed to cross the fence, the land on the other side was private and out of bounds to horse riders. But they always went this way, because once across the fence, they could take a shortcut through the gorse and trees which led out to a glorious stretch of clifftop riding.

The wind blew strong off the sea, howling in their ears. Together they slowed the pace and Valentine turned sharp left along a narrow path through the woods. It was a stony, uneven track and he had to pick his way carefully along until gradually it became a wider trail between tall trees, the grass underfoot nibbled short by rabbits.

He picked up speed again. This was the run up to the start of the clifftop gallop. She sat forward and called to him over the sound of the wind, 'Go, Valentine, Go.'

The slope was levelling out and he ate up the ground. She saw the end of the trail, no more than fifty yards away now, leading out to the grassland on the top of the hill. She felt a blast of pleasure, anticipating the best bit of the ride just ahead.

Laura had no idea what hit them. One moment they were galloping out of the woodland towards the open ground, the next she was thrown from Valentine's back with the force of a giant catapult. She hurtled through the air, instinctively curling her body into a ball, knowing that if she put out an arm to break the fall, she would break the arm.

She landed hard against the hillside with all the breath knocked out of her. She lay still, gasping for air then doubling up with the sudden pain of it. She felt a stab of fear. A fall like that could kill her, she thought stupidly, could break her neck.

She tried moving her head. She remembered a blow on her riding hat when she'd hit the earth, but luckily it hadn't been a big one, hopefully not enough for a head injury or concussion. But what about her spine? Her backside and left side of her body had jarred heavily against the ground.

She twisted her neck slowly from side to side. She couldn't feel any pain. Gently she shrugged her shoulders up and down and then, very tentatively, raised the top half of her body from the earth. She sat up, heart racing, breathing heavily. Her ribs screamed and a jolt of pain shot through her left thigh and up her back.

She stretched out her legs. They seemed to be working properly but the movement sent another wave of pain up her back. And then she saw something, something which made her forget all about herself. Her stomach churned.

He was lying on his side about fifteen feet away, his head towards her. He wasn't making a sound but she knew he was scared, very scared. She could see the whites of his eyes. As she watched, he struggled to get to his feet. He didn't make it. He crashed back down to the ground.

She stood up and went over to him, not noticing her own pain. She looked in horror at his left foreleg. A length of barbed wire was wrapped around the top of it, the spikes embedded in the leg; the skin was torn and bleeding.

'Oh Valentine,' she whispered, panic rising. With an effort, she stifled the sobs that were building in her chest. They would only make him more frightened.

She sat down beside him, tears filling her eyes, and without thinking, put out her hand to stroke the white star on his forehead. In his terror, the movement startled him. He recoiled from her, his body thrashing, and he tried desperately to stand up.

Again he fell back, the vicious wire gouging deeper into his leg. A pool of blood gathered on the ground. He lay still and the panic spiked in her again.

'Don't give in,' she told him, 'just don't give in.'

She took off her riding jacket, wincing at the pain in her shoulders and back. She found a sharp stone and tore out the lining. Slowly, so as not to scare him again, she knelt beside his injured foreleg and tied the lining firmly round it to try to stop the bleeding.

She had to get him on his feet and she had to do it fast. She knew about horses, how easily they could give up the fight if they couldn't stand. A phrase came back to her from a long ago riding lesson, 'if they're down, they're out'.

She crept round to the top of his head, put her hands underneath it and lifted gently. Then she took the reins, brought them over his head, and pulled his head towards her making him push himself up with his hind legs.

'Come on, old boy, you can do it,' she encouraged.

He made it on the third attempt and Laura's spirits soared, briefly, before sinking again.

He was standing, yes, but only on three legs. He was holding his right foreleg, the one without the barbed wire, suspended in the air. She guessed it was broken.

Reluctantly, she pulled her mobile from her jacket pocket. He was looking at her with those wild eyes of his and, she thought, he knows what is going to happen. She wanted very much to tell him that it wouldn't, that he would be all right, but she didn't because she knew it was a lie. She had an urgent desire to make the call in private, some place he couldn't hear. Absurdly, she backed away a few feet from him.

She made the call, choking out the words, but the line was bad and the wind was rattling through the trees and Grace, the stable girl who answered the phone, didn't seem to follow what she was saying. She repeated it all at the top of her voice but even then

Grace was confused. She kept asking exactly where they were and why they had left the proper route.

Laura started to lose it, shouting at Grace to 'get the fucking vet out here now'. Abruptly she stopped, forced herself to give clear instructions, to make certain Grace understood. When the call was over she put her head in her hands and sobbed, replaying the accident in her head, trying to work out what had happened. It occurred to her then that she should take photos of the scene. Holding her mobile in shaky hands, she focused, half blind, through weeping eyes.

She knew she must stop crying as it would only upset Valentine more. She must grit her teeth for him and stay quietly with him until the vet arrived. She couldn't do much for him but she could do that. She could try to comfort him, make sure nothing startled him, stop him from moving about and making his injuries worse.

She wiped her eyes with her sleeve and stood next to the horse, waiting, all the time talking softly to him and trying to put from her mind thoughts of the inevitable – the vet arriving, seeing the horse, fetching the gun from his bag …

Valentine trembled, nostrils red and flared, ears flat. Sweat poured off his flanks and neck and head. But she didn't need to see these signs. She could feel his fear, and however much she tried to hide it, she thought that he could feel hers. She looked at her watch, wished that the vet would arrive, then wished that he wouldn't. Just a few more minutes, she said out loud, then wished that she hadn't.

CHAPTER THIRTEEN

Joe lay in bed and watched her sleeping next to him. She had put him on cloud nine and he was in no rush to come down. She was beautiful in a way he found it hard to describe. It was not a classical, regular beauty but a striking and overpowering one and it took his breath away. She had a long face with a strong chin, full lips and startling green eyes set far apart so that sometimes, in the half dark, she looked like a cat. But it was more than her looks that excited him, it was her whole nature. Her passion, her sense of fun, her interest in every little bit of his life and the way, when he talked to her about it, she listened as if he was saying the most fascinating things in the world. She made him feel good, like a drug – a drug he couldn't get enough of.

She opened her eyes, saw him looking at her. He smiled, raised an eyebrow at her in that hot, suggestive way that so many women had found irresistible.

'I love your smile,' she purred, touching her fingers to his lips, drinking him in. He kissed her and she pulled him down towards her, putting her hand behind his head and twisting her fingers in his hair. He felt her tongue on his teeth, in his mouth, and he closed his eyes, totally lost to her.

Of course, he had missed the business meeting and he was annoyed with himself for doing so. Why he had thought he could visit her and still make it, God alone knew. Things had not worked out that way, of course they hadn't. Once he was in bed with her, he never rushed away.

He and his brother were due to see some American tour operators who, if handled right, could deliver a lot of custom to the Greene hotel chain. Joe was good at chatting up clients. His looks, his charm and his ability to put on a show, paid dividends. The Americans were on a tight schedule and Saturday morning was the only time they had free, so now brother Peter would have to do it on his own and it was not his strong point.

Joe texted Peter with the excuse that he was coming down with flu. Peter replied immediately, furious, calling Joe unreliable, saying it was a pity that he couldn't even deliver on one of his few assets, his PR skills. Words like erratic, useless and disappointment were sprinkled through his angry texts. Joe switched off the phone. He really shouldn't have to put up with this.

'My brother needs to be a bit more savvy about being a salesman,' he said, frowning, 'Spend some time learning people skills instead of being pissed off at me.'

She trailed her fingers through the hair on his chest and gently stroked his neck. 'He shouldn't be pissed at you, sweetheart, he needs you. You can get him more business than he knows what to do with because you,' she kissed his chin, 'can charm the birds off the trees."

He looked down into the sparkling green eyes. No-one had ever made him feel this special. So, he had missed the meeting, upset Peter, but there were compensations. She had told him she was free until early evening. Laura would be at the stables for most of the day and he didn't think she would miss him. It meant they could spend the afternoon in bed together.

'I love the way you believe in me, honey. Makes me feel I could do anything in the world.'

'You can do, Joe. You can do whatever you want. And I will always be there to help. Always.

'In that case, I can never go wrong,' his blue eyes sparkled.

'Don't laugh,' she said, 'But I feel like we're soulmates.'

'Body as well as soul,' he said, kissing her hard on the lips.

It was nearly five when he looked at his watch and told her he should get going.

'You take care, honey,' he murmured, stroking her hair.

'Tell me you love me,' she said, hugging him close.

'You know I do. You know I'd do anything for you.'

When he had gone, her full lips curved into a wide smile. He had missed his important meeting because of her; he loved her and would do anything for her, anything at all. He was such a wonderful man, everything she had hoped he would be.

CHAPTER FOURTEEN

For Jeff Ingham it was one of his worst case scenarios. A badly
injured horse that should be put down as soon as possible, and a
traumatized woman refusing to let him do it. He had been here
before. He sighed.

As soon as he arrived he knew she was trouble. She spotted him
walking up the track and headed him off well before he reached the
horse. She shouted at him that she did not want the horse killed,
that before she would even consider it he would have to prove
beyond a shadow of a doubt that there was no other way. She made
him feel like he was in the dock, on a charge of horse-slaughter.

She was a mess herself, covered in mud, with her riding jacket
ripped at the shoulder, and blood down the left side of her trousers. Her hat was askew and her face streaked with dirt and tears.
She limped towards him, putting all her weight on her right leg,
looking very young and vulnerable. One hand clutched her ribs.
Clearly, it had been a bad fall for her too.

Reluctantly, she let him near the horse. He saw at once that it
was badly hurt. There might be a chance if it had only been the
one leg damaged by wire. The injuries there, though bloody, were
at the top of the leg where there was dense muscle. If infection
didn't set in, the wounds might be repaired with careful stitching.
But the other leg looked as if it was broken. The horse could put

no weight on it at all. Together, in his opinion, the injuries were a fatal combination.

Gently he explained it to her, ran through what he had to do and why he had to do it. Pauline, the veterinary nurse who had come out with him, put her arm around the woman's shoulders.

'Best to get it over with,' she said, 'He'll just suffer otherwise.'

The arm was furiously shaken off. The woman's hazel eyes glared at him and she said in a barely controlled voice: 'How bad is the break?'

He couldn't tell her that, not without an X-ray. Valentine was relaxed now with sedatives and painkillers and he examined the leg again. There were no obvious odd angles to indicate where the fracture was, or that any bones were displaced, but the skin was broken above the fetlock, a few drops of blood marking the spot. A place for infection to strike.

A sour ball of dread filled Laura's stomach as she watched the vet inspecting Valentine's injuries, his curly brown hair flopping over his forehead. He swept it back with his hand and straightened up, a set look on his open, freckled face. Laura thought, desperately, it was a kind face with kind, soft brown eyes. He would give Valentine a chance, surely. But that was a stupid thought. He was a professional, he would be used to this kind of situation, he would make a pragmatic decision.

She took hold of his arm, apologized for shouting at him earlier, apologized to the nurse for being rude. Then she politely introduced herself and told him that he probably thought her hysterical and unable to make a decision that would be best in the long term for Valentine, thought her too emotional to be objective.

It was so exactly what he did think that he had to smile.

'Please,' she said, 'I just have to be sure. Please let's take him back, X-ray him, treat him and then, if it's hopeless, I won't argue. I won't keep him alive if his life is a misery. I'm not that selfish.'

It was a difficult call. Until a few years ago a fractured leg was an automatic death sentence. It wasn't possible to put a horse's leg

76

in a plaster cast because of its size and the weight of the animal. But now that could be done and there were options.

The vet knew the chances of recovery were slim and that the process would be extremely stressful for the horse. The very things necessary for healing – confinement, inactivity, and drugs – could drive the creature mad. But there were success stories and Valentine was young, young enough to heal if the break was not too bad.

'All right,' he said, 'We'll see. One thing. Are you insured? This could cost a lot. Thousands probably.'

She nodded, hope pulsing, not trusting herself to speak in case the tears came. It was true she had insurance though she knew it would be no use. She had been trespassing so it wouldn't pay out, but she wasn't going to tell him that. He looked around, searching for a route to bring in transport for the horse. Laura told him they would have to bring the trailer in across fields then down over the clifftop.

'It's all private land, Jeff, ' Pauline said. 'Grace at the stables said they shouldn't have been riding here. She was worried about it. Seems there's been some trouble between the landowner and the stables. Should we get permission?'

'No time,' he told her, 'We're taking too long as it is. Get the trailer here as fast as you can.'

The nurse set off down the path. Laura stood talking quietly to Valentine. Jeff Ingham went and stood beside her, holding his vet's bag. He put it down, opened it, took out the splints and bandages. Beneath them lay the gun, the gun that would have ended Valentine's life. He saw her eyes flick over it, saw her flinch.

'How did the accident happen?' he asked.

She stared at him blankly for several seconds, 'I just don't know. It was so sudden. The wire … ' she trailed off.

'It must have been on the ground and got caught round his legs'

'Yes, I suppose so.'

'Not the usual riders' route is it? You never know what's been left lying around.'

As soon as he said it he regretted it. He hadn't meant to sound like he was blaming her but he could see from the hurt look on her face that she had taken it that way.

Together they began splinting the broken leg and he explained how it was done. He would have liked to talk to her about what lay ahead, to make it clear that she needed to make hard decisions. Even if Valentine could be saved, and that was a very big if, she could not afford to be sentimental.

He wanted to say that horses were meant to spend their lives in motion. It was their nature, their design. A horse kept alive but unable to move freely or take more than a few steps at a slow walk, had no quality of life. Valentine would hate the vulnerability that came with lameness and pain, the terror of being on insecure footing, of being unable to run away from possible threats. Mother Nature wasn't kind – horses with broken legs were not meant to be hospital patients, but dinner for local predators.

But he said none of it because he sensed she already understood and didn't need a lecture.

It took them more than half an hour to finish the splint. There was more equipment in the trailer and they did a thorough job. He couldn't be certain there were no displaced bones and he took great care to make sure there would be no chance of further damage on the journey back. He used two lengths of half rounded guttering pipes to make up the splint and wrapped around them a small mountain of cotton wool, bandages, bits of old towels and sheets, self-sticking veterinary wrap and nearly twenty rolls of various elastic tapes. At the end of it all, Valentine's lower leg was immobile, encased in a giant, many layered column.

Laura had seen these bandages before but had never been involved in making one. It was a 'Bob Jones' bandage, named for the World War One doctor who developed it, and it had used more materials than she had ever thought possible. Each layer, on its own, was not enough to stabilise a serious injury, but as successive layers were added and the padding was pulled tighter and tighter, the eventual result was a stiff cast. It was a first aid technique that could save a horse's life and increase the chances of long term recovery. She put all other thoughts aside and concentrated on getting it right.

After Pauline arrived back with the trailer and started helping with the bandage, Laura's job was to hold Valentine and keep him still. He'd been heavily sedated and cooperated well at first but as the wrapping continued he became panicky and it was hard to calm him.

When the splint was done, Jeff Ingham turned his attention to the other leg. As best he could, he cleaned and covered the wounds. He cut away the barbed wire as close to the leg as possible but left in the spikes – he said that if he pulled them out, the bleeding would get a whole lot worse.

Then they had to get Valentine into the trailer. Laura pulled him by the reins while the other two joined hands across his hind quarters. Using brute force they dragged and shoved him up the ramp.

She had been holding it together while she had work to do but now she couldn't stop the tears rolling down her face. The vet drove slowly across the bumpy ground, watching her in the rear-view mirror. She was slumped in the back seat, white-faced, leaning over to the right to try to minimize the pain from her ribs. She'd taken the painkillers he offered her but refused the sedative. He wanted to drop her at the stables so she could go to hospital, but she had refused that as well. Pauline argued with her but it did no good. She insisted she was going with them to the big veterinary clinic near Lewes where Valentine would be treated. They had given up trying to talk her out of it.

CHAPTER FIFTEEN

Joe had met her eight months ago at the nursing home by the sea where his mother was. Not the most romantic of meetings – she had been pushing a man in a wheelchair, an old neighbour of hers, she said, who she visited occasionally because his only relative, his son, lived in Canada and never came. She had lost control of the chair for a moment and it had run into the side of his mother's.

It had been one of those lovely, early spring days when you know for certain that winter is on the way out. Sunny with a light breeze but not enough to be cold and so he had taken his mother out into the gardens to sit and watch the sparkling sea. The chalk cliffs of the Seven Sisters towered above it, bright white in the sunlight. The blue of the water and the green of the downland stretched their rough sea beauty as far as the eye could see.

He had been entranced by her from the start. The sun gleamed on her blonde hair as it fell full and soft on her shoulders; she was slim but with an hourglass figure. She was wearing black figure-hugging jeans and high heels and he thought she would not look out of place on the catwalk. Later, when he thought about her, and he thought about her all the time, he described her in his own mind as 'stunning'.

After the wheelchair collision he had stood, staring at her, forgetting to speak. She had thought he was annoyed.

'I am so, so sorry,' she said, bending down to talk to his mother. 'Are you all right?' And then, looking up at him, she said shyly, 'women drivers' and he laughed. She always did make him laugh.

She had made a fuss of his mother and he liked her for that. So often his mother was ignored, as if, because she was in a wheelchair, she was no longer a human being capable of comprehending the world around her. Instead, the speaker would address him, across his mother's head, speaking of her in the third person. Not that his mother put up with it – she didn't, not for a second.

They had sat together on a bench looking out to sea, the wheelchairs parked on either side. The old man said nothing. He was deaf, she said, and suffering from dementia. The nurses had told her he was increasingly disturbed by frightening visions. He did not seem to know any longer who she was and she was worried her presence might upset him and make him anxious. She wasn't sure she should carry on visiting, but didn't like the idea he would have no one if she didn't come.

Joe had noticed her lips. They were gorgeous lips and he wondered what it would be like to kiss them and what colour her eyes were behind her sunglasses. He felt guilty to be thinking these things and to be fantasising about her, but he couldn't stop himself. At the time, and for months afterwards, he could think of nothing but how much he wanted her. There was no room in his mind for anything else.

Of course, he had asked to see her again and she had agreed. And there had begun the most intense, most intoxicating love affair of his life. She was emotional and unpredictable, he knew that, but she was also vulnerable, exciting, and loving. She made him feel powerful and alive.

It was a very different relationship to the one he had with Laura. Not just from the relationship now, which had been tainted for him by his affair, but from the one he'd had at the beginning, in the good times, when he wanted to stay with her forever, have children with her, grow old and wrinkled with her. How he had admired her; successful, determined, always together, Laura. She knew what she wanted and went all out to get it.

That was how it had been with him. She had come to see a play he was in, had recognized his name in the programme and talked to him afterwards. They'd met years ago, she said, when they were both still at school, had dated a couple of times. It made her laugh that it took him so long to remember. Clearly, the seventeen-year-old Laura hadn't made much of an impression on him, she joked.

It was only when she mentioned that he'd wanted to take some rather too sexy photos of her, that he'd smiled and the penny had dropped. He recalled that she had refused and he'd lost interest in her. He'd had other girlfriends who were more obliging.

After the meeting at the theatre she had been the one to get in touch, to chase. He was used to that. He was a good looking man and women came easily to him. But this had been special. Never before had he been chased by a high flying, high earning and highly desirable lawyer. He was flattered and pleased and he chased her back.

Laura worked hard for her success, worked the longest hours, took the cases that no one else wanted … and won them. He'd known her for six months before he realized why. She told him one night when she'd had too much to drink. It was a way of burying her demons, the guilt and self-doubt that had come to her with the knowledge of what her mother had endured while she had been blind to it. The harder she worked on other people's problems, the less she focused on her own; the higher she climbed up the greasy legal pole, the more chance she'd start believing in herself and her confident shell would morph into her real self. It had been a choice, she said, between work and the vodka bottle.

After a year or so, he had moved in to the house in central London that Laura owned. Two years after that, when his mother had her stroke, Laura had been keen, more than keen, to leave London and head for Sussex so that Joe could take up his new role with Greene's. The demons were in retreat and she was ready to move on with her life.

They married, sold the London house, and bought an old Sussex farmhouse just outside Rooks Green, a few miles from Brighton. Laura loved it – the change of pace, the countryside, and best of all, catching up again with friends she had almost lost touch with in her frenetic London life. He loved it too; it had given him a new start on a more equal footing with his wife.

Gradually, almost without realizing it, Joe had grown less enamoured of Laura's success, less willing to bask in her reflected glory, less willing to accompany her to the legal functions she needed to attend. As his own career went nowhere, it became an irritation. But once they were out of London and he had a business to run, it stopped bothering him.

It was a very different problem now. He had loved Laura, had never meant to cheat on her. He had not wanted to, he told himself, it had just happened and there was absolutely nothing he could have done about it. It wasn't his fault.

One thing was sure, it could not go on much longer, this double life. He might be an actor, albeit an unsuccessful one, but it was a part he couldn't play anymore. It was well past time for the curtain to come down.

In the last few days Laura's life had done a rare thing – it had skittered a little bit out of her control. She had been scared, put on the back foot and she'd needed his support. It had made him think hard about what he was doing.

He stared at himself in the mirror. 'What am I becoming?' he muttered. Only a monster would behave the way he was. And he was not a monster. Was he?

CHAPTER SIXTEEN

Blood bubbled from the holes as Jeff Ingham wielded a pair of pliers and pulled the spikes of barbed wire from Valentine's flesh. He stitched and dressed the wounds. There was a lot of tissue damage and he was worried about infection.

All the time that he and the rest of the surgical team worked Laura stayed with them, assisting wherever she could. She didn't say much, just asked a few details about what they were doing. In her mind, lurking behind her immediate fear and grief for the horse, was suspicion: suspicion that what had happened was not an accident at all, an uneasy, intuitive feeling that would not go away.

The vet had done the X-rays and she watched him studying the pictures that would show how bad the break was, nervously awaiting his verdict. He ran a hand through his unruly hair, turning the pictures around, frowning in concentration.

'I can't be sure,' he said. 'There's some good news. No evidence of a major break or a multiple break or a shattered bone. With a bit of luck it might be a fairly simple fracture, maybe even a hairline one. But there's some serious swelling near the knee where the skin is broken.'

He guessed any fracture was hidden by the swelling, saying it was often difficult to see the break straight away. After ten days or so, when it started to heal, it would be easier to spot on an X-ray because the new bone forming at the fracture site would show up.

'We should wait then?' she asked eagerly. 'Give him a chance.'

His answer was brutally frank.

'I have to tell you that Valentine is a very sick horse. Because of the number and combination of his injuries there is a high risk of infection in one or both of his legs. Even if he avoids that, there are other major complications that may occur. His road to recovery will be hard and it's likely to distress him badly.

'He'll need at least eight weeks of box rest for his cut leg. As for his fractured leg, on the best outcome, it's likely to be a year before he can walk on it properly again. He'll be immobile and probably on painkillers for much of that time. It would not be the wrong decision to put him to sleep. You shouldn't feel guilty about it.'

'Would it be the wrong decision to keep him alive?' she asked quietly.

He hesitated. 'No, I wouldn't say that. As long as you're willing to pull the plug if things go badly, if he's suffering and can't stand the strain.'

Laura imagined Valentine going crazy because of her misguided effort to save him, because she was too stubborn and too self-centred to see sense.

'I understand and I will do that,' she promised.

She stayed with them another hour. Valentine had had a full anaesthetic and to get him upright again, and keep him upright so that the fracture could be joined, he had to be put in a full body sling. She watched as 560 kilograms of unconscious horse was hoisted into the air and gently manoeuvred into the sling. It was a strange and unnerving sight and it left her full of doubt.

It seemed to take forever to get it right. His hindquarters must be properly supported so he would not tip backwards out of the sling. His weight must be evenly distributed and the multiple straps adjusted to avoid pressure points on his abdomen. He would be in the sling for some time and there were many dangers: his lungs could get compressed and congested; his digestion could be upset giving him colic; he could develop bad pressure sores. He would have to get used to sleeping in the sling and having his meals fed on a platform.

When it was finally done Valentine stood immobile, dead to the world, his abdomen and chest supported by the contraption. The team began to unravel the Bob Jones bandage, then they would put a plaster cast on his leg.

Laura stood up to go. On tiptoe, she kissed the white star on Valentine's forehead.

'You'll make it,' she whispered to the unconscious horse, swallowing hard on the lump rising in her throat, and limped out of the stable.

CHAPTER SEVENTEEN

The clinic's receptionist, relaxing after the morning surgery, saw Laura coming towards her and smiled. The arrival of Valentine and his battered rider, determined to save him, had been a major excitement. The receptionist was keen to hear full details of the drama straight, so to speak, from the horse's mouth. She was disappointed. Laura, in pain and obsessed by the suspicion nagging at her mind, just asked if she'd mind calling a minicab then rapidly disappeared into the ladies toilet.

Her left hip and her back hurt like hell and so did breathing; if she breathed in too deep her ribs shrieked in pain. She took off her riding hat and washed the dirt from her face. Her hair was tangled and sweaty. She found a gash on the side of her leg which had bled a lot on her jodhpurs. It looked quite deep but it wasn't bleeding much anymore, so she cleaned it with some toilet paper and forgot about it. There was something she had to do and none of these injuries was going to stop her.

She called Joe again, and again he didn't answer. She texted him and left another message telling him about the accident. That word again. When the vet had said it, out on the hillside, it had hit her like a jet of cold water. Suddenly she had known, without any doubt whatsoever, that it had been no accident. But the certainty had faded and now she couldn't be so sure. She was left with a feeling of unease and misgiving and an urgent need to know the truth of it.

She scanned through the photos she'd taken of the scene, wincing as she saw the stricken horse. There was nothing obviously suspicious but she realized there were no detailed photographs of the exact spot where it had happened. Valentine's momentum had taken him some way further on and her pictures were mostly of the place where he had fallen to the ground. The rest were too general. She needed to go back for another look and she needed to do it now.

The minicab driver was the chatty type and the bedraggled state of his passenger interested him. He was full of questions and when he heard her answers, told her she should be looking after herself instead of traipsing round the countryside again. It would be better if he took her to hospital for a check-up – she said no – better if he took her home – politely, she refused – where was her husband then? Good question, she thought.

She asked him to drop her by the side of a narrow road across the top of the Downs from where, she judged, it was a short walk to the scene. He had given up arguing with her. He drove off, rolling his eyes in disapproval.

Laura looked around. There was no one in sight so she climbed over the fence, gritting her teeth at the pain from her ribs and her hip, and headed across the field towards the clifftop.

She found the place easily enough. There was no mistaking the dark patch of ground where Valentine's blood had spilled. It made her a little queasy. She began searching the area, examining the ground methodically, moving slowly back from the dark patch down the track into the woods.

Nothing. There was nothing to show that the fall was anything but an accident caused by her own stupidity. She knew she had been reckless to ride on private land where any kind of danger could be waiting. There was always a chance that a piece of barbed wire like the one that had brought down Valentine, would be left lying around. It was her own fault and she would have to accept it.

The afternoon was dark, getting darker all the time, and it would not be long before it was too dark to see. Adrenaline had kept her going but it was wearing off fast and tiredness was setting in. She'd eaten nothing since breakfast and her legs were like jelly. She leaned back against a tree and slid dejectedly down to the earth. Poor old Valentine, was she being crazy to keep him alive?

It was then that she saw it, half invisible in the growing dark. A piece of black rubber hosing tied around the trunk of a tree near the end of the track about two feet from the ground. Protruding from its end was a length of barbed wire. Across the track, around a tree on the other side, was another piece of black rubber hosing encasing another piece of barbed wire, a longer length this time with its end hanging loose on the ground. Laura's heart jolted in her chest and she shot to her feet, weariness forgotten.

Someone had strung the wire tight across the path. Someone had taken the trouble to put the ends in rubber hosing. Valentine had galloped full pelt straight into it and it had broken under his weight. Most had wrapped itself around his leg but the rest remained tied to the trees.

Fear pulsed through her. Who could have done such a thing and why had they done it? Her heart raced as she felt again that the fall had been no accident. Her intuition was back, telling her, loud and clear, that the barbed wire had been meant for her, had been meant to take her down.

She struggled to stay objective, took hold of her conclusion and tried to overturn it. What other reason could someone have for putting up that wire? Perhaps to stop motorbikes using the path, to deter poachers or other trespassers like herself. She could think up reasons but none of them satisfied her. It was a callous, thoughtless act and whoever had done it hadn't cared about the consequences, hadn't cared if they killed someone. Maybe they had wanted to kill someone. Maybe that someone was her.

She asked herself how it could possibly have been aimed at her. No-one knew she rode there – for obvious reasons she had never mentioned it at the stables. A creepy feeling came over her, one that made the little hairs stand up on the back of her neck. Could someone have been following her, watching her? She came this way every Saturday after all. She thought about the car chase, the troll on the website, Harry Pelham. He was in hospital but that didn't mean he couldn't have put up the wire a couple of days ago or got someone else to do it for him.

Her cold hands fumbled for her phone in her jacket pocket. She needed photos of the wires on the trees if she was going to prove anything.

In her jittery state, the angry voice behind her made her jump a mile high. She spun round to find a large, middle-aged man with a stick and an Alsatian, confronting her.

'Oi, this is private land,' he jabbed a finger at her. 'Clear off.'

Laura showed her palms defensively, 'I'm sorry, I'm not doing any harm, I'm just looking for something.'

He looked her over and what he saw seemed to make him more annoyed.

'Are you the silly cow who's caused all the fuss today?'

'Yes, I guess I probably am, I'm really sorry.'

'What are you doing back here again?' He came a step closer, 'Don't you know you've got no right to be here?'

'I do and I'm sorry but … '

'Donoghue told me what happened, told me it was one idiot rider who will be barred from the stables. I told him, and I'm telling you now, if you or anyone else ever comes here again, I'll prosecute. Do you understand?'

'I almost died this morning and my horse probably will die and I wanted to find out what made us fall,' Laura was unable keep a tremor from her voice.

'It's your own stupid fault for riding where you shouldn't. Now I've asked you to leave. I won't ask politely again.'

'There was barbed wire strung up between these trees,' she persisted, pointing to one of the wire ends. 'We galloped into it. Do you know how it got there?'

He looked at the wire then crossed the track and bent down to examine the other one.

'Damn kids, I suppose,' he muttered to the dog and she only just caught what he said.

'Does that mean you don't know anything about it?'

'Of course I don't,' he said, inspecting the rubber casing.

Laura took out her mobile, 'I just need to get some pictures.'

He moved quickly towards her and knocked the phone from her hand. 'No photos. Get out, get out now,' he raised his stick. The dog growled.

She grabbed the phone off the ground and backed off fast taking a couple of hurried shots as she went.

He watched her go then turned his attention to the wire. He had no idea how it had got there but he didn't want to be blamed for it. He removed the wire ends from the tree trunks and pocketed them. He noticed the rubber meant no marks had been left on the trees. Now, if anyone else came snooping, there would be nothing for them to see.

CHAPTER EIGHTEEN

Harry Pelham stood in front of the nurses' desk demanding to know why the man, 'that nutter' as he called him, had been allowed to get into his room. Harry was big and chunky and his heavy black brows were drawn together in a scowl. The nurse was looking at him nervously. He thought she might call security so he stopped barking at her.

'Typical police,' he said, more quietly and winked at her. 'Never around when you want them.'

The police guard had left late on Friday afternoon and Harry made no secret of how pleased he was to see the back of them. The consultant had told them Harry was being kept in for observation for a few more days. The doctors originally thought he'd had a mild heart attack, but test results had not confirmed this. Still, they wanted to keep an eye on him for a bit longer. The policemen reported back to Barnes, and a few hours later, Harry was granted bail. There had been conditions though and they'd made him furious. He was not to contact his wife and child, directly or indirectly; he was banned from going anywhere near them; he must live at a specified address and sleep there every night so the police knew where to find him; he was not to access any computers so there was no chance of him re-offending.

The conditions were vindictive, he thought, and they had Laura Maxwell's fingerprints all over them. He protested loudly to Ronnie but Ronnie said impatiently there was nothing he could do about any of it, at least not until the computers had been examined. He told Harry the police would want to finish their questioning, probably on Monday if the doctors said he was fit enough. He warned Harry not to leave the hospital in the meantime.

The nurse didn't like the wink and she didn't smile. She didn't say anything either in case it set him off again. The police wanted to question him about some unexplained offence, rumoured to be something horrible, he'd just finished yelling at the man who'd come to visit him and now, here he was, kicking off at her. He was dangerous and she wasn't taking any chances.

'OK,' he said, 'I know it's not your fault. Just tell me about the guy.'

'I don't know anything about him.'

'He talked to you when he arrived. What did he say?'

'He just said he was a friend of yours and he wanted to know where he could find you.'

'I've never seen him before in my life. Like I say, he's some sort of nutter.'

She flushed. In fact, Ben Morgan had asked her if the police were still around and when she'd told him 'no', he'd marched straight off to Harry's room. She remembered how he had come in the day before, and when she'd gone to tell one of the policemen that he wanted to give Harry a note, he had disappeared in record time.

'I wasn't to know that,' she said, stiffly.

Harry Pelham put his elbows on the desk. He was right in her face, his moustache bristling at her.

'Look are you sure that's everything he said? Nothing else that might give me a clue?'

'He said he was an old friend and he wanted to see you, and, um, he asked if the police were still here.'

She waited for an explosion but it didn't come.

'So he knew the police were here,' Harry muttered, pretty much to himself, not considering that the nurse might have supplied the information, 'and what did you say?'

'I said they'd gone and before I could say anything else, he just shot off to talk to you.'

The elbows and the moustache withdrew and Harry Pelham went back to his room.

The visitor had upset him. Badly upset him. The little creep had been watching him, sticking his nose in where it wasn't wanted, where it had no business to be. It was clear that Morgan knew a lot, far too much, about him. He needed to be taught a lesson and Harry had every intention of doing so.

The man had burst in the door, announced that his name was Ben Morgan and that he was a 'friend'. He was very hyped up, like he was on something. When he sat down, his right leg jigged restlessly on the floor. His eyes kept shooting all over the place and he talked a mile a minute. He was speaking softly but there was something wild in there too. He grabbed Harry's hand, told him he'd come to help, knew all about his troubles and felt drawn to him like a brother.

'I know what's going on, see. All of it. I've been watching, getting myself the full picture. Checking stuff out. You know what I mean. No worries though, I want to help.'

Harry's eyes narrowed. He would have told him to piss off there and then but for the mention of his daughter's name. It silenced him.

'Martha loves you, I know, and you're not going to lose her, no way, not like I did. That Maxwell scum isn't going to get away with it, not anymore. She's toast. I know what she's up to, I can see it coming. She lives in my head, see. Tried to shut her up but it didn't work. On and on I hear her talking, saying I'm crazy, not fit to be a father. Haven't slept for three days, my brain won't turn off. Reason is it's full of her voice. I've got to fucking shut her up. Got to. No problem.'

Ben Morgan continued without a pause. He was speaking so fast that Harry found it hard to follow. There were long rambling references to his own daughter, Millie, tirades against secret and unaccountable family courts, against judges and psychiatrists, but most of all against Laura Maxwell. He was going to stop her before she did any more damage. He was on her case. She was not indestructible and if she thought she was, he would teach her different.

Ben Morgan jabbed a skinny finger in the air. 'She worked for my wife for free. A lawyer – for free. That's a joke, eh? So ask yourself, why?'

He left no room for an answer but supplied his own. 'Because she was out to get me. She singled me out early on, oh yes. She knew I'd seen through her and had worked out what kind of a spiteful, man-hating bitch she is and that meant she had to destroy me. Now I want payback. Would feel so good, wouldn't it? Bringing the bitch down.'

Harry wanted to laugh, the man was talking like a third-rate gangster, but what he said next wiped any idea of laughter from Harry's mind.

Ben Morgan had been watching Harry carefully and had seen he needed help to deal with Laura Maxwell. Harry was a man suffering the same agonies Morgan had been through, a man trapped in the same nightmare situation. Harry was bipolar, he knew, was on medication, was unfairly accused of all sorts of things, was in trouble with the police. Morgan understood all that only too well and he understood that none of it was Harry's fault.

'Where the hell did you get hold of all this crap?' Harry snarled.

'She wants to be with you, you know,' Morgan said. 'Martha, she's heartbroken, she cries herself to sleep, she says you're her best friend.'

Harry Pelham stared at the man, feeling his chest grow tight. Rage filled him so intense that it clogged his throat. He reached out, grabbed Morgan's forearm, began to bend it sharply backwards.

'Who the hell are you?' he shouted.

At last there was silence for a moment, then Ben Morgan said, 'Take it easy, will you?'

'I am taking it easy. Believe me.'

'Please, you're really hurting.'

'I asked you a question. I want an answer.'

'I told you. I'm a friend.'

Harry increased the pressure. The man gasped, stifled a cry. His eyes had stopped darting around. Harry had their full attention. They were wide. They watched a vein pulsing in Harry's forehead.

'You want me to break your fucking arm?' Harry asked.

'Look, I can help you. I know what to do about that lawyer,' he paused, 'Martha talks to you through her favourite teddy bear, you know, she misses you so much.'

Almost unconsciously, his mind taken up by this new piece of outrageous information, he twisted the arm back further. There was a yell of pain.

'Shut up! Just shut up about my daughter. You understand?'

Harry let go of the arm before the man could yell anymore and bring people running. Ben Morgan clutched it, rubbed at it frantically.

They were sitting next to each other at the side of Harry's bed and now Harry moved his chair round in front of the other man's, to block his exit.

'Right, you little shit, you're going to answer some questions.'

Ben Morgan didn't want to fight. It was bad for him, brought him down to a bad place, he knew that. The conversation had not gone as he expected. It had gone all wrong. Harry had got so angry. He hadn't expected that but he realized he should have done. Of course, Harry was angry. Wasn't he angry himself? Angry beyond belief.

He had woken up full of energy and confidence, pumped up – today was the day he would see Harry and explain that he could sort out his problems. No-one was going to stop him this time. He would talk to the police guard, persuade them to let him through, no trouble at all. When he discovered that the police were gone, he had taken it as a sure sign he was destined to succeed.

It should have been easy but it was falling apart. He was handling the whole thing badly. He hadn't thought it through properly. Not properly at all. He needed to run.

Harry Pelham was shouting at him again, demanding information. He had to get away. Harry leaned across and shoved his hand in a pocket of Morgan's scruffy jacket. He pulled out a town centre map, a biro, and a Brighton and Hove bus saver ticket. Disgusted, he threw them on the bed, reached for the other pocket. But Ben Morgan had had enough. He jumped up from his chair out of Harry's grasp, leapt across the bed and ran, almost colliding with the nurse on her way to see what all the fuss was about.

The speed of his flight took Harry by surprise. Too late, he tried to grab hold of the man's legs. But he was gone, taking his secrets with him, leaving Harry Pelham cursing himself for letting him get away.

CHAPTER NINETEEN

As soon as she was a safe distance away, Laura sat down to rest. She looked at the pictures she'd taken but they were blurry and dark and the wires couldn't be seen. She thought about waiting around for a while and then going back but she was nervous of running into the landowner again, and in any case, the light was almost gone.

She must find a witness, someone who would come back with her and verify the wire on the trees. She headed for the stables where her car was parked. She tried to run but the pain of breathing made her give it up.

It was obvious, she thought, that the landowner knew nothing about the wire or who had put it there. By the look on his face it had been as big a surprise to him as it had been to her. Someone then, someone unknown to both of them, had deliberately placed it there, on the route she always took. Three days ago, the car chase, now this. Her suspicions grew large. Someone out there wanted to hurt her; didn't mind if they killed her. Someone out there had been watching her, maybe was still watching her. She looked around nervously in the cold, dark afternoon.

Michael Donoghue was waiting for her when she reached the stables. He was in a very bad mood and he read her the Riot Act. There was no excuse for trespassing, he told her, and causing trouble for him with a difficult neighbour. He'd only just sorted out a boundary dispute with the man. She was a lawyer, weren't they supposed to stick to the rules? He didn't wait for an answer but simply told her that she could no longer use the stables. She was barred.

Donoghue was an easy-going Irishman and although she knew he had every reason to ban her, she still felt as if he'd slapped her in the face. Her shoulders slumped in the torn riding jacket.

'Hey,' he said, softening and putting his arm around her. 'You know I have to do that, for now anyway. Come back when it's all blown over.'

'Thanks.' Laura attempted a grin.

'I'm sorry about the horse. I heard you're trying to save him but with those kind of injuries … ' he shrugged, 'what I mean is you shouldn't feel guilty.'

It was exactly what the vet had said; a gentle way of telling her she should put Valentine out of his misery.

'I just want to give it a try, you know, in case … ' her voice wavered.

'It's going to cost you. The insurance won't pay out, not when they find out you were trespassing.'

Laura nodded. She gave up the idea of asking Michael to come with her to see the wires; it was plain he wouldn't want to get involved and limped away towards her car. He watched as she manoeuvred herself painfully into the driving seat of the Audi. Some people, he thought, had a lot more money than sense.

It was shortly after five when she arrived at the police station in John Street in central Brighton. She walked through the reception area, feeling a bit light-headed, towards a row of bulletproof screens behind which the police dealt with the public. At one of them stood three sullen looking teenagers dressed in hoodies, baggy jeans, and trainers. A young policeman was booking them in and they looked bored by the whole exercise. They stared at Laura with interest.

Her mobile rang. It was Joe, at last, and just the sound of his voice brought such a rush of relief that her legs went weak. She veered across to a bench by the wall and dropped down on it. The teenagers waved, calling to her across the room.

He'd rung as soon as he'd got her messages, he said. How badly hurt was she? Had she been to the hospital? Where was she now? He was so sorry he'd been out of contact. He had gone out and left his mobile behind, the way you do sometimes when you're in a rush. He was on his way to her right now.

She told him she was at the police station and she told him why she was there and he sounded shocked. He also sounded incredulous. How could she be sure it was deliberate? It was pretty unlikely wasn't it? Maybe when she'd had time to calm down, things would look different. Through her relief, she felt a spark of annoyance. She had been keeping her voice low, trying to avoid the teenage audience, but now it rose higher as she emphasized her worries. The boys laughed, started to repeat bits of her conversation.

Another policeman, a sergeant, appeared behind the screens. He told the boys to shut it, glanced at her impatiently as she talked on the phone. As quietly as possible she assured Joe she was fine and he needn't come and get her. After talking to the police she'd drive straight home and then it would be great if he would take her to hospital.

'Tell your old man not to bother because I'd love to take you,' called one of the boys. They all sniggered.

She stood up, went to the screen farthest away from them and waited as the sergeant rather slowly headed in her direction. He was in his fifties, balding with his remaining grey hair cut very short and he looked like he had seen it all. There was a sceptical, slightly amused expression on his face as he listened to what she said. She could tell what he was thinking, that she was hysterical and imagining things, and she told her tale with increasing frustration.

It was always going to be difficult to convince him. She had known that. But there were ways of presenting things, persuasive ways which she knew all about, which she used regularly at work,

100

with success, but was failing to use here. She was handling it badly. To her own ears the story sounded weak and she sounded neurotic.

'I think someone may be trying to kill me, certainly to injure me.'

She said this early on and knew at once it was a mistake. It sounded like the start of a bad black and white movie and his lips set in disbelief. Dutifully he wrote down the details she gave him. She wondered if he had entitled them 'drama queen'.

She told him about the car chase; pointed out that it had been serious enough for her to report it to the police, but it didn't seem to have any effect. Certainly it did not wipe the doubting look from his face.

He scratched the sparse bristles on the top of his head and said: 'Just to be clear, you say you left the usual riders' route and crossed onto private land. Let's put aside for now the fact that you were riding where you shouldn't have been, and just explain to me how anyone else could have known you'd be there?'

'Because I ride there every Saturday. At about the same time, on the same route.'

'So every Saturday you trespass on someone else's property. Do they know you do that?'

'It's not for long, just a shortcut to the top of the Downs,' she said defensively.

'Maybe the landowner takes a different view. Maybe he put this wire up to teach you a lesson.'

'This has got nothing to do with the landowner,' she said, exasperated, 'I told you he knew nothing about it.'

'I'm probably being a bit thick, Mrs Greene, but how do you know that?'

'It was obvious. From his reaction when he saw the wire.'

'So who do you think is responsible for this deliberate attack upon your person?' he asked with heavy sarcasm.

Laura hesitated, uncertain whether to mention Harry Pelham. She thought it could be him but she had no evidence. It was something she would rather raise first with Detective Barnes.

'I'm not sure. But whoever it is knows my habits. They must have been following me and ... '

She stopped again, aware that it sounded melodramatic. He was making another note on his pad. She didn't think it was a good note.

He studied her. She was a nice-looking woman if a bit dishevelled. She'd had a traumatic day that had been too much for her. It was a shame. Still, he wasn't a nurse or a psychiatrist. He was expecting another hectic Saturday night full of drunks and punch-ups and he didn't want any more of his precious downtime disturbed by her nonsense.

'All right' he said looking down at his notes, 'I've got all the details. Someone will be in touch.'

'No,' she said hotly, 'that's not good enough. 'Will you send someone to look at that wire?' She was almost shouting at him. She glanced towards the boys to see if they'd heard, then was angry with herself for caring. They had lost interest anyway. The young officer had finished with them and they were shuffling off towards the exit.

The sceptical look on the sergeant's face was replaced by annoyance.

Know your enemy, she thought, that was the first rule in court, and she had broken it. She had behaved in exactly the wrong way. She was being aggressive and strident. He was not the kind of man to like that, she thought, he would make a point of not being pushed. Nor, she guessed, was it likely that he would be swayed by tears.

'We're very stretched at the minute,' he told her in a wooden tone of voice. It implied that if they had nothing at all to do they'd still be too busy to attend to this.

Laura could see that he was practised in the art of getting rid of nuisance members of the public and he had put her firmly in that category. She'd blown it and she wouldn't get any further with him. It had been an exercise in how not to get your point across.

'Look,' he said, in a trying to be helpful tone, 'you've told me you were riding on private land when the accident happened. That means it's a civil matter and really has nothing to do with us unless there's some hard evidence of criminal intent. I would advise you to see a solicitor. We have a duty one here you can speak to if you don't have one of your own.'

She wanted to shout in his disbelieving face, to tell him that since she was a solicitor she may as well go and talk to herself as that would be more productive than talking to him. Instead she smiled and told him what her job was.

He had the grace to laugh and she wished she had tried humour on him from the start.

She asked if he'd mind checking for her if Detective Inspector David Barnes was working that weekend and available to talk to her.

'He'll know me as Laura Maxwell, my work name, from Morrison Kemp solicitors.'

She wondered if the name would ring a bell with him, wondered if he was the same sergeant she'd spoken to when she was tracking down the officer in charge of Harry Pelham's case.

If she'd hoped to make him take her more seriously, she was disappointed. He couldn't give details of officers' whereabouts, he told her, but if she left a phone number he'd make sure the detective knew she wanted to speak to him. He'd also make sure, she thought, that Barnes was fully aware of his opinion of her.

She wrote down a number for him and said goodbye. He watched her leave with the same cynical expression he'd had all along.

All of a sudden, she felt very sore indeed. Now there was no urgent action driving her on, her brain was registering the pain. Her back and hip had stiffened up, every move and every breath hurt.

She pushed open the glass doors of the police station and walked out into a clear night. It was very cold but the earlier wind had dropped and a brilliant full moon hung over the sea. She'd had to park a few streets away, down near the front, and she shivered, hugging the tattered riding jacket to her.

The town was getting busy now, evening revellers gathering in force, milling about noisily with a hint of lunar madness under the huge moon. Later they would head for West Street and the heart of clubland. On a typical Saturday night there would be three and a half thousand of them out for fun. Laura felt a flicker of sympathy for the sergeant.

She was threading her way through the crowd, trying to shield her body and walking with her head down to make it easier to breathe, when two young guys barged into her. There was a stab of excruciating pain from her ribs and she looked up, annoyed. They were laughing, enjoying themselves, and with a shout of apology they moved on. She was so preoccupied with the pain that at first she didn't register the face of the other man not far behind them who was staring at her. She walked on and then it hit her and she stopped in her tracks. She turned around and caught sight of him disappearing fast up the street.

It was years since she had seen that face but she remembered at once who he was. Ben Morgan. She had acted for his wife in their divorce. She shivered again and this time it was not with the cold. He suffered from bipolar disorder, supposedly only in a mild way, but it turned out to be severe. He had been violent, unpredictable, out of control, and his wife had been terrified of him. He hadn't been able to deal with the court process and his manner in court had bounced from suicidal gloom to adrenaline-charged exuberance. Towards the end of it, convinced he was about to lose all contact rights to his young daughter, he picked her up from school, took her to the flat he was renting, barricaded the door, and threatened to kill her and himself if anyone tried to take her away.

There had been a short siege during which he had stood at a window brandishing a knife and shouting threats at the negotiators below. Eventually, at four in the morning, police had broken the door down. Ben Morgan had been wide awake and waiting for them and one of the officers had been stabbed and badly hurt.

Later, Morgan's defence lawyer claimed the stabbing was accidental, had happened when the officer threw himself on his client who was holding the knife. Morgan had been lucky to get away with a conviction for grievous bodily harm rather than attempted murder. Instead of going to jail, he'd been sectioned for hospital treatment. He had lost contact rights to his daughter.

It was while he was in hospital that he wrote Laura the letters saying the world would be a better place if she were dead. He sent three of them before she contacted the hospital and they put a stop to it. The letters were rambling and repetitive but that didn't make them any less threatening. She had never again heard anything from, or of, Ben Morgan. Until now. Now here he was in this Brighton street. Now, when she was sure that someone was out to get her, here he was, right up close.

CHAPTER TWENTY

Harry Pelham was about to leave and the nurse wasn't intending to make any more efforts to stop him. She'd told him he couldn't go until the consultant had declared him fit for discharge and the consultant wasn't there. It was Saturday evening and he wouldn't be in until Monday morning.

He glared at her. He was red in the face, seriously pissed off. She decided not to remind him that it wasn't only the doctor he was supposed to wait for, there was also the small matter of the police. She would alert the nurse in charge to the fact that he was discharging himself; that was the best she could do. The police would have to catch up with him later.

'If anyone's asking for me, you can tell them I've left the building. Better still, tell them I've left the country,' Harry barked and headed for the exit.

His mind was full of theories about Ben Morgan but none of them made much sense. He wondered if Morgan had been sent by his wife, or by Laura Maxwell, or by both, to worm his way into his confidence and get him to confess to the crimes he was accused of.

Outside, the sharp, cold air helped to clear his head. He had a lot of unfinished business to take care of, but before he did anything else he intended to track down Morgan and get the truth from him. If necessary, he would beat it out of him.

He decided against going home to pick up some things because it was possible the police would be waiting for him. Unlikely, he thought, they'd move that fast, even if they had been told he'd walked out of the hospital – after all, it was Saturday night, and he wasn't exactly top of the wanted list. But no point in taking the risk; he couldn't afford the police getting in his way.

Harry checked the cash in his wallet, took a bus into the town centre, and drew out the maximum he could from various bank machines. He would not use his cards again in case the police tracked them. For what he was planning, he would need to keep off the radar. He paid cash for a pay-as-you-go mobile, which he could buy without giving any personal details; that way it couldn't be traced to him.

He checked in to a big hotel on the sea front where he could stay anonymous and then logged on to one of the computers in the lobby. He googled Ben Morgan and up came some press articles detailing his case. Then he read Morgan's own account, given in graphic detail on a website for divorced fathers.

The story was a bit disjointed, as if parts of it had been removed, but it made clear that he blamed the lawyer, Laura Maxwell, for what had happened to him. She had driven him over the edge, hounding him to the point where he could not bear it anymore. Harry Pelham read it, and nodded his head, almost unconsciously. It struck a chord, a deep chord. Dear God, did he need to get that woman off his back!

Morgan had been his own worst enemy. He'd been unable to cope, his medical history and his behaviour had combined to seal his fate, had made him easy meat for Laura Maxwell – she had chewed him up and spat him out. Well, she would not do the same to Harry Pelham. He would make sure of that. He would do whatever it took.

He concentrated on finding the man. All he had was a name, maybe not even a real one. He tried to recall everything Morgan had said, sifting it for clues. It wasn't easy because the narrative had been all over the place and there were gaps in his memory caused, he supposed, by the anger he'd felt at what he was hearing.

He guessed Morgan didn't live in Brighton or anywhere nearby; if he did, he wouldn't need to carry around a map of the town. He might be staying with a friend – but who would have him – most likely he was at a hotel or a guest house. Harry found more than 150 of them listed on TripAdvisor; he needed a way to narrow them down.

Judging by the state of the man, he decided to rule out the expensive places. Morgan's clothes were shabby; he had a mangy beard and an uncared-for look. Harry remembered the bus ticket. Probably no car then. The chances were he'd come to Brighton by train and used buses to get around.

He began searching for cheap accommodation within walking distance of the station. He found a booking site which listed the places on a map, and he could adjust the distance to pinpoint those that were within a mile of the station. It had separate lists for hotels and for guest houses. He began with the hotels nearest the station and worked his way outwards. He tried more than thirty before switching to the guest houses, just for a change. Needle in a haystack, he thought, and perhaps Morgan wasn't in any of them. He looked at his watch, it was getting late; he would give it another half hour. He got a bottle of brandy from the bar and carried on.

He was ringing a cheap guest house in the back streets when he got lucky. A bored-sounding woman eventually picked up the phone. He asked her his usual question and waited for the usual answer.

'Hang on,' she said, 'I'll put you through.'

It took a moment to register – he was expecting the monotonous negative he'd got used to. He waited, the phone to his ear, and then he heard Ben Morgan's voice, anxious, wary, slightly nasal, unmistakably his. Harry Pelham put down the phone.

CHAPTER TWENTY-ONE

The doctor in accident and emergency stitched up the gash on Laura's leg. He told her she had a cracked rib and serious bruising to the left side of her body and her back. He wanted to admit her to hospital for a few days' observation, but she refused.

He thought she was being stubborn and foolish but he also considered how busy the hospital was and decided not to push the point. Instead, he turned to Joe in the hope that he had better sense. He told him that if his wife developed a persistent headache or felt dizzy or found any blood in her urine, he should ring at once for an ambulance to bring her in. Then he prescribed pain-killers, sedatives, and lots of rest and moved on to the next patient.

Laura woke up late on Sunday morning. She hadn't wanted to take the sedatives but Joe had insisted and she hadn't felt like putting up much of a fight.

Fear returned as soon as she awoke. Perhaps it had never been away, had been there while she slept, curling through her, seeping into her subconscious mind and growing roots. No longer was it giving out a subtle warning signal; it was waving a huge red flag in her face. Something was wrong, very wrong; she felt it in her bones.

Joe was sitting in a chair beside the bed. She watched him through closed lashes. He was texting on his mobile, a smile on his face.

'Hi', she said, yawning and turning towards him. Bad idea. There was a jolt from her rib and she gasped in pain.

'Laura, honey, are you OK?' he asked, putting the mobile away in his pocket.

'I think so, just have to be careful,' she smiled and sat up gingerly in the bed. He kissed her, adjusted the pillows, smoothed out the duvet, asked if he could get her any breakfast.

Laura shook her head, what she wanted more than anything else was to talk; she needed to go through what had happened and try to understand it. She had unloaded it all on Joe the night before but he hadn't said much. He had seemed too anxious about her injuries, and getting her to the hospital, to pay much attention to what she was telling him.

Now she began again but almost at once he put his finger to her lips, stroking her hair with his other hand.

'Laura, you have to rest. Just put it out of your mind for today at least.'

'Not much chance of that.'

'I know it's hard, but you need to relax, get some distance from what's happened, try to get things in perspective.'

'In perspective,' she said, 'what do you mean?'

'I mean, it was just an accident. A horrible accident, but hey, at least you're not too badly hurt.'

'How can you say that? This was deliberate. Someone put up that wire to get me and didn't care if they killed me. Maybe they wanted to kill me.'

'Come on, anyone could have been riding there. Nobody could know it would be you. In fact, thinking about it, no one does ride there do they? It's private land, so that makes it even more unlikely.'

'That's the whole point, Joe. I go there every week. Me, just me, and probably no one else. Someone must've been watching, following me. They laid a trap, don't you see?'

He said nothing and she pulled away from him.

'I told you about this guy Ben Morgan,' she went on, 'he was crazy all those years ago and he's probably still crazy. He nearly killed a policeman and he blamed me for losing his kid. And now he's here, right next to me. Maybe he's decided it's time for revenge.'

'OK, calm down. That is a bit weird but why didn't he just attack you in the street instead of some half arsed idea of knocking you off your horse? And why wait all this time then suddenly decide he's coming after you? Doesn't make any sense. You thought Harry Pelham might be out to get you, now it's this Ben Morgan.'

'I know someone is out to get me. There's nothing might about it.'

'There's no evidence. Listen to yourself. You're sounding totally irrational.' There was a note of impatience in his voice.

She stared at him and his eyes slid away.

'Irrational. I could have died yesterday and I could have died in that car chase, and all you can say is I'm being irrational.'

'Don't get me wrong, I can see why you would be, but you're taking a set of events and reading them the wrong way. Sometimes life throws a whole lot of crap at you. It doesn't mean that anyone is out to get you.'

'Oh I see. All this crap is one big coincidence is it? And Ben Morgan is in Brighton on his holidays.'

'All I'm saying is to keep an open mind.'

'Well thank you for your support,' she said icily.

'What does that mean? Of course you have my support.'

'Well it doesn't feel like it. In fact, it never feels like it anymore.'

The words came out hot and angry and she knew they sounded childish and a little mad. But they wouldn't stop. There was a whole steaming torrent of them forcing their way through her lips.

He heard her out without saying another word. Then he left the room. She sank back on the pillows, exhausted.

Thoughts came into her mind. Thoughts that had come in before and been rigorously expelled. This time they were crowding in and they wouldn't be sent away.

Joe. She felt there had been a change in him. Nothing she could put her finger on exactly. The best way she could describe it was as a withdrawing from her. She had told herself it was nothing to worry about; it was just what happened to all couples when the intensity of first love began to wear off. It hadn't happened to her yet, but she could accept that it had happened to him.

Lately, though, she had worried it might be more. Sometimes she would catch him looking at her as if she were a stranger. An irritating stranger. She would try to talk to him but everything she said, every subject she tried, would turn out wrong, as if the lovers' wavelength they had both been using had been switched off.

He turned to her less often in bed, and when he did, he was different. Less passion, as if, for him, the edge had gone. There had been a time, not so long ago, when he could not keep his hands off her but now she had begun, almost unconsciously, to count the times they had sex. Once a week, maybe twice if she was lucky. She tried to interest him, excite him, but the effort wasn't a great success.

Then there was the baby. He had been so keen, but these days when the subject came up she sensed hesitation, or thought she did. Their plan had been to wait a little longer, until she was made a partner at Morrison Kemp and her position was secure. That had turned out to be more complicated than expected. Morrison was tricky; he blew hot and cold. He enjoyed dangling the partnership in front of her, but she was not certain when, or even if, he would actually deliver.

Their plan. She thought of it as 'their plan'. But was it? Wasn't it her plan designed to fit around her life? After all, they had enough money, they had the hotel business, they didn't really need her partnership. She had suggested waiting, maybe she had waited too long.

It was an odd thing about love, she thought. It made you feel like you knew everything about the other person, that no one could ever understand them better. Then later you discovered that perhaps you didn't know them quite as well as you had imagined.

Taking small, shallow breaths, Laura got out of bed on shaky legs and went into the shower. She examined her body. Most of her left side was turning purple. It was shocking; the violence of the colour against her pale skin.

She turned up the heat and the hot jet of water soothed her body but it didn't soothe her mind. It fizzed with the terror of yesterday. Joe had said her fears were irrational, but her instinct told her that wasn't right. It also told her time was short; there would be a next time and it would be soon. In the heat of the shower, an icy fear pierced her chest.

Much later, though she had no idea how much, she heard Joe's voice asking if she was all right. Yes, she said, she was fine; she would be out in a minute. She turned off the water, stepped out of the shower and began, painfully, to dry herself.

When she checked her mobile there was no message from Barnes. No surprise there then. She was sure that even if the sergeant had got around to contacting him, the version of events he would have been given was not going to galvanize him into action on a Sunday. At best it would be on his list for Monday. Call Laura Greene/Maxwell (neurotic). It would be at the bottom of his list.

But there were two messages from Jeff Ingham, and with a pang of guilt, she remembered. She should have rung back; could not believe she had forgotten. The first message had been left the previous evening while she was at the hospital. She had listened to it on her way home. The laborious process of putting a plaster cast on Valentine's leg had been successfully completed. He had come round from the anaesthetic all right but he wasn't happy. Jeff Ingham wanted to discuss what would happen next.

He had left a second message early that morning. This time his tone was abrupt. Would she call him, please? Valentine had had a bad night. He was distressed and fretful. She guessed the vet had sat up with him for most of the time.

She rang his number hoping he wouldn't pick up because that might mean the crisis was over, that he had been able to leave

Valentine quiet at the clinic and go home to bed. He answered at once and she braced herself.

'I've been trying to get you,' he said crossly. 'You need to come down here. Things are not going well.'

'What's wrong?'

'Didn't you listen to my message?'

'Yes, sorry, of course I did. I'm being stupid. You said Valentine was upset.'

'Upset is not the word,' he said tersely, 'He's a highly strung horse. He can't move and he's in a strange place. Result, he's terrified and very distressed. It may be best to end this now.'

'Hang on,' she said miserably, 'I'm on my way.'

CHAPTER TWENTY-TWO

The guest house was less than a fifteen-minute walk from his hotel and Harry Pelham set off for it early on Sunday morning. It was fairly small, no more than ten rooms he thought, and it had definitely seen better days. He gently pushed open the door. No-one at reception, no sign of life at all, just a smell of fried bacon. It was 9.20 a.m.

He considered walking straight in and knocking on every room until he found Ben Morgan. But he thought it might cause a fuss and he didn't want that. Morgan was unpredictable, who knew what he might do when he saw Harry at his door – panic, try to run, shout out for help. Harry wanted to question him in private and it would be better if the rest of the guests were not already alerted. That was if there were any; it didn't look the sort of place to be packed out.

There was some stationery on the reception desk and he took a piece of it, wrote a note, then folded the paper in half and rang the bell. Nothing happened. He leaned his elbow on the bell until a voice came from a back room.

'All right. Keep your hair on. I'm coming.' A middle-aged, overweight woman appeared, wiping her lips with the back of her hand.

'Sorry to keep you,' she said, in a tone that made it clear she wasn't.

He handed her the note.

'Can I leave this? It's for one of your guests – Ben Morgan.'

There were nine numbered pigeon holes on the wall behind her. Harry waited, hoping she would put the note in one so that he could see which was Morgan's room. She didn't move.

'At least,' he said, smiling at her, 'I'm pretty sure he's staying here. Ben Morgan.'

'Yeah. He's here. I'll give it to him.' Still she made no move towards the pigeon holes, 'You a friend of his?'

'Not really.'

'Actually I'm a bit worried about him.'

There was a pause. Obviously she wanted him to ask.

'Why's that?

'Is he a bit … ', she made a circling motion with her index finger at the side of her head, 'you know, screw loose?'

'Like I said, I don't know him well.'

The woman carried on, 'he's a real oddball. Been here for weeks. Never says much but gets all twitchy and wound up like he's going to burst. Never has any visitors, 'cept you of course.'

Harry gestured towards the note. 'I have to run – if you would make sure he gets that.'

She shifted her bulk and put the note into hole number '9'.

'He's going to have to clean up his ways if he wants to stay here any longer. His room was a tip when I went in the other day. You ask me, he needs someone to take him in hand,' she leaned against the desk. 'You want me to call his room? Let him know you're here?'

'No thanks. Afraid I can't stop.' He turned away, walked to the door, waving goodbye.

He stood in the street outside pretending to be checking his texts but really looking in through the front window of the guest house. Almost at once he saw the woman leave the reception desk and disappear into a back room. He gave her another minute, then slipped back inside and up the stairs.

It was as scruffy inside as the outside had promised it would be. Nobody had used a paintbrush here for years and the place smelt of mildew. As he climbed to the third floor he wondered how the torn stair carpet had evaded health and safety. He reached door number '9' and waited, listening, but he couldn't hear any sound coming from inside. He rapped hard on the door. Silence. He tried again.

'Who is it?' Ben Morgan's voice. Nervous, hesitant.

'Harry. Harry Pelham. I need to talk to you.'

No reply.

'I'm sorry I got angry before.'

'How did you find me?'

'I rang round the hotels.'

'How did you know which one to ring?'

'I didn't. I guessed you'd be in one near the station.'

'Someone told you I was here, didn't they?'

'No, of course not.'

'I can't see how else you would know.'

'I just told you, I rang round. You took some finding.'

'You were tipped off, weren't you?'

The man was paranoid, Harry thought, exasperated.

'Please, can we talk,' he tried not to sound irritated. He didn't want to frighten Morgan, not yet, not before he'd opened the door.

'You hurt me last time.'

'I'm sorry. What you said about Martha, it upset me.'

No reply.

'You said you wanted to help.'

Still nothing.

'I need help, Ben. I really do. I want you to help me deal with Laura Maxwell, the way you said you would.'

He heard the door being unlocked. Ben Morgan opened it a little and stared out at him. He looked pale and edgy. Harry shoved the door wide and strode into the room, pushing Ben Morgan to one side. The fat woman was right; it was a mess. There were dirty

117

clothes and papers all over the place, foil tins from old takeaways crackled under his feet.

'Right, now you're going to tell me who put you up to this,' he demanded.

Ben Morgan's anger took him completely by surprise. The man was suddenly beside himself with fury, yelling abuse, screaming that Harry had it in for him just like everyone else. Then Morgan lunged at him, swung back his right fist and hit him hard in the face. Harry Pelham reeled backwards, blood pouring from his nose.

'OK. Calm down for fuck's sake.'

But Ben Morgan didn't calm down, not at all. It was like a switch had been pulled and there was no off button.

He was shouting that he'd had no contact with his daughter for six years, not even supervised contact – no court had been willing to allow it, claiming it would put Millie at risk. And it was all because of Laura Maxwell. She had driven him insane, driven him to do something crazy. He hated her. She should have never been born.

The door to the room was still open and people had heard the commotion and come to watch. It looked like Harry had been wrong in thinking there were not many guests as quite a crowd had gathered. A man rushed up the stairs, followed more slowly by the chubby receptionist.

'What the hell's going on?' the man asked.

'Hey, what are you doing here?' the woman puffed out as she reached the landing. 'He's the guy I told you about – must've sneaked up here when I wasn't looking.'

The audience made no difference to Ben Morgan. His tirade continued non-stop. His fists were clenched and his thin frame shook with emotion.

Harry saw he had no choice but to give it up. He would get nothing now out of Morgan and he didn't want anyone calling the police. He wiped the blood from his face with the sleeve of his coat.

'That's it, show's over,' he said, pushing through the crowd and stomping off down the stairs.

CHAPTER TWENTY-THREE

Laura abandoned her Sunday afternoon plans to go shopping with Emma and went to visit Valentine instead. They arranged to meet afterwards at a café in the North Laine area of town. It was where Emma loved to shop, with lots of small, independent traders that weren't too expensive. The place was colourful and vibrant with a studenty, Bohemian feel. It was the style Emma had always liked and now, at thirty-four, it was still reflected in her clothes and her curly, red hennaed hair.

Laura was late getting to the café and Emma had been waiting almost an hour when she finally arrived. It was after 6 p.m. and the shopping crowds had all gone home. Emma was sitting on her own at a corner table, surrounded by bags, examining a pair of handmade silver earrings she'd bought. There was a half full glass of white wine in front of her; a bottle of wine was on the table and one empty glass.

'Hiya.' Emma stood up and hugged Laura, then pulled back as she saw her wince with the pain from her cracked rib.

'God I'm sorry. I forgot. Are you OK?'

Laura nodded, sinking down in the chair opposite.

'Well you don't look it. You're white as a sheet.' She poured wine into the empty glass and pushed it across to Laura.

'Sorry I'm so late, Em. I know you need to get back.'

'Actually, I don't. I've texted and they're fine. They're back from Speedway and Steve is making the boys' tea. So, no problem.'

Laura was grateful though she didn't believe it. Emma and her family were flying off to Majorca tomorrow to spend half term week at Steve's parents' apartment in Puerto Pollensa. Emma must have a thousand things she needed to be doing.

'How was Valentine?'

'Not good,' Laura said dejectedly.

Jeff Ingham had not exaggerated. Valentine was in a bad way. Physically, of course, he was bound to be but it was his mental state that would kill him. He struggled in the sling, wild eyed and crazy. It was the worst thing he could do, and if he continued with it, he would not survive. His broken leg needed rest and he had to stay calm so that his weight would be kept evenly on all four legs. The sling helped – it meant that most of his body weight was partially supported off his legs – but on its own it couldn't save the day. The struggling unbalanced him and risked injuring his other legs. He had to help himself, she knew, and so far he wasn't doing that. It had been all she could do to persuade the vet to give it a few more days.

'Do you think I'm being selfish?' Laura asked, close to tears. 'Keeping him alive like this?'

'No, of course not. I know you'd only do what's best for him.'

'I feel so guilty. I mean is it fair to put him through all this? Am I just doing it for myself and not in his best interests?'

'If you feel it's right then I'm sure it is. You've got to give it a try.'

Laura looked at her uncertainly and managed a weak smile.

'Come on, I'm starving, let's order,' Emma said, anxious to distract her friend from tormenting herself over Valentine. She waved at a waiter and ordered a pizza for two with mushrooms, red peppers, and anchovies, then asked Laura to tell her everything that had been going on.

'I know it sounds crazy but I think someone's targeting me,' Laura said, gulping down wine. She searched Emma's face for a reaction, steeling herself for signs of disbelief. But all she could see there was concern.

'I can't get it out of my head that it's all connected. I've got this horrible feeling that he's going to try again.'

'You think it could be this guy you saw, Ben Morgan?' Emma said.

'Yes I do.'

'And he's been following you?'

'I think so. The way he ran off when I turned round to look at him. If it was coincidence he wouldn't have reacted like that, he'd have been as surprised as me. It was like he knew I was there.'

'But if he wanted to hurt you, why didn't he do it then? I mean why run off when he had a chance to get you?'

Laura shivered, 'I don't know. Maybe he didn't want to do anything when there were witnesses around.'

Emma looked at her, appalled, 'You have to go back to the police. Tell them about this man, get them to track him down. Why not do it now? Come on, I'll come with you.'

Emma did not doubt her, Laura thought, didn't think she was being irrational. It was a relief to be believed, but it left a bitter taste as well. Emma was taking her fears seriously, was being supportive, whereas Joe …

'That's so kind of you, Em,' Laura felt tears start again in her eyes, 'but the policeman I need to talk to won't be in until tomorrow so I'll do it then. There's no point in going back now. They won't do anything.'

'What about Harry Pelham?' Emma asked her. 'He sounds a nasty piece of work.'

'He is, and I'm suspicious about him. That's the thing, I can't be sure who it is, just that there is someone.'

'You say the police are letting him go free even though he's threatening his wife?'

'They've put conditions on his bail, not much else they can do. He hasn't actually been convicted of anything violent.'

'So they just sit back and wait until he's killed somebody,' Emma said, angrily. 'And what about him being a paedophile? They have to act over that, don't they?'

'Yes, if it's proved, but he won't go to jail unless it's really serious.'

'I can't believe this,' Emma frowned, her sharp brown eyes examining Laura. 'I'm worried about you, Lau, you look really stressed out.'

'I shouldn't have unloaded it all on you,' Laura said, feeling guilty for bothering Emma with her troubles when she was about to go on holiday. 'Don't worry. I'm OK. Maybe I'm overthinking it anyway, maybe there's nothing in it and it's just a lot of random bad things all coming at once. Shit happens, as Joe would say.'

'Is that what he thinks?'

'He thinks I'm being neurotic; irrational was the word he used.'

Laura drank the rest of her wine. The bottle was empty and she ordered herself another glass. She would have got another bottle but Emma said she needed to get home without being totally pissed.

'It's not like it used to be. Joe's different,' she said, and told Emma her worries.

'Sounds like it's just what happens to everyone after a while.'

'Yeah, maybe,' Laura said.

'Wait until you have a kid, that will really put sex on the back burner,' Emma said, grinning, then told what she hoped was a funny story about one of the ups and downs of her own fifteen-year relationship with Steve.

Laura was only half concentrating. She kept glancing towards the door and out of the window to the street outside. Maybe her attacker was waiting for her, ready to strike again. Her fingers picked at the pizza in front of her, slowly shredding it to bits.

'You're supposed to eat it, not mutilate it,' Emma said.

Laura gave a weak laugh. She took a bite of the pizza but it seemed to swell up inside her mouth and she needed some wine to be able to swallow it.

She looked at her watch. Gone 8 p.m. 'Em, you should get going. I shouldn't have kept you so long.'

Reluctantly, Emma gathered her bags together.

'I wish I wasn't going away. You take care and try not to worry too much. Make sure you text me what happens with the police.'

Laura promised that she would and Emma kissed her goodbye, remembering not to hug. She set off to catch the bus that would take her home to Saltdean. Laura watched her go then stood looking nervously round the street, staring at the faces coming towards her and peering into the shadows.

Her head was fuzzy with the white wine but fear was clearing it fast. A wave of threat hit her like a blast of cold wind blowing up the road. Her enemy was here, somewhere close by, she knew it in her gut, and terror filled her. This time he wouldn't care that there were witnesses; she saw herself stabbed and dying on the pavement, her blood running into the gutter.

Laura started running towards the taxi rank, regardless of the pain, blessing the lights from the Royal Pavilion that lit the way to safety.

CHAPTER TWENTY-FOUR

There was an atmosphere. Definitely hostile. Definitely involving her. Laura noticed it as soon as she walked in on Monday morning. Monica, on the front desk, was definitely off with her. Laura knew that if there were any office gossip Monica would know about it because she always made it her business to find out.

Monica was in her early fifties and had worked at Morrison Kemp for thirteen years – full time for the last six since her children were now grown up. With a lemon-sucking face she had watched Laura arrive from her big London job, knowing, before meeting her, that she would be too big for her boots. Now her lips were set in disapproval, her needle-sharp nose lifted in distaste. She could hardly manage a curt 'Hi' before turning away to talk to her colleague.

Mid-morning, Laura attended the weekly review meeting. Morrison chaired it and made sure there was the usual sky high level of praise and self-congratulation for the firm's overall performance. No mention was made of the Hakimi debacle. Morrison simply remarked, casually, that Sarah Cole had now 'gone to pursue career challenges elsewhere.' No-one said anything but Laura sensed frosty eyes upon her and felt herself blush.

Shortly afterwards she ran into the young, studious trainee, Alex Marshall, who had shared an office with Sarah, and his manner towards her confirmed her feeling that something was wrong. Alex was only twenty-five but he was going on forty. He loved legal textbooks and obscure facts and he always tried to follow the exact letter of the law. It got him into trouble with Morrison who often ticked him off for being too pedantic and for getting so hung up on legal details that he couldn't see the bigger picture. As Laura knew only too well, Morrison was a man who cared about the end result and was none too fussy about the means of achieving it.

She attempted to chat to Alex about a course he'd been on recently. It was entitled 'overcoming probate challenges' and mention of it and its fascinating mix of up-to-the-minute facts about wills, trusts, and inheritance tax planning would usually have guaranteed his attention. Probate and wills were one area of the law that Laura would have gone a long way to avoid, but she knew Alex found it interesting. He could become quite animated discussing it. But not today. Today he couldn't wait to get away from her.

He mumbled that it had been fine and hurried back to his office and she wondered what Sarah had said to him on Friday afternoon as she'd cleared her desk. She guessed it had been about her and it had not been nice.

Laura had forced herself to go into work. She'd woken up stiff and in pain, wanting nothing more than to stay under the bedcovers and swallow another sedative. But the tear from the night before still clung to her, and the worry that she had no time to lose nagged insistently at her.

She called Detective Inspector Barnes first thing and got through to him without a problem though she thought he sounded wary. Yes, he said, the sergeant had contacted him and he had been going to ring her. He had a note in front of him to do so.

She did it much better this time, told her story matter-of-factly; not neurotic, not melodramatic, she just stated exactly what had happened and left him to think about it. No assertions that someone had been following her, that someone was out to get her, no apparently crazy assumptions, no demands for action. To begin with he said nothing, but as she continued her unemotional account he interrupted with the occasional question. By the end, when she related how she'd recognized Ben Morgan in the street, he even sounded moderately interested.

Without her having to ask, Barnes said he would check out Ben Morgan with a view to finding him and interviewing him. Laura was encouraged and decided to push a little further, asking if he would go and look at the wire on the trees. He hesitated, said he'd see what he could do. It was the best she was going to get and she thanked him.

One other thing, he said, sounding uncharacteristically sheepish, on the matter of Harry Pelham. He had discharged himself from hospital on Saturday evening. His present whereabouts were unknown.

Laura felt alarm explode in her chest. Harry Pelham was on the loose, had been on the loose on Sunday evening when she'd felt sure she was being followed. Her scalp prickled.

'We're checking his house regularly to see if he's there,' Barnes said quickly, 'and we're letting his wife know, but please can you tell her anyway? I'll keep you both informed.'

'Please do. Can you phone me as soon as you find him?'

Barnes promised he would. He gave her his mobile number and the fact that he volunteered it made her more worried still.

Laura had rung Anna at once with the bad news, telling her to call Barnes immediately if she heard from Harry or was worried he might be watching the house. Anna hadn't said much because Martha was with her, but asked if she could come in for a chat around lunchtime.

She had just arrived, looking anxious and defeated, and Laura invited her up to her office.

'He just walked out of the hospital and no one tried to stop him,' Anna said, spreading her arms in a hopeless gesture.

'I know.'

'The police told him to stay put. How bloody stupid is that? As if he was ever going to take any notice.'

'The thing now is to find him. Can you think of anywhere he might go?'

'Apart from coming after me and Martha?' Anna gave a thin laugh. 'Thank God, Martha's going away for a few days over half-term to stay in London with a school friend's auntie. She's home on Saturday though, and he was due to see her then. He'll still try to, that's for sure. He won't give a shit about the bail conditions.'

'I'll ask Barnes if he can put a watch on your house on Saturday,' Laura promised.

Anna was sitting with her hands limp on her lap, her head and shoulders shaking nervously.

'It's me,' she burst out, 'I'll always be a victim, I always have been and I always will be. Right back from when I was a kid at school. It's never, ever going to change, is it, however hard I try?'

Anna covered her face and began to sob as she let the memories flood back.

CHAPTER TWENTY-FIVE

Christmas 1997
Anna wanted very much to kill herself. She tried first with her mother's sleeping pills and then with a razor blade.

She had grown tall early on and she had grown heavy. At the age of twelve she was five-foot-seven and weighed thirteen stone. She felt huge and ridiculous and ugly next to her petite classmates, and they made it clear they felt the same about her.

She remembered it all vividly; remembered the bullying, remembered Maria Burns and Jennifer Fleming and Michelle Cullen and Lisa Handley and all the rest of them who had made her life hell for years.

Afterwards, when she'd been taken away from the school and was being treated in hospital, the psychiatrist had explained to her about bullying. She didn't need it explained, she was already a world expert, but he liked the sound of his own voice and she was a captive audience. He told her theories about why it happened, about who did it and who they did it to. He told her that all sorts of people were targets, for all sorts of reasons. She mustn't think that she had brought it on herself, had somehow invited it by being the odd one out. He gave her some case studies to look at. She read them and found what she already knew.

Girls can be mean. Girls can whisper. Girls can gossip, manipulate, isolate, target the weakest spot. Boys use physical strength to bully but girls are far more frightening. They use psychological warfare. They can destroy you from the inside.

There's always that one person in every school. The one who gets made fun of and judged, even though no one really knows much about them. That person was Anna. Right from the start, she had been different. She had wanted desperately to fit in, but, try as she might, she never managed to.

The boys simply ignored her and the group of girls she tried to hang out with laughed at her and then persecuted her relentlessly. They sneered at her clothes, her hair, her weight, her face. They glared at her, refused to talk to her, called her names, gossiped about her and spread rumours. They would sit whispering to each other, staring straight at her. Every day she ate lunch by herself.

They failed to invite her to parties, sleepovers, get-togethers. She would sit in class listening to them talk about funny stories from the times they had spent together. She spent a lot of her school day locked in the toilet cubicle, crying. One day when she couldn't stand it anymore, when she was so tired of being bullied and ignored, so sick of fighting back tears and being told by teachers to just ignore the other girls, she called her mother and asked to be collected from school.

It was a sign of weakness, and from it, she learned never to show weakness again. They knew she was upset and their bullying fed off it. They knew, too, that her mother suffered from depression because once, as part of a doomed attempt to fit in, Anna had talked about her family and her mother's problems. They began to act as if she was crazy. When they saw her coming they would make gestures, pretend to slit their wrists. Some would call her 'pyscho' and tell her they daren't speak to her in case she messed them up and made them crazy too. If she sat down at the same table they would gather their things together and leave.

It went on like that for about three years and then, gradually, life began to improve. The group had its own fallings-out and realignments. New friendships were made, and a larger, wider circle formed. Although the bullying continued it was not nearly so bad, and gradually Anna became tolerated, if not wholly accepted. She even felt that a few of the girls: Maria and Jenny and Lisa, she might one day be able to call friends.

By December 1996, soon after her fifteenth birthday, Anna was enjoying life for the first time that she could remember. Other girls phoned her with invitations. She knew she was never their first choice, she was more a last resort person who they would call when no one else was around, but at least they called her. She even went to a couple of parties, stood silently next to Maria or Jenny, clutching a glass of fruit juice that lasted all evening. No one ever offered to get her another and she was too timid to help herself. It wasn't exactly the height of social success but at least she was there.

It was soon after one of these parties that Anna made a mistake. It seemed a small enough thing at the time but it had big consequences.

She was trying to get more friendly with Maria Burns because she wanted Maria to become something she had always craved but never come anywhere close to – a 'best friend'. Anna had learned by now that the surest way to put someone off you and to end up being ridiculed was to appear needy and clingy and desperate for a friend.

She had also discovered that girls liked you to be interested in them, liked you to make them feel superior, liked you to confide in them. And so she did all of those things and Maria, who was not the most popular of girls herself, began to see that a best friend like Anna, although a bit of a loser, might not be such a bad thing. Certainly she wouldn't threaten Maria's position or steal attention away from her. In fact, she would show up all the better by contrast. Maria started to include Anna in everything she did, and for a while it looked as though Anna would get what she wanted.

It was April and the general election was looming. John Major's government pinned its hopes on the 'feel-good factor', hoping the economic prosperity that had followed the recession of the early nineties would be enough to distract voters from all the sleaze and the in-fighting over Europe. There was no feel-good factor for Maria. That month her father lost his job and the family were faced with selling their house. They would lose a lot of money; the house was in negative equity.

Maria tearfully confided all this to Anna one evening when they were babysitting Maria's four-year-old brother. The following morning at school, in a weak moment, a moment designed to show off how close her friendship with Maria had become, Anna related the details to two other girls. By lunchtime everyone knew.

Maria came up to her, furious: 'You cow, I can't believe I ever wanted to be friends with you. Oh, and never forget how much I hate you.'

That was all she said. No shouting, no screaming or recriminations, just an understated fury. She never spoke to Anna again, on that subject or any other. Instead, she said a lot about Anna, behind her back, and the results were soon clear. The bullying came back, big time, worse than it had ever been.

She went to her locker and found pictures stuck all over the front of it; pictures of her with a group of her former friends but with her face cut out. She sat down at lunch and they moved away and threw food at her, taunting her for being fat. They would stare as she came towards them in the corridor and make mooing sounds as she walked past. There was always a laugh, a cough disguising an insult, a whisper or a rude gesture. She found a note left on her desk, which read, 'leave, like seriously, just die.'

Phone calls at home were never for her. Friday nights and weekends she stayed in watching television or sitting in her room. She was an only child and had no one to confide in. Her mother had problems of her own and she wasn't close to her father. She got on his nerves, she knew that. He made it clear that all she'd

131

ever been was trouble and he had enough trouble already with his wife. Even if Anna had tried to talk to him, she thought he'd have had no idea how to help. She sank into depression.

It was around that time that she first noticed him. She'd gone shopping – on her own as usual – when she'd seen a crowd of boys, arguing. She stopped to watch, saw that one boy was being picked on by the rest, saw that he was thin and geeky looking, saw that he was crying. He was the one, she thought bitterly, the one they would instinctively target. He may as well have had the word 'victim' tattooed on his forehead. She winced with fellow-feeling as he was knocked to the ground.

Then a boy on the edge of the crowd moved forwards, stood in front of the victim waving his arms and pushing away the aggressor. There was a moment when it could have gone either way, when the 'saviour', as Anna always thought of him afterwards, could have been challenged and swept aside. She held her breath.

The saviour was yelling and a boy was yelling back and the victim was cringing on the pavement. Then it was over. The boy who had led the attack turned away and the crowd began to shuffle off. The victim shot to his feet and ran off at top speed.

She let out her breath. From across the street she gazed at the boy who had intervened. He had stood up for one of life's victims, had stood up for someone like her. Fascinated, she followed him home. From that moment on she couldn't get him out of her mind.

Anna had never had a boyfriend nor ever considered having one. They were one of the things she accepted a girl like her could never have. She belonged to an invisible group, the ignored girls; a group that boys didn't seem to notice. But now she started to wonder what it must be like to be the sort of girl who was wanted by boys, who was competed for by boys, in particular, by boys like him.

Usually she didn't have a lot to do with her spare time. That all changed. Every moment was precious because every moment was spent on him. She amassed information, gathering it stealthily, secretly, watching and following him.

He lived three miles away from her and went to the boys' school on the other side of town. She learned about his friends, his family, his daily routines, discovered his passion for photography and films, and those things she made her passion too.

She didn't dare speak to him. She was too convinced of her own grossness to do that. She lived in terror of actually meeting him. Instead, she wrote down her feelings in a notebook:

To me he is the perfect man. I adore him, almost like he is a god. If I could only make him notice me, make him like me just a little bit. No, that's not quite right. If I'm honest I'm scared of him noticing me because if he did he would see all my faults. He certainly wouldn't want me, or think I'm attractive in any way or even think of me at all for more than two seconds. Much better if he doesn't notice me. Not yet, anyway, not until I'm ready. Imagine if he knew how they bully me, what they say and do. Then he'd feel sorry for me. Pity me. How awful would that be? I'm happy just to stay near him. To know that he exists, and that I can look at him, is enough for now.

One day she would be ready to meet him, she told herself, but not yet, definitely not yet. Her love for him was no less strong because it was silent. Perhaps it was stronger because he could never fall from his pedestal by making some crass remark. In all her schooldays, she had never spoken a single word to him.

Anna may not have talked to the boy but she talked with him. Imaginary conversations in her head that grew ever more real. They were written down in the notebook, a solid record of their relationship. And if sometimes she needed more, she would call his home, hoping that he answered, hoping for the brief thrill of hearing his voice before she put down the phone.

She had found his phone number in the dustbin along with all sorts of other personal information. There were two bins by the side of his house and some evenings, after dark, she sneaked across the back fence and went through the contents. She knew it was a bit crazy, but what harm did it do?

She aimed for Wednesday nights because the refuse men called on Thursdays. She fished out household bills, junk mail, discarded catalogues. Anything he might have touched, anything addressed to him, she treasured, locking it away in a suitcase under her bed. To have something that he'd owned, even if he didn't want it, made her feel she was part of his life. One time she struck gold. She pulled out a shirt ruined with ink from a broken biro. She knew it wasn't his father's or his brother's because she recognized it immediately as one of his. It became the centrepiece of the shrine that she built to him.

He loved photography and so she became an expert. She took hundreds of photos of him. She waited for hours with her camera outside his house, outside his friends' houses, outside anywhere she could track him down. Sometimes she would see him come out of his house, three cameras strung round his neck, heading for the beach or the town centre. She would creep along behind, out of sight, and when he took a picture she would take the same one, studying the light and the composition in the same way she saw him do it. By doing so she felt that she was growing ever closer to him.

It was on one of these days – a blistering hot Saturday afternoon in August – that he spoke to her. Brighton seafront could have doubled for the south of France, were it not for the pebbles and the smell of burgers and onions. Visitors packed the town, sunbathers packed the beach, and in the middle of them, set up between the two piers, was a bungee jumping machine.

It made a good picture taken from the promenade above – rows of bodies lying prone in the sun, others lounging in the ubiquitous striped deckchairs, and then another body plunging down into their midst. He spent a lot of time taking photos and when he finally moved away, Anna took his place. She was leaning on the rail, camera poised, waiting for the next man to jump, when she heard his voice.

'Great shot eh?'

She froze, terrified, unable even to press down her finger and snap the picture as the man fell towards the crowds below.

'Did you get him?' the boy asked.

She could not answer. She stood, the camera clamped to her face, wishing that the burning sun would melt her and she could ooze away unnoticed into the ground.

'Hey, did you get the picture?' he asked again, louder this time, thinking that she hadn't heard him above the noise of the crowd milling around them.

'I can take one for you if you want. I do a lot of this,' the boy said.

She could bear it no longer. She squeezed herself under the lower railing, dropped down onto the beach and ran off, scattering shingle as she went.

In her mind, and in her notebook, she endlessly replayed and rewrote the events of that day. And as she did so she came to believe that he liked her. Why else had he spoken to her and offered to take a photo for her? The incident inflamed her feelings and during the next few months, as she thought about it continually and followed him at every possible moment, she became convinced that, not only did he like her, but he wanted her and returned in full the feelings she had for him.

Why else did he go back so often to the beach and stand by the railings looking at the sea? In the hope of seeing her again, of course, in the hope that she would come by with her camera.

Once, on a stormy day in early winter, he went on to the Palace Pier to take pictures. She didn't like to follow him because the pier was empty and she would be conspicuous so she waited nearby on the beach. White horses rode the water, crashing through the legs of the pier and down on to the shingle. There was a crowd of people watching the wild sea; she stood among them and someone must have had some food, because, all at once, they were buzzed by a squadron of screeching seagulls. To her surprise, and intense delight, she saw the boy turn his camera towards her. He was taking her picture, he must be, what other explanation could there be?

The more disordered her life became, the more isolated she felt, the more she believed that he cared for her. By thinking about when she would next see him, she could endure the bullying. She inhabited a world where he loved her and so she was able to escape from her own dismal existence.

CHAPTER TWENTY-SIX

Lisa and Luke Handley were having a birthday party. Lisa would be sixteen on the 13th December 1997, her brother would be seventeen three days later. Their party was on the Saturday at the end of term. The Handleys went to Anna's school and both of them were popular – it seemed like everyone had been invited. Everyone but Anna. She hadn't really expected to be, but it still upset her for she had once counted Lisa Handley as a friend. It hurt, especially as Lisa had never taken much part in the bullying, seemed not to enjoy it. Lately, though, Lisa hardly ever troubled to speak to her.

As the party night grew closer, Anna was forced to overhear endless chatter about it. She was forced, too, to endure taunts and mockery because she wasn't going. Girls who had been discussing it would suddenly stop talking when she came near, then say something like: 'Shh. She's coming. Ugh. We'd better shut up or she'll go and tell her friends what we've been saying. Oh hang on, she doesn't have any!'

It was the last day of term and the morning's lessons had finished. Students headed for their lockers, and when Anna arrived, there were large groups standing about chatting. She was making her way through them when she spotted the card taped to her locker door. She stood before it, a hard lump in her throat and a sick feeling in her stomach.

Slowly she pulled the card from the door. It had a picture of a hugely fat girl with a doctor in his consulting room. The caption read, 'It's partly glandular and partly 8,500 calories per day'.

She opened it.

'Sweetheart', it said, 'I love the way your fat spills over when you wear those tight jeans. Will you come to the party with me? A secret admirer.'

She heard sniggering behind her back. Big, tearing sobs filled her chest and as she tried to stifle them, she let out a strangled howl of pain. The buzz of conversation around her stopped, all eyes turned towards her. In the few moments before she ran from the scene she saw through her tears the smiling, smug face of Maria Burns.

She ran but there was nowhere to hide. She ended up where she had ended up so often before, locked in a cubicle in the girls' toilets, sobbing her heart out. But this time was different. Something else was mixed in with her distress, something that had been growing in her and was finally raising its head; a determination not to let them win, not to be a victim anymore.

She gritted her teeth. Her enemies had hurt her, yes, they had seen her cry, yes, but she would get up again, they would not keep her down. In the afternoon she was back in class as usual. She said nothing, as usual. The teacher took no notice of her, as usual. A couple of the girls stared at her and she stared back. Maria Burns and her friends would get no more satisfaction from what they'd done.

At last it was over. End of term. She hurried out the door, and then an amazing thing happened: Lisa Handley came up to her, thrust an invitation card into her hand, said, 'You're welcome, if you want to come', and walked off before Anna had time to reply. She couldn't have replied anyway, she was too choked up to speak.

She knew at once that she would go. No doubt Lisa had witnessed the locker incident and felt sorry for her. But she didn't need pity. She would show them all, show them that they could not crush her.

She had not forgotten the message in the card and she chose to wear a pair of loose, black trousers. For the first time in a long time she studied herself in the mirror. The spots, which had infested her forehead and chest, were clearing up; she had grown taller, five foot ten at least, and she didn't look so fat. Her large breasts were now in proportion to the generous swell of her hips, her belly no longer resembled a sack of potatoes. She would still be called 'a big girl', but she wasn't so sure she would still be called ugly.

It was an exciting discovery and maybe the reason her judgement deserted her. She put on a tight, low-cut Lycra top and squeezed her body into it. She thought with a thrill that her large eyes might almost qualify as attractive. She smothered them in heavy make-up, unconsciously ruining their natural charm. She persuaded herself that she looked good. It never occurred to her that she might look like a slut.

Her mother should have told her but her mother was ill. Her mental health was fragile and she felt only relief that her troubled daughter was finally behaving like a normal teenager. Her father dropped her off at the party.

Anna summoned up her courage and rang the doorbell. A boy she didn't know let her in. She pushed her way down the packed hallway searching for a place to get a drink. Someone cannoned into her, spilling lager over the too tight blouse. It clung forlornly to her stomach. She was painfully conscious of her size. With dismay she spotted the gang of girls clustered round the kitchen doorway: the usual suspects. In their midst, Maria Burns.

Maria had recently made great strides in the popularity stakes and was holding court. Maria saw her, stopped talking for a moment, and then began again. The gang of girls turned towards her. To her surprise they began waving, beckoning her over, and although the music was too loud for her to hear what they were saying, they were clearly being friendly.

She moved nervously towards them. They welcomed her, put their arms round her, and somebody shoved a glass into her hand.

'You look fab,' shouted Jennifer Fleming.

Anna wasn't sure, it might have been 'flab' and Maria Burns might have sniggered. On the other hand she might simply be paranoid. She took a gulp from the glass. She wasn't used to alcohol and the cheap red wine relaxed her almost at once. Michelle Cullen asked her where she got her 'fantastic' blouse and a glow of happiness inside her fed the glow from the wine.

'Come on you lot. Why aren't you dancing? It's our birthday!' Lisa Handley was bellowing at them. She was standing with her brother Luke, arms around each other's waists, looking out from the living room where the DJ and the dancing were. The crowd parted to let the pair through and they marched down the hall, scooped up the girls, Anna among them, and, shouting and laughing, they headed for the dance floor.

It was not something that Anna would ever have done. Dancing. She just didn't – couldn't. It was way out of her comfort zone. But the wine made her brave, the apparent friendliness of the other girls buoyed her up and she decided it could be done and she would do it.

No-one was more surprised than Anna by the result. For all her bulk she turned out to be a good dancer. There was nothing clumsy about her and if Maria and her friends had looked forward to a good laugh, they didn't get it.

Anna was doing something right for a change, doing it so that she couldn't be mocked or criticized. She closed her eyes, lost in the music and the dance. When she opened them again he was standing there. The boy from the beach. The saviour.

CHAPTER TWENTY-SEVEN

Laura was worried by Anna's breakdown and wondered if it meant she was going to cave in to Harry, give him everything he wanted, just to try to get some peace. Of course, it wouldn't mean peace, Laura thought, it would only encourage her husband, make him think she would come crawling back in the end and he could continue abusing her just where he left off.

A voice message from Jeff Ingham had arrived while Laura was talking to Anna. He'd already called early that morning to say that Valentine had spent another restless night. He wasn't eating properly either.

'We'll keep trying, little and often, with the things you told us he likes, but he needs to pick up soon … ' the vet had said.

Laura listened to the new message with a thumping heart, trying to brace herself. Valentine just would not calm down, Jeff said, they were going to have to sedate him. He wanted her to be prepared for that when she came in later to visit.

It left her in an agony over whether to take the awful decision to put Valentine out of his misery. Wouldn't that be better than making him fight for his life, and putting him through all this extra suffering?

Her gloomy thoughts were interrupted by a knock on the door and when she called out 'come in', she was surprised to see Morrison appear. She couldn't remember him ever knocking before, let alone waiting for an answer.

'Laura, could we have a little chat?'

He was smiling and for once it didn't look patronising. He was being friendly.

'Wednesday night,' he said, handing her a white printed card, 'you should approve of the venue: Greene's hotel.'

It was the Law Society dinner. Inwardly, she groaned.

'Good to see they're supporting the family firm. Thank you. I'll look forward to it.'

Perhaps he would go away now, she hoped. But, no, he wasn't going, he wanted a chat. He sat down in the chair opposite, silent, considering what to say. If she hadn't known it was an absurd idea, she would have said he was nervous.

'I've had a call from the Legal Ombudsman,' he began, 'one of their case workers. A Mrs Asha Patel. It seems there's been a complaint about our handling of the Hakimi case.' He told her that Mrs Patel had been informed by the complainant that Laura Maxwell had put forward a scheme to forge the letter but it had been vetoed by Sarah Cole. Laura started to protest but Morrison held up his hand. He continued, 'She said, bearing in mind the serious nature of the allegation, she might have to bring in the SRA.' His lip curled as he said the initials.

Laura was well aware of his opinion of the Ombudsman and especially of the SRA, the Solicitors Regulatory Authority, which would investigate any possible misconduct. He hated them both, but he also feared them, for they had extensive powers to investigate and their decisions could not be easily challenged. He regularly complained that they were unaccountable to anyone.

There was also the original mistake to consider, Mrs Patel had said. Of course, any resulting negligence claim was a civil matter and nothing to do with the Ombudsman, but they did have a duty to investigate whether there had been inadequate professional service to the client and they would be doing just that. She had faxed over a copy of the complaint and given Morrison fourteen days to put in a response.

In true Morrison fashion he had told Mrs Patel that he knew very little of the matter but he would look into it fully, right away, and get straight back to her.

He studied Laura. 'Of course, I realize it was not your idea to write the letter, in fact, it was because of your good sense that no such letter was handed over but you'll understand I couldn't correct Mrs Patel's version without admitting the initial fault. Better not to comment at this stage.'

He paused, as if he was expecting her to agree or approve the fact that he had not immediately cleared her name.

'I would like it made crystal clear to Mrs Patel that I had nothing to do with it,' said Laura hotly.

'Absolutely. No question of that,' he said then coughed awkwardly. 'Could I have the Hakimi file, please?'

She opened a drawer, took it out, and handed it to him. He flipped it open, read through Sarah's letter, which was pinned to the top of the pile of correspondence.

'I've spoken to Sarah Cole this morning and left her in no doubt about the very serious position she's in. Her name is on this and whatever she may say about being ordered to write it, she has signed it and is accountable.'

He stared hard at Laura, all trace of a smile gone from his face.

'We agreed that it's best for all of us that this never happened, that no such letter was ever written.'

He unpinned the letter from the file. 'As far as the file is concerned this letter never existed. But I won't destroy it just yet in case Sarah becomes unhelpful. I'll keep it somewhere safe.' He folded the letter and put it in his jacket pocket, 'I trust you have no problem with that?' Unusually, it was a question, not a statement. He badly wanted her cooperation.

'But surely Sarah must have supplied the information on which the complaint is based so it's going to be pretty difficult now for her to say it never happened,' Laura said, confused.

'She says not. She says she hasn't told anybody. She says she was so traumatized by losing her job that she spent the whole weekend in bed. She hasn't felt up to talking to anyone. Not even her mother. Must say, I felt rather sorry for her.'

A small part of Laura found time to be astonished at the nerve of the man. He spoke as if he were an innocent bystander in no way responsible for what had happened. The rest of her was struggling to understand the implications of what he'd said.

'You believed her?'

'Of course not. She's lying. How else would Clive Walters have known if she hadn't told him? But the good news is she now realizes she needs to save her own skin and cooperate.'

'Clive Walters made the complaint?' Laura asked.

'Yes and I know you're going to say he's not the client so technically he's got no right to complain, but he seems to have got round that by saying it's on behalf of his sister who is too upset to do it herself.'

Laura hadn't been going to say any such thing; her mind was running in quite a different direction. She was puzzled by Morrison's account of what Sarah had said. It sounded authentic. Sarah would be shattered by what had happened and she wasn't stupid. She knew Clive Walters was trouble; if she wanted revenge she'd realize that involving him was not the way to get it. Any formal complaint was bound to backfire on her. Morrison had dismissed what she'd said as lies but Laura found it hard to do so. But then, she told herself, he must be right. There could be no other explanation.

'So are we agreed on the best way to proceed?' He was still there wanting a commitment.

'I'll be very happy to say that I never suggested, or took part in, the forging of any letter,' she said, hating herself for even half colluding with him. It was not the wholehearted rebuttal of the complaint that he wanted but he would have to be satisfied with it. She was not going to tell any outright lies though neither would she volunteer information. But if Mrs Patel pressed further she would only answer truthfully.

The expression on his face was an odd mixture of relief and resentment. She had not displayed the total dedication to the well-being of Morrison Kemp that he would have wished for. Her commitment was lukewarm.

'We need to stick together over this, there's no 'I' in team,' he said, waspishly, 'And there's still the original error to be dealt with. A very serious one, Laura.'

He was rapidly returning to his old intimidating manner. He stopped short of trying to blame her outright for the mess, but, she thought, only because he needed her support over the forgery complaint.

'We have to accept there was no letter advising Mrs Hakimi it was her responsibility to tell us to renew the order. Clearly we can't produce one now. It's an oversight that could cost us one hell of a lot of money.'

'I'm doing my best to get the boy back. I don't think Mrs Hakimi wants to pursue a claim anyway, certainly not at the moment when she believes we can help her. It's her brother's idea. He's after a pay-out.'

"And he's very likely to get one," Morrison snapped, "Let's hope you can persuade his sister that we'll do a better job for her if she gets her brother off our back."

"I'll speak to her."

He stood up to go, looked down at her coldly. 'This will be a challenge for you Laura. How you handle it will help me decide what sort of contribution you can make to this firm in the future.'

The superior smile was back on his lips: 'I have every confidence you'll be able to deal with this in your usual competent manner.'

'Good of you to say so,' she murmured, but Morrison was immune to irony.

CHAPTER TWENTY-EIGHT

After Morrison had gone, Laura rang Mary Hakimi on the excuse that she wanted to update her on the search for her missing son. It was not much of an update and Laura was honest enough not to exaggerate it. She said that she'd called a contact in Tunisia, given him details of the boy and his father, and he had agreed to alert the immigration people there. She didn't say any more, didn't try to explain what she hoped might come of it, but if she had single-handedly rescued Ahmed from the jaws of death, Mary Hakimi couldn't have been more grateful. Clutching at straws had nothing on this, Laura thought unhappily.

Mrs Hakimi sounded her usual stressed and dazed self and when Laura gently raised the subject of the complaint there was no reaction at all. She tried again, saying they would deal with it as quickly as they could and they understood her concern. Laura was careful to keep away from any mention of the actual allegation but she needn't have worried.

'I'm sorry, I don't know what you're talking about. I haven't made any complaint,' said Mrs Hakimi.

Laura explained that the Legal Ombudsman had been contacted about the handling of her case and was now conducting an investigation.

Silence from the other end of the phone, then an intake of breath that sounded like a sob.

'Oh my God. It'll be Clive. It must be. He'll have done it.'

'I see.' It was all Laura could think of to say.

'It'll only make things worse, won't it?' She was trying hard to hold back the tears.

Morrison would have pounced. He would have subtly but assuredly left the woman in no doubt that, yes, the complaint would make things a whole lot worse, especially her chances of ever seeing her boy again. He would have made it clear that the smart thing for her to do would be to get on to the Ombudsman at once and withdraw it.

'It won't make any difference to the search for Ahmed,' Laura told her.

At the mention of the boy's name Mary Hakimi began to cry. 'Clive talked about it, but I never thought he'd do it. Not without my agreement.'

'I'll let you know when there's any news. We'll talk again soon.'

There was no answer, just sobbing.

It was not a performance Morrison would have approved of, she thought as she put down the phone, not the sort of 'contribution' he was after. She could imagine him hissing at her, telling her it had been an opportunity to save their skin and she had let it slip away.

She picked up her mobile to text Joe and tell him how she was. He'd wanted her to stay at home to rest for another day, at least. He'd told her he had nothing much on at work and could probably get away soon after lunch and come back to look after her. They would talk everything through – he knew she wanted to and he would listen and try to be constructive. Then they would visit Valentine together. It had been a sweet interlude after the harsh words and it reminded her of old times.

He had sent her a couple of texts during the morning. They were full of 'honeys' and sweethearts' and they made her happy. He did still care for her then, maybe as much as ever.

She was writing him a message when another text came in.

Next time I'll get you, you fucking bitch.

She stared at it, trying to take it in, feeling the blood drain from her face. The text alert buzzed again.

Not much time left you piece of scum. I'm coming for you.
And again.
You've been lucky so far but understand this, you're going
to die.

They were anonymous – no name – just an unknown number. Of course they would be.
Buzz.

You deserve everything you're going to get.

The sour taste of fear filled her mouth. She had been right all along. Someone was trying to kill her; she had not imagined it, here was the proof, someone out there wanted her dead.
Buzz.

You'll be dead by the end of the week.

With a trembling finger she pressed the button to clear the night-mare away.
Buzz.

Want to know what I'm going to do to you before you die?

She waited, heart galloping, ice along the nerves.
Nothing. The mobile stayed silent. She clutched it in front of her.

The phone on her desk rang and she jolted with fear. It was Monica. Detective Inspector Barnes was on the line, would she take the call?

'Please, Monica, please put him through,' her voice cracked in her throat.

'I'm getting death threats,' she burst out at once. 'On my phone. Texts. He says he'll kill me by the end of the week.'

She read him the texts. He would have to take her seriously now. Buzz.

She shouted down the phone at Barnes. 'There's another one.'

'OK. Read it to me'

'Hey, hun … ' she stopped abruptly as her brain caught up with what her eyes were seeing. It was from Joe, asking how she was and if she was coming home early.

'Sorry. False alarm. My husband.' she said, shakily.

She stared at Joe's message, its normality mocking her, wishing she could go home to him without the certain knowledge that someone hated her so much they wanted her dead.

Barnes was asking questions, could she think of anyone, apart from Ben Morgan or Harry Pelham, who might be doing this, enemies from her professional life, vengeful ex-boyfriends, what was her relationship like with her husband?

'Fine,' she said, 'I mean it's good.' The question rocked her.

All the time she talked to Barnes she stared at the mobile, braced for another text.

'If we're going to trace the texts we'll need the phone,' he said.

'You think you can trace them?' she asked, hopeful.

'There's a chance. Depends how much effort's been made to hide the trail.'

'I'll bring it in straightaway.'

'One thing,' he said before ringing off, 'don't try to reply. It's never a good idea.'

Buzz.

Have you been waiting, bitch? Are you scared? You need to be.

She would ring Joe to tell him what was happening, then she would switch off the mobile. Forever. She never wanted to touch it again.

He didn't pick up. She tried him at the hotel, he was out, they didn't know where. Back to the mobile, texted him, *please, ring me very urgent*, then left him a message; a worrying, alarming message but she couldn't fuss about that.

Buzz.

Paralysis. Read it or turn it off and never know. Her finger hovered over the screen. But she had to know. Of course she did.

You said I was crazy, you were right. Want to know how you're going to die?

Skin crawling on the back of her neck. Ben Morgan. He was out there, stalking her, preparing for another attack.

Buzz.

Painfully. Very painfully. And very soon.

CHAPTER TWENTY-NINE

When Laura stood up it was as if the nerves in her legs had been cut and there was no strength left in them. She leaned against her desk like an old woman. The mobile was switched off and now she put it in an envelope and sealed it, relieved not to have to touch it again.

There was a fuss going on when she reached the front office. For once, the usually reserved Alex Marshall was centre stage. He was relating a story to Monica and Elaine on reception, and three of the firm's legal staff were standing around listening. Morrison himself had just arrived through the door and Monica, wiping tears of laughter from her eyes, demanded that Alex begin the tale again.

'You've got to hear this, Marcus. It's a hoot,' she told him.

Laura was frantic to be gone, to get the phone to Barnes without a moment's delay. But she saw that Morrison had stopped and Alex, looking a little flustered at having his boss in the audience, was preparing to start again. Morrison spotted her and waved her over.

Laura hesitated. If she walked through the crowd and out the door it would look rude, as if she wasn't interested, as if she wasn't a team player just as Morrison had led them all to believe. Monica, for one, would know she was not off to see a client or any other urgent work appointment. It was just gone 2 p.m. They would assume she was taking a late lunch and had no reason to rush. As it was, she was not flavour of the month; it would be stupid to make things worse. She waited, it would not be for long, she thought.

Alex had been on a home visit. He'd gone to see an elderly couple who couldn't get out much, so that they could sign their wills. When he arrived the wife had let him in and told him her husband was still in bed. She offered him tea while he waited.

'Well I didn't have much choice,' he shrugged his round shoulders, 'so I said yes and sat down.'

'I hope you told her the taxi meter was running.' It was Morrison, ever concerned about money. There was a ripple of amusement but Morrison was poker-faced. It was not a laughing matter.

The young trainee paused for a second, could think of no satisfactory reply and carried on with his story.

'After about ten minutes I asked if she would mind going up and finding out what was happening.'

The woman didn't budge. She was disabled and found walking difficult, she was in no hurry to tackle the stairs. He'd made several more efforts to get her to chase up her husband but all had failed. He described these at length, in his laborious, exact manner, determined to make the most of the attention he was getting.

Laura fidgeted with the envelope in her coat pocket.

Alex had also explained to the woman that she must get her neighbours round, as previously agreed, because they would be needed to witness the wills. He took some time outlining the procedure for will signing, keen to demonstrate his expertise to Morrison.

Laura squirmed in frustration. Would he never get to the point? Was there a point? She supposed there must be. Monica had said it was 'a hoot'. She glanced around; a couple of the faces were looking a bit bored. But Morrison's wasn't and while he stayed, they all would.

'I really couldn't hang on any longer. After all time is money,' he stopped, looking towards his boss for approval. A wintry smile crossed the thin lips.

'So I decided to go upstairs myself and find him,' he said it with a note of triumph at his own daring as if he'd had a James Bond moment, 'and when I got there. What do you think?' He looked at them all self-importantly. Of course, most of them knew already because they'd been here first time round. The act was for Morrison. He hurried on in case any of them replied and stole his thunder. 'I went in to the bedroom and he was lying there. On the bed with his mouth open, not moving, looking like he'd had it. I shook him by the shoulder, and I kept shaking him, really hard in the end, but he didn't wake up. No sign of life at all. "He's dead," I shouted out.' He stopped, suddenly aware that it might not have been the best way to break the news to the man's wife. 'I was so shocked,' he added defensively. 'I couldn't help myself.'

Laura looked at her watch. Eight minutes. Eight precious minutes had ticked by.

'I ran down the stairs at top speed and there she was, still sitting in the chair drinking tea. So I told her again, straight out. "I'm very sorry but I think something's happened to your husband. We need to call an ambulance".'

Alex drew himself up, straightened his shoulders, and puffed out his chest.

Please, thought Laura, please might this mean he's coming to the punchline.

'And you know what, she just laughed. Actually laughed. And then she said to me, "he does that all the time" and started talking about the weather. Asked if it was still freezing cold outside, can you believe it?'

'Not as cold as your husband, Madam.' Morrison said. The audience giggled dutifully, wondering if the joke wasn't in rather bad taste.

'I thought maybe she was in denial, you know, so I said I would get help and stay with her until it arrived and make sure she was OK. I wanted to be as caring as I could.'

'Good for you, Alex,' chipped in Monica.

'I phoned for an ambulance and for their daughter who'd arranged the appointment and lived round the corner. They arrived about the same time and they all rushed upstairs while I stayed with the wife. She wasn't bothered by any of it and I thought she was gaga.

'Eventually, the daughter came down and said the paramedics had managed to wake up her dad. Then she apologized and said she'd meant to warn me this could happen as it had happened before just the same – paramedics and all!'

Everyone laughed and Laura laughed too but the smile froze on her lips. She was facing the door to the street, and at that moment, it opened and a man came in. A gaunt, shabby-looking man. He stood surveying the group before moving forward towards the reception desk. It was then that he caught her eye. They stared at each other. Ten seconds, maybe, before he turned abruptly on his heel and left.

Alex was still talking; she vaguely registered his voice droning on in the background. Her jelly-like legs would support her no more. Reluctantly, they took her as far as the row of chairs set out for waiting clients. They were over where Morrison was standing and he glanced at her as she sat down heavily.

'Then to cap it all, the husband comes down the stairs and into the room as if nothing is wrong. His wife is still cackling away and she says to me, "Gave me a terrible fright too, young man, the first time it happened". The daughter told me her dad had narcolepsy and that's what caused it. It was incredible, really. He just wouldn't wake up, however much I shook him and shouted. It was like he was in a coma, dead,' he frowned, 'that's not strictly true, of course, when you're in a coma you're not actually dead. In fact … '

'Get on with it Alex. Everyone who works here knows all about comas!' this from Monica. Another burst of laughter, Morrison excepted.

'The neighbours had come in by this time and so the man and his wife both signed the wills and he apologized for keeping me waiting and for giving me such a shock,' he finished rather lamely.

'Great story, Alex. I can't imagine why anyone thinks wills and probate are dull.'

More laughter for Morrison.

He turned to Laura in the chair beside him. 'How about you, Laura? Have you got any amusing anecdotes from your heady days in London?'

Slight sarcasm in his tone but it was lost on her. It was all she could do to register that he was talking to her and had asked her a question. Her mind was filled with Ben Morgan and his hostile eyes watching her from across the room.

She sat, unable to answer. A wild part of her wanted to tell them her story, the one she was living through now, the one about the madman from her past who was out to kill her, who had tried twice already, who was, at that very moment, threatening to kill her, who had, just a few minutes ago, walked through the door. No laughter, no funny endings.

'Not really off the top of my head,' she stuttered out. 'Can't think of anything terribly exciting.'

It sounded feeble and a bit remote. Nil points scored in the popularity stakes. Morrison was talking again though she couldn't have said what about. She was concentrating on breathing. Deeply. It was hard, it hurt, and her hammering heart kept getting in the way. But it had to be done. It was the only way to get oxygen to her legs so that they would stand up and take her to see Barnes.

CHAPTER THIRTY

It was good to be out of the building at last, but it was bad to be out in the open where she was vulnerable to attack. She looked around for Ben Morgan. The man who is waiting to kill me, she thought. Her nerves crackled with fear.

If he was here, he would be hard to spot; there were numerous places to hide where he could spring out at her. If she screamed would anyone help her or would she be dead before they took any notice? She stood, paralysed, eyes scanning wildly up and down the busy street. The restaurants, the karaoke bar, the car park, the Black Lion pub, Jamie's Italian restaurant. He could be sheltering anywhere, watching her, waiting for her.

She thought about going back into Morrison Kemp and calling Barnes again but she knew there wasn't much he could do. Morgan had gone and she couldn't stay holed up in her office forever. The sun was out, but she didn't feel it. She was in a world of shadow; cold and menacing.

Laura forced herself to start walking to the police station. It wasn't far, no more than ten minutes if she took the back route, but she didn't go that way. She stuck to the main roads where there were fewer alleyways, where she could see farther ahead. Immediately, she had that creepy feeling again that someone was following her. She began stopping suddenly and turning round quickly, ducking into doorways, trying to see if she was being stalked. Her cracked rib screamed in protest and she pushed another painkiller into her dry mouth.

By the time she reached the police station in John Street she was clutching her chest like an old woman having a heart attack. She hadn't spotted Ben Morgan or anyone obviously suspicious, but the feeling that she was being followed never left her. As bad luck would have it, her favourite sergeant was manning the desk. The cold and the fear had made her nose run and she didn't have a tissue. She wiped it on her sleeve but it kept dripping. The sergeant looked at her, that same cynical expression on his face.

'Hello again Madam, what can I do for you?' he asked.

'I'm here to see Inspector Barnes,' she managed a smile.

'I'm afraid he's not available,' said the sergeant.

'I think you'll find he is. I spoke to him a short time ago and arranged to see him.' Her smile was dying fast.

'Sorry, Madam, it's not possible.'

'He's expecting me, I told you,' she snapped out.

'As I said, he's not available. He's ... '

'Look, will you just tell him I'm here!'

'Please, stay calm,' said the sergeant.

'I am calm,' she shouted.

Suddenly, shockingly, she started to cry, not gentle tears filling her eyes and rolling down her cheeks, but great violent, heaving sobs, which made her chest burn with pain. She couldn't believe it. Not here, she thought. Not in front of him. Please.

She had been wrong about the sergeant. He wasn't immune to tears and he could see her distress was genuine. His manner changed, the hardness gone, and he guided her to an interview room. Laura sank into a chair, wiped her nose again. He brought her tea and a box of tissues.

'I'm sorry,' she said.

'No problem. Would you like me to call someone? Your husband, maybe, who could make sure you're all right,' he said, carefully.

'I really do need to see the Inspector.'

'He had to go out on an urgent call. Just before you arrived. I was about to tell you.'

'I see,' she said, blowing her nose, disgusted that some weak, frightened part of herself had taken over. This wasn't meant to be her, this scared, defeated woman.

'If you want to give me any information I'll make sure Inspector Barnes gets it as soon as he gets back. Or you're welcome to stay here and wait for him, but I don't know how long he'll be.'

She thought about it. She wanted very much to stay put. She felt safe in the police station and there weren't many places left that she could say that about. But it was only a temporary haven. She wasn't likely to get police protection on the basis of a few threatening texts and some nasty incidents that might or might not be connected.

She pulled out the envelope with the mobile from her coat pocket, handed it to the sergeant, and asked him to give it to Barnes when he returned. She told him about the texts and about Ben Morgan and how horrified she'd been to see him walk in to Morrison Kemp. The sergeant noted it all down, and this time, she hoped he might not have added the words 'drama queen'. His attitude had changed and he seemed to be taking her seriously. But then again, she thought, maybe it was just the tears that had wiped the doubting look from his face.

The sergeant arranged for her to be dropped back at work. The breakdown in the police station had shocked Laura, and as she sat in the back of the police car, the stubborn, single-minded streak that had helped her to succeed in the past kicked in. She was not going to cower away in dread, she was going to fight back. Like Anna Pelham, she would not let herself be a victim.

Monica pounced as she came through the door: 'Laura, I've been trying to get hold of you. Joe's been calling. I said you'd gone out but I didn't know where. He sounded a bit frantic, wanted to know if you were all right.' She paused for breath, eyeing Laura closely: 'There's nothing wrong is there?'

'I'm fine, Monica. Bit of a headache, that's all.'

'Hmm,' she said.

Laura attempted a smile and tried to hurry past.

'Oh and Anna Pelham came in for you. She waited for a bit but then she had to go. Nothing important, she said, she'll call you tomorrow.' Monica lowered her voice confidentially, 'That husband of hers is a total shit, isn't he?'

Laura didn't wait to answer and headed up the stairs to her office. She called Joe and for once he answered on the first ring. He was appalled when he heard details of the texts, said he had one more meeting and then he was coming straight over. She told him he didn't need to, told him she could handle things, but he said he was coming and that was that. He wanted to take care of her.

For the next hour she concentrated on Ben Morgan. She called a friend at her old firm and asked for a copy of the Morgan divorce file to be sent over. It was a thick one, she remembered, and contained the three threatening letters he had sent her from the psychiatric hospital.

The newspaper coverage she found on the Internet was familiar, but she wasn't prepared for 'Ben's Story' as he had written it on the divorce web site. It had been posted only three months ago. It began: *I have a daughter, Millie, who I haven't seen for six years now* … It shook her and she realized how much of a grudge he had. She was staring at it when Joe arrived. He came rushing in and hugged her close. Pain spiked from her rib.

'You OK?'

She nodded, biting her lip and pointing at the screen, 'Take a look at this.'

Joe began to read.

'Wow,' he said after a while, 'he certainly blames you a lot for what happened, but he also blames the system.'

'He sees *me* as the system, Joe. We're the same thing. I represent the system that screwed him and took away his daughter. That would make him hate me quite a lot, wouldn't it?'

Joe turned from the screen to look at his wife, his bright blue eyes scanning her face. It was wearing a brave little smile, but the smile looked fragile and dislocated.

'I'm so sorry, honey, I should've taken your word on this. I should've realized you weren't imagining things.'

'You weren't to know. It could all have been coincidence. Some of the time I doubted myself.'

'I haven't been there for you, Laura,' he stopped for a moment, 'but I'm going to be.'

CHAPTER THIRTY-ONE

He wasn't struggling anymore but that didn't mean good news. He wasn't struggling because he'd been sedated again. He was sluggish and his eyes were dull.

Joe and Laura stared miserably at Valentine trapped in the sling while a frowning Jeff Ingham explained that they'd tried to put the sedative in Valentine's feed but he'd refused to eat it. In the end, they'd had to syringe it into his mouth as a paste; the whole operation had been highly distressing for everyone involved.

He pointed to a haynet hanging in front of Valentine's nose. 'He should be grazing on that all day long because he needs the fibre. He's hardly touching it at the moment. Without it, his gut is starting to dry out and he's likely to get colic.'

Laura winced. Colic, a serious threat to a healthy horse, would be a certain killer for Valentine.

She climbed up on to the platform beside him where there was a bag of feed. Carrots, apples, molasses were mixed in to tempt him to eat. She took a carrot from the bag and stroked the horse's head, whispering to him, coaxing him. To her huge delight, the carrot disappeared.

Her smile of triumph irritated the vet and his usual gentle manner deserted him.

'You have to realize what's happening here,' he snapped. 'So far he hasn't been able to cope with life in a sling and also he's not eating properly. If that doesn't change, even if he avoids colic, his body will start to feed off itself and it won't be long before his muscles waste away.'

Laura took a handful of feed and held it under the horse's mouth. He began to eat, slowly, without enthusiasm, but he was eating.

'Visiting him for an hour a day,' the vet paused trying not to be rude, 'well, you may not get the full picture.'

'How much longer should I give it?' Laura stroked Valentine's flank. Her hand came away sticky from the polymer gel that coated the sling to try to prevent bed sores.

'If he's not eating reasonably well and we can't get him off the sedatives by the end of the week, there's no point in putting him through any more.'

'Is there anything else we can do to help his chances?' she asked anxiously.

'Maybe another nurse. It's a pretty much around the clock operation. Depends if your insurance will stretch that far.'

'Yes. That's no problem. Please do get another nurse.'

'Laura, I hate to say it, but this is really going to cost us,' Joe said. She felt a sting of disappointment in him.

Jeff Ingham looked at her sharply. 'No insurance?'

'I don't know yet,' she said curtly.

'I thought you said they'd turned you down flat,' Joe again.

It was true, the insurance company had confirmed what she already knew, that she didn't have a claim. No question. Private land, out of bounds, not even arguable, they'd said gleefully. But she didn't want Jeff Ingham to know – in case he tried to save her money.

'No, they just said it wasn't clear cut, they'd have to look into it.'

The vet wasn't fooled. 'You've already got a bill for thousands of pounds. For a week, I don't know, maybe if he means that much to you, but if it goes on after that you're going to need to take out a mortgage.'

'It's what I said, honey. He's a great horse, but we have to be realistic. I think another nurse is pushing it.'

She glared at him. He had a strange idea of being there for her.

'I have the money,' she said in a frosty voice, 'I would like to employ an extra nurse, and,' she turned towards the vet, 'after four days, as you suggest, we will review.'

Jeff Ingham nodded and said no more. He'd made the position clear and now he would just get on and do his best for Valentine and for the woman. He liked her strength and stubbornness and wondered why she'd ended up with such an arse of a husband. Self-regarding, mean-spirited, he stopped himself adding to the list of faults, surprised by his own strength of feeling.

On the drive back from the clinic Laura sat huddled in the passenger seat of Joe's car trying to stop her rib from being jarred by the journey. Her head was bent over and she looked at Joe from the corner of her eye. His face was tight and she knew he was annoyed by her unilateral decision to spend more money on Valentine. It was a pity; she'd hoped for more from him.

'OK,' he broke the silence, 'which way do I go?'

She directed him to the narrow road over the Downs. Earlier, he had suggested going back to the place where Valentine fell to get photos of the wires on the trees. Laura had been pleased; it showed that his attitude had changed. No longer did he dismiss her fears as fantasy.

'Great. How about going first thing tomorrow?' she'd said. 'Doesn't matter if I'm a bit late in to work.'

'Can't do that,' he shook his head. 'Meeting at nine. Let's go tonight.'

Laura had been doubtful whether they'd get any decent pictures in the dark but Joe assured her his camera would have no trouble, and the full moon would help.

She recognized the spot where the minicab had dropped her and Joe parked at the side of the road. They set off together over the clifftop and down towards the wood. A cold wind was blowing and clouds came and went across the face of the moon, but its light still shone bright and she easily found the way.

'There it is,' she whispered pointing ahead, 'the wire's on that tree.'

Joe unslung his camera and walked quickly towards it. He bent over, examining the trunk.

'Can't see anything on this one,' he said as she caught up with him.

She saw at once that he was right. There was a whooshing from the wind in the tree tops and the light from the moon was dimmer here. Joe took a torch from his pocket and played its beam up and down the tree and on the surrounding ground. Nothing. There was no wire and no sign that one had ever been there.

'You sure this is the place?'

'Positive.' She walked across the track to the other tree. Nothing there either. The wires were gone.

'Someone's taken them away,' she said, returning to Joe's side.

He was examining the trunk again. 'There's got to be some damage,' he muttered. 'You and Valentine whacked into that wire, must've left a mark.'

'That was the point of the rubber casing, Joe. So there would be no tell-tale marks on the trees.'

He straightened up and looked at her, one eyebrow raised, that disbelieving expression she'd seen too much of recently. He began talking but she had to tune him out, either that or bite his head off. He was saying things about 'accidents' and 'not getting carried away'. She turned from him and walked further into the wood, straining her eyes for the wire.

The clouds cleared and the moon blazed down through the trees and Laura thought she saw something ahead, something that might be black rubber hosing. She began to run, and almost at once, she tripped on a rabbit hole and fell to the ground, letting out a yell of pain. She lay on her face taking shallow breaths, then turned and looked up. Joe loomed over her, his face pale and set in the bright moonlight.

Panic spurted in her chest. He was going to attack her. Suddenly, it was obvious to her that Joe was the one who wanted to kill her. Barnes's question flashed through her head, *what sort of relationship do you have with your husband*? She knew the answer now, how stupid she had been not to realize it before.

She tried to back away but it was too late, his strong fingers gripped her arm and he pulled her roughly to her feet. She yelled again, this time in terror, and then his mobile started to ring.

'Oh God, I'm sorry,' he said, 'I forgot about your rib. Are you OK?' He silenced his phone, put his arm gently round her shoulder and started kissing the top of her head.

Laura felt the tension rush out of her. Ridiculous, she was being ridiculous. Of course it wasn't Joe. What the hell was wrong with her; was she losing her mind? She felt tears close to the surface and didn't trust herself to speak.

'Honey, are you OK?' Joe said again, urgently.

Instead of crying, she began to laugh. It was a shrill, manic sound in the night and Joe put his finger to his lips and shushed her. It hurt her chest but she couldn't stop.

'You're making one hell of a noise. What's so funny?' he demanded.

'Shh' she snorted at him. 'This is supposed to be a covert operation.'

'I think we might've blown that,' he said, laughing himself. 'Let's hope your angry old man isn't on the prowl.'

CHAPTER THIRTY-TWO

They found no trace of the wires or the hosing and walked back to the car in silence. Joe would be doubting her again, Laura was sure, and she kept quiet because she didn't want to hear him say it. When she got home, she found a message from Barnes waiting for her. He apologized for being out when she had come to the police station; he'd been called away to an emergency. The sergeant must have told him how upset she was because he said she was welcome to ring him on his mobile any time that evening. She rang at once and listened while he gave her a progress report. He spun it out, trying hard to make something out of not very much.

'We're still looking for Ben Morgan,' he told her, 'I'm sure you understand it's no easy thing to find someone in a town as big as Brighton with so little to go on, but we'll keep at it.'

'Yes,' she said, 'I realize it's difficult and thank you. How about his home address? Have you had any luck tracing it? He used to live in Reading, I told the sergeant that.'

'And he still does live there. Reading police have been round to his flat,' Barnes said in a tone of admiration for police efficiency, 'but there was no sign of him, and the neighbours hadn't seen him for weeks.'

That's because he's been here trying to kill me, Laura thought, but stopped herself from saying it. The detective seemed less sceptical now and she intended to keep it that way. He addressed her as 'Laura' rather than 'Ms Maxwell'. She wasn't going to panic him with an outburst of emotion.

'What about the phone?' she asked.

They had traced the number of the mobile sending the texts. They'd got it from Laura's company, O2, which had a record of the texts she'd received and where they'd come from. That was as far as they'd got. Tomorrow they would contact TalkTalk, where the mobile was registered, to find out more. It was possible to pinpoint its position to within about thirty feet, he said, even if it was switched off. But he didn't want to get her hopes up because usually, in cases like this, the phone was dumped after the texts had been sent.

Barnes went on to tell her that a considerable amount of child pornography had been found on Harry Pelham's computer as well as the death threats sent to his wife. There was, however, no trace of the 'marcus.morrison3' email address used for the website posting. Pelham, himself, had not yet been found but the detective was hopeful they would find him before much longer.

The Morgan divorce file arrived at Morrison Kemp early on Tuesday morning and was waiting for Laura when she got to work. She'd lain awake most of the night, thinking about the texts, thinking about Valentine, and was at her desk ploughing through the thick file, feeling exhausted, when Monica called to tell her that a Detective Inspector Barnes was in reception for her.

'There's a police car outside and he's in a rush and … '

Barnes took the phone from her before she could finish.

'Are you alone?' he said sharply.

'Yes. Why?'

'Please come to reception now.'

Laura's tiredness lifted. He must have made progress if he was here in person. Hopefully, she hurried down to see him.

Barnes had on his poker-face. Laura smiled as she walked towards him but his face didn't crack and she couldn't tell if he was pleased or not. There was a man with him, another officer, who he introduced as Detective Constable Andrew Fox. He asked if there was somewhere private they could talk.

Laura led them to the conference room.

'We've got a fix on the phone,' Barnes told her as soon as they were inside.

'Great,' she said and stopped. The policeman didn't look like he totally agreed.

'Isn't it?'

Barnes nodded towards his colleague.

'I liaise with the phone companies,' the constable said, enthusiastically. 'You see, a mobile is giving out signals all the time, even when it's turned off. Those signals are picked up by base stations in the area where it's located. In fact that's why the Americans call it a cell phone because it's covered by these base stations in small areas, in other words, cells.'

Barnes frowned at him and he took the hint and got to the point. 'I've checked with TalkTalk. They say it's a pay-as-you-go and they don't know who owns it but it's here, in this building, and it's switched on.'

She felt her stomach clench with fear. In this building. What the hell did that mean?

'Does Morrison Kemp occupy all three floors?' Barnes asked.

She nodded. 'Are you saying Ben Morgan is here, in this building?' she asked, horrified.

'Have you any idea where the phone might be?'

Laura stared at him, her mind slow and stupid. It was stuck on the awful thought that Ben Morgan was no longer out there, he was right in here with her.

'Have you any idea who might have it?' Barnes persisted.

Why was he asking that? It was obvious who had it, surely.

'Ben Morgan … he must be here, somewhere,' she said again.

'Have you seen him?'

'No, but if his phone's here then he must be, mustn't he?'

Barnes gave her an odd look.

'Just run me through the people who work here and who's on which floor,' he said.

What was the matter with him, she thought. Why was he wasting time asking pointless questions when he should be searching the building?

'Excuse me saying so, but is that relevant? Shouldn't you be trying to catch him?'

'There's a car outside. If he's here and he tries to leave, we'll pick him up. Now please answer the question.'

The confusion clogging her mind lifted, leaving behind a cold, hard, terrifying thought. What if it wasn't Ben Morgan? What if someone else, someone here at Morrison Kemp had sent her those texts? Was that what Barnes was getting at?

She pulled herself together and answered him, trying to work out as she went through the staff if that particular individual could possibly have some kind of grudge. It would have to be a damn big grudge.

'Are you thinking that one of my colleagues might have sent the texts?'

Barnes shrugged and didn't answer.

Through her fear, Laura felt a stab of irritation with him. He was scaring her badly, he should at least explain things to her properly so she knew the worst, instead of leaving her to try and guess.

'I'll do this as discreetly as I can,' the detective said, taking his own mobile from his jacket pocket. 'I'm going to call the number and see if we can hear where it's ringing. Andrew, can you take the first floor.'

The constable went off up the stairs leaving the door open behind him. Monica appeared, offering tea, eager to find out what was going on. She was disappointed. Her tea was refused, and Barnes waited until she had retreated to reception before dialling.

Laura felt sweat start on her forehead. Listen for the phone; don't think about what it means.

Barnes made the call but she could hear nothing. Was the number actually ringing? She didn't know, he didn't say, just sat there with his impassive face, the phone to his ear.

A loud shout came from upstairs and she almost jumped out of her skin. So much for discreet. Barnes shot off towards the first floor, nearly colliding with Monica, who'd either been lurking in the corridor or was extremely quick off the mark. Laura followed, less eager, held back by a feeling of dread. Monica was ahead of her at the top of the stairs with Barnes; he was pointing towards an office, asking whose it was. Laura assumed it was where they'd heard the phone though there was no longer any sound of it ringing. By the time she arrived the three of them were inside the room. She stood in the doorway staring in shock and surprise.

Monica had her back to her, her body craning towards the two men standing by the shelves of law books on the far wall, listening to what they were saying. There was a gap in one of the shelves and a few books were lying on the floor. The constable was examining a mobile and talking to Barnes. He stopped abruptly when he saw Laura appear.

'We understand this is your office, Ms Maxwell,' said Barnes in a tight voice.

It wasn't a question and she didn't reply.

'The mobile was hidden behind the books,' he gestured at the shelf.

Laura stared blankly. She felt light-headed.

'Can you tell us how it got there?'

This time it was a question, a big question, and she had no answer.

'Can you explain how Ben Morgan, as you allege, could have used it to send you threatening texts,' he stopped then added, 'or anyone else for that matter, Ms Maxwell?'

The 'Laura' was gone. She knew what he was thinking – that she was some kind of nutter; a flake who wanted attention, for what reason he could not begin to guess and didn't much care. He suspected that, as a way of getting it, she had sent the texts to herself.

She walked unsteadily into the room. 'I have absolutely no idea what's going on,' she said, leaning heavily against her desk.

CHAPTER THIRTY-THREE

Barnes made it clear he wasn't going to continue to look for Ben Morgan or anyone else in connection with the texts. He referred to them as 'alleged threatening texts' and, with a sardonic look on his face, gave her back her mobile. He thought she'd been wasting police time.

Rather belatedly, he asked Monica if she'd mind leaving the room while he talked to Ms Maxwell in private. She did mind but she had no choice; in any case, she had a fair amount of gossip to be going on with. Laura Maxwell had complained to the police that someone was sending her nasty texts; they had investigated and found the offending phone hidden in her office. Laura couldn't explain how it came to be there; they suspected she'd been making the whole thing up.

Monica was hardly surprised. Laura Maxwell was neurotic, no doubt about that. From the minute she'd arrived as some hot-shot from London, it was obvious she was highly strung with an over-inflated idea of her own importance. The way she'd treated poor Sarah Cole was heartless and shocking, blaming her for her own mistakes then getting her fired. Monica's pinched face had a rare, satisfied look.

Laura recovered enough self-possession to try to persuade Barnes to think again. It was true she had no explanation for the phone being here in her office, but everything she had told him was true. Why, after all, would she make it up? She saw him raise an eyebrow at that as if he might be expecting her to provide the answer.

'If I sent the texts to myself', she protested hotly, 'why would I be stupid enough to hide the phone in my office where you would be bound to find it?'

Barnes looked at her speculatively, 'I don't think I'm the person who can answer that, Ms Maxwell,' he said.

She was scared, she told him, very scared, frightened for her life. Please, at least would he keep trying to track down Ben Morgan? No go. He had better things to do. She wanted to yell at him then, to yell that he was making a big mistake and that mistake would kill her, and when it did, it would be his fault. But she said nothing because she thought it would only make things worse. She remembered the website posting and that the police had found no evidence it had come from Harry Pelham's computer – probably Barnes thought she had sent that to herself as well. She knew his attitude was not unreasonable, that he might have grounds for his scepticism, but the knowledge didn't help, just filled her with a hopeless, directionless fury.

When the policemen had gone, Laura's anger drained away fast, replaced by dread. She wanted to ring Joe and tell him what had happened but she shied away from it, knowing that when he heard where the phone had been found, he, too, would doubt her.

Would anyone believe her, she thought despairingly. Would Emma believe her or would even Emma think she had gone nuts? It was academic anyway because Emma was away and couldn't help her. There was no one to help, she realized, her insides churning with fear, she would have to deal with this on her own. She was alone with whoever it was out there who wanted her dead, had promised she would be dead, painfully, by the end of the week. She wondered if this was the day she would die.

Shut up. Stop scaring yourself. Concentrate on what you can do about it.

She made a big effort to get a grip and work out what to do. She was no further forward than she had been a few days ago, when it all began. Except it didn't seem like days, but like months and years, an eternity of dread. Another injection of fear, fast and terrible, shot through her. Of course, she was further forward because she knew now, for certain, that none of it was chance. She was being relentlessly targeted by a killer, a killer who liked to play vicious games.

Was it Ben Morgan? Had he somehow got past Monica and sneaked up to Laura's office to hide the phone without anyone seeing him? But why, if he'd got so far, hadn't he just waited and attacked her when she came in? Was he worried it was too public, that she'd scream and people would come running, that he could not be sure of killing her? And what was the point of leaving the phone? Easy question, she could answer that one – to discredit her with the police, to leave her vulnerable, to panic and confuse her.

There was something very calculated in what was happening that didn't really fit the Ben Morgan she remembered. He had been highly emotional, on the edge of coping. He had lashed out because he thought he would lose his daughter, but that had been the crazy act of a sick man. She tried, without very much success, to picture him as the perpetrator of this purposeful, ruthless campaign against her.

But if not him, then who? Someone who had access to her office. Someone close by then. Her eyes flicked nervously towards the door. Someone out there wanted to kill her and now that someone was in here, in her own office. Nowhere was safe for her anymore. Not out there, not in here, not anywhere.

CHAPTER THIRTY-FOUR

Harry Pelham had spent Monday evening spying on his wife and daughter. He had taken a risk and gone home to collect his car. He reckoned he had a good chance of getting away with it so long as he was careful and he needed the car if he was going to watch her. A taxi dropped him at the end of his road and he walked, very cautiously, towards his house. It was possible the police would be waiting for him, but he doubted they had the manpower to stake out his home all the time. Most likely, they checked now and again to see if he'd come back.

The house was detached and well screened from its neighbours, and, so far as Harry could tell, the coast was clear. He avoided the house itself, made straight for the garage to the side of it, and within a couple of minutes, had taken his car and was gone. He checked the rear-view mirror; there was no one in pursuit.

He drove to the country lane where his wife and daughter lived, leaving his car a few hundred yards short of their cottage where the lane widened and he could park anonymously among residents' cars. He walked towards the cottage, passing a couple of houses and arriving at the gate without seeing anyone. He crept inside, stood in the cover of the boundary hedge, and waited.

It had turned out to be a cold and fruitless exercise. All he had got from it was a glimpse of Martha through the kitchen window.

Later that night, he had walked down to the sea front and sat on a bench in the chill, bright night. But it was not the cold that made his hands tremble. He had stayed a long time, staring out at the sea glittering under the moon, considering his next move. Then he went back to his hotel. Hard to sleep. Uneasy dreams.

He's collecting Martha. She's in a building, on the twelfth floor. He's waiting by the lift, waiting for a long, long time. He's getting impatient. At last it arrives. The doors open but there's no lift; just thick ropes hanging down covered in bright red jelly. A security guard walks over to him, hands him one of the ropes, tells him he must climb to the twelfth floor if he wants to see his daughter.

He starts climbing, but he's afraid. His hands keep slipping on the jelly. He looks up and sees two men dressed as clowns laughing at him from the twelfth floor. He carries on, gets halfway up the lift shaft, then realizes it's not jelly at all. It's blood. Bright red blood. He lets go of the rope in shock and he falls ...

Harry woke up urgently needing to see his daughter. He could not wait a moment longer. Ben Morgan's words were in his head, eating away at him, 'She's heartbroken, she misses you so much ... she cries herself to sleep and talks to you through her favourite teddy bear.'

He told himself the man was deranged, perhaps so traumatized by his own experience that he was muddling up his daughter, Millie, with Martha – putting her words into Martha's mouth. More likely still, it was all a product of Morgan's unhinged imagination. In any case he was a fool to let it bother him. Harry told himself these things but his heart rebelled.

It was half-term week and Martha was going away on Wednesday to stay with a school friend. She would be back at the end of the week and he was due to take her out for the day on Saturday. That was all organized before the bail conditions, of course, he thought bitterly. Now he was not due to take Martha out at all, not ever.

On Tuesday morning Harry texted his daughter, asked if she was free any time that day to meet him, just for half an hour or so. It was a stupid thing to do, he knew that, a deliberate breach of his bail, and if his wife and her lawyer got to know about it, he was in trouble. But he was desperate so he did it anyway.

Martha replied that she was spending the day with her friend, Jessie. Her mum was about to drop her there and then Jessie's mum was taking them shopping in town and then bowling. She supposed she could meet him but it couldn't be for long, before lunch maybe. Did he want her to keep it a secret?

Her message sounded so grown-up that it made him wince. Mixed emotions. Pleasure that he could see her, guilt that he was involving her in something she thought of as a deception. It astonished him how she picked up the vibes, how instinctively she knew she should keep quiet about meeting him. She was only eight but already she was wise in the ways of adults. It scared him like a lot of things had recently.

He waited for her outside a doll and teddy bear shop in The Lanes. Not so long ago it had been a favourite place but, lately, she'd made it clear she was far too old for it. Unlikely then, he thought unhappily, that she would talk to him at night through her favourite bear. He realized then that it was not something he would feel able to ask her.

He saw the three of them approaching and his heart squeezed. Martha was tall for her age and thin. Almost too thin, Harry thought, though she liked her food well enough. But Anna was strict. No daughter of hers was going to be overweight, she said. Anna had told him she had once been fat herself and had suffered badly for it.

He was relieved to find that he didn't recognize the woman or Jessie, the other child. Martha ran the last few yards, threw her arms around him and hugged him in her usual enthusiastic way. She smiled up at him with his own dark brown eyes. In looks, at least, she resembled him a lot.

The woman was friendly enough; she seemed to have no problem with the meeting and asked no awkward questions. They agreed that he would bring Martha back in an hour's time to the Italian place round the corner where they were having lunch.

'I told her you had to go away for work and I wanted to see you now,' his daughter announced proudly when the other two had gone.

Harry put his hand on her head, stroked her long, dark hair. She was lying for him now and it made him feel awful. He said gently that it wasn't really a good idea to make things up.

'But Daddy I had to tell her something or she might have rung Mummy to check. I thought she might anyway so I said Mummy knew about it and it was like a last minute thing.'

He sighed and she asked him if anything was wrong. He understood then that she was anxious, that his text had been out of the ordinary and it had upset her. He wished he hadn't troubled her. What purpose had there been in it anyway, except his own selfish desire to see her and to reassure himself that the things Ben Morgan had said were not true? A gloomy helplessness descended on him, these days he seemed to call everything wrong.

'Sweetheart, everything's great. I just wanted to see you, that's all. You know how much I love you, don't you? And I miss you.'

She gave him the 'look', the one that, even though she was eight-years-old, was always dead on and never missed. He remembered that he never could fool her.

'I love you too, Daddy,' she said in a serious voice and his heart twisted.

He sat with her in a café for the next hour in a state of forced cheerfulness, her dark eyes watching him over the top of her strawberry milkshake. He talked of anything but what he wanted to say. At the end of it he hoped he'd set her mind at rest but his own was still in a mess. He could not be sure that tonight she would not cry herself to sleep, could not be certain that the teddy bear was a fiction.

'Is Joe a friend of yours too?' she asked him. It came out of the blue just as they were about to leave.

'I don't think so. I'm not sure I know him,' he said carefully, then with a sudden flash of intuition added, 'but maybe I do. Is he a teddy bear?'

She looked at him as if he was a total idiot. The scorn in her young face withered him.

'Of course he isn't,' she said sternly, 'he's a friend of Mummy's. He came to see her yesterday.'

CHAPTER THIRTY-FIVE

For almost three hours they'd kissed and touched and tasted and pressed their bodies together and still Anna Pelham had not had nearly enough of him. His beauty overwhelmed her and she experienced, for just a few moments, a total joy. But then the maggot of doubt was crawling back into her Eden, bigger than ever, feeding off her insecurity and terror – the terror of losing him, the unshakeable fear that she was on borrowed time.

Just the thought of his arrival had given her a tremendous high, a buzz all through her body. Even now, after months of knowing him, her heart beat a little faster, butterflies fluttered in her stomach, and the palms of her hands were damp. She checked herself in the bedroom mirror. Did she look good enough? Good enough for him.

She had washed her blonde hair twice and it shone. Long legs, flat belly, lots of curves, waxed all over. Joe Greene found all these things hot and she made sure she didn't disappoint. She kept herself fit and slender, relentlessly expelling any hint of fat. She exercised with a personal trainer twice a week and whenever she could, which was nearly every day in term time, she swam fifty lengths at the pool.

She loved the cottage because everything in it reminded her of him. His smell was on the sheets, on the duvet as she hugged it to her face. Before leaving Harry, she had searched long and hard for a place to rent; a place not just for herself and Martha, but for herself and Joe, where his visits could pass unnoticed, where nosy neighbours could be kept at arm's length, where one day they could be together, forever, as they were meant to be. As they had always been meant to be.

He visited mainly during the day when Martha was at school but sometimes, if Martha had a sleepover at a friend's house, Joe would come in the evening. There had been two heavenly occasions when he'd stayed all night. On one of them, while he was sleeping, she had taken a photo on her mobile of the two of them in bed together. She knew it was reckless because they mustn't be found out, but she couldn't resist it. She needed it, needed something definite to cling on to when he was not with her, something to look at, and love.

In Anna's subconscious, though, he was with her all the time. She felt his presence in every room. In the early evening watching TV with her daughter, he was sitting there with them like a proper family; when she took a bath he would slide down with her into the warm water; at night he slept with her in the double bed. She would desire him, reach for him, imagine that he held her close and it would light the fire inside her. Later, when her hand lay flat on the empty sheet, she would feel a pang of disappointment at the realization that he was not actually there.

Anna had reread her schooldays' notebook many times in recent months and now she looked through it again. Joe Greene. The saviour. She had been so right about him twenty years ago – about how much she wanted him. It had been no simple infatuation. It had stood the test of time.

It had been there, bubbling away inside her, all those years. A dormant volcano waiting to erupt. He had been there, constantly there, at the back of her mind. But the chances of ever having him had seemed so utterly remote that she had resigned herself, or imagined she had, to forgetting him. What nonsense that had been, a total delusion. She had never resigned herself. Of course not. She could have no life without him. That was so clear to her now. Why else did she have Joe's collection, with everything she had taken from the dustbins all those years ago, buried in a locked briefcase in the garden? Why else had she kept it safe and cherished it?

Two years ago, when she and Harry moved house, she had taken it out again. She had not looked at it since her marriage, had locked it away out of sight, out of her life, because she knew how badly it destabilized her. It had lost none of its potency. She searched for him then on the Internet, couldn't help herself, and the thrill of discovering that he was an actor had been extreme. His picture stared out from the computer screen. It was like a time bomb going off, reawakening all the old feelings of love as if they had never slept. Intense. Overwhelming. Uncontrollable.

It rattled, close on blew away, the flimsy structure of her relationship with Harry. Anna had found marriage difficult and having a family even harder. She had put off getting pregnant as long as she could, not wanting the commitment, but Harry had become insistent, and in the end, she had gone along with him. Why not, she thought? – after all, no other life, no other man would be much better because the only life she had ever wanted, the only man she had ever wanted, was Joe, and he was gone.

Now she had found him again and her world shook. She searched for news of him, constantly, on every website she could think of, but it was a disappointing quest for there was not much to find. One day, one very special day, she found him on Facebook. She could access only a few basic details but his photo was there and she stared at it, spellbound. She ached to ask him to accept her as a 'friend' but she didn't dare to. She could not face possible rejection.

Then came a heart-stopping moment when she read that he was appearing in a play by Tom Stoppard called *The Real Thing*. It was on at a fringe theatre in East London. The thought of seeing Joe, glorious on stage, took her breath away and she knew at once that she must go.

The play was about love, and Joe had the lead part. The script was complicated, and as she sat there gazing at him, she wasn't sure she fully understood it. It seemed to be trying to pin down the nature of love – what is real love and how do you know when you have it? But she didn't need to follow the words because she already knew the answers to the questions. She simply stared at the man who was saying them. She felt the yearning for him, deep and strong.

Anna cursed herself for marrying Harry; what had she been thinking of? Now she had Joe again, life with Harry was unbearable, sex with Harry intolerable but she had to bear it because Harry would not be denied, would not leave her alone. She gritted her teeth, tried unsuccessfully to blot out his face and replace it with Joe's.

It was a couple of months after the theatre visit that it happened. She was searching the websites again with keen anticipation, hoping for something thrilling, perhaps a new play she could see him in. As she entered Joe's name on the screen, a rush of excitement ran through her.

She believed she had a sixth sense about him, that she could tell if he was happy or sad, that she would know instinctively if he were to undergo any life-changing event. It made the shock ten times worse. She had no premonition, no sense that something bad was going to happen. It was a bolt from the blue.

There was nothing on the websites that she hadn't seen already, so she checked his Facebook page. It was still closed to her but she looked anyway, just to see his face.

There was an update. A dreadful, one-line update that everyone was allowed to see. It said that he was married. It said that the name of the woman who had become his wife was Laura Maxwell.

For a while she was too paralysed to move. Her eyes stared, unbelieving, at the screen. Then, hardly aware of what she was doing, Anna typed in Laura's name and there, in the Law Society Gazette under the title 'Heading South', was the information that high-powered divorce lawyer Laura Maxwell was leaving her post at Lloyd Wingate to join the firm of Morrison Kemp in Brighton. There was a brief résumé of her career highlights but Anna didn't see them. She could see nothing through the white-hot anguish in her brain.

It was beyond belief; surely, beyond endurance.

CHAPTER THIRTY-SIX

The shock had been tremendous and Anna's hands shook as she forced herself to read about Laura Maxwell. There were articles charting the progress of Laura's illustrious career. In 2006, she had been named as one of the ten 'most-promising lawyers under thirty', in 2007, she joined the prestigious London office of Lloyd Wingate; always, Laura was a rising star.

Laura's divorce clients got ever more important, and if she'd carried on the way she was going, it wouldn't have been too long before she represented the very rich and famous. As it was, there were no celebrities or princesses and her name didn't make the front pages but it did occasionally appear in the middle pages linked with cases involving ground-breaking settlements or topical points of law.

Laura had made a point of doing pro bono work for 'deserving' clients who couldn't afford her firm's fees; no doubt, Anna thought sourly, so that she could get extra points in the league table of promising lawyers. Having a social conscience, or appearing to have one, always ticked a useful box.

It was one of those cases that blew up in her face. Laura Maxwell had been representing Georgina Morgan for free, and she had done an excellent job. But when the distraught father, who suffered from bipolar disorder, took the law into his own hands, some of the press coverage questioned whether the system put those with mental health problems at a disadvantage. She had operated that system and the whole thing had left a nasty taste behind it. For once, and once only, Anna enjoyed the coverage.

Now Laura Maxwell had married Joe. It was grotesque. But Anna had learned to control her mind and any thought that she had lost him was ruthlessly banished. There would be no negatives. They made a fool of you, made you vulnerable, made you a victim. Instead, she decided to find a way to meet him and the decision both excited and terrified her. All day, every day, she plotted how to do it, made a hundred plans to make it happen.

She was a good-looking woman, she knew that, probably very good-looking, and she knew how to attract men. The ugly girl had grown naturally into her large body, morphing into a tall, striking, curvaceous woman. Anna had helped the transformation along. Ever since her late teens, when she had come out of the psychiatric hospital determined to turn her life around, she had focused on improving her looks. Her mousy brown hair became blonde, her diet was merciless, she worked out rigorously at the gym, spent money on stylish clothes and beauty treatments. She had worked on her mind, too, with yoga and meditation classes to give her self-control. And she had worked on learning how to make people like her.

She could be charming, lovable, demure, exciting; independent or hanging on their every word; a chameleon, ready to fit whatever she judged was wanted. She could adapt, could give people what they were looking for; tell them what they wanted to hear. And so she had travelled a million miles from the ugly, introverted teenager that Joe had once spoken a few words to on the beach.

Joe was living just a few miles away, had come right back into the centre of her life, smack into it. The thought that he was here, and so close, made her tremble with excitement. The thought that he was here with Laura Maxwell made her tremble too, but with a different emotion.

In the end, meeting him had been ludicrously easy. Deliciously so. The trick with the nursing home had worked like a dream.

She had found out where he lived by waiting outside Morrison Kemp for Laura to appear, and then following her home. The sight of her, even from a distance, had made Anna's stomach churn. If she had felt jealousy at seeing a photo of Laura on the Internet, that was nothing to what she felt at seeing her in real life.

She was brutally honest with herself. The woman was attractive, she had a petite prettiness, and her milky skin and high cheekbones gave her a stylish look that was also very natural. Her black hair was tied back and she was wearing a pair of thick spectacles, but in an odd way, that all added to her air of elegance. It was a brief, awful glimpse, and it detonated an explosion inside her. Laura had driven off in her white Audi and Anna had followed in her own car, her knuckles white on the steering wheel, the palms of her hands sweaty from adrenaline.

She tracked them both for months weighing up her best chance. To start with she focused on Joe's workplace – the Greene House Hotel in Hove – it should be easy to meet him there. But she worried he would be busy and distracted by other things. She needed a place where she could have time with him, where she could make a good impression. On Thursday mornings he usually visited his mother at her nursing home out on the cliffs near Rottingdean. She followed him there and waited for her chance.

It came on a crisp sunny day, which brought the year's first touch of spring and the first real opportunity for the nursing home residents to enjoy sitting out in the fresh air after a long winter. The home had large, leafy grounds overlooking the sea. She was standing among a group of conifers, half hidden from view, when she spotted Joe come out of the double doors pushing his mother's wheelchair.

There was a lot of activity. Those without visitors to assist were being taken out by the staff. She watched as one old man was wheeled towards her. The nurse stopped the chair close by, spoke to the man in a loud voice and Anna guessed he must have trouble hearing. The nurse pointed out the sunlight sparkling on the sea, the yachts below working hard to catch the light breeze. It would make a good painting, Anna heard her say. The old man didn't reply, just stared ahead with an anxious look on his face.

Anna moved out from the trees towards the wheelchair, an idea forming in her mind. She caught the nurse's eye.

'Good morning,' she said, 'fantastic spot, isn't it? I'm looking round for a nursing home for my father. He's a keen artist and I think he might like it here.'

'Perfect for him.' The nurse nodded towards the old man. 'This gentleman, he used to paint, but sadly not since his stroke. I'm afraid he can't speak anymore so he can't talk about it but I'm sure he still loves the views.'

Anna said something sympathetic, felt excitement inside her. The nurse patted the man's arm, told him she would leave him to enjoy the beautiful day and be back in half an hour.

She waited until the nurse was out of sight then seized the wheelchair. She smiled at the old man but got no response.

'Would you like a tour of the grounds?' she asked, to test him.

No reply. No change in his anxious expression. She decided to take a chance.

She wheeled him away towards Joe and his mother. They had reached the edge of the grounds and he was standing beside his mother's chair as they both looked at the view. Anna took a parallel route and then turned right down a slight incline, which joined the path Joe was on.

Anna heard them coming before she saw them. Joe's mother was speaking. She had a loud, bossy voice, one that had clearly been used to giving orders. She was telling her son about a famous guest who had regularly stayed at one of the Greene hotels. Joe was making interested noises but Anna had the idea he'd heard the story before.

As they came level she pushed the old man's wheelchair forward, letting it run gently into the side of Helen Greene's. She was hugely apologetic. How stupid of her. Were they all right? She fussed over the occupants of both wheelchairs.

Joe had been attracted to her at once, it was written all over his face, and she was thrilled to the bone to see it. He gazed at her and seconds ticked by, then he asked the old man if he was OK. Anna played safe, just in case, and explained that he was unlikely to answer; he rarely spoke and when he did he said strange things. He suffered from delusions.

They sat down together, she and Joe on a bench with a wheelchair on either side. It had been heaven. The sweetest moment of her whole life. She was with her saviour, beside him, talking to him. And it was for real.

His presence next to her made her legs tremble, her throat dry, and her head dizzy. She had to concentrate hard to take in what he was saying. But she didn't fall apart; the lessons in self-discipline paid off, the centre of her stayed cool and calculating. She was in control, for she had information that would help her. She knew his likes and his dislikes, his hobbies, his birthday, his middle name. She knew these things and many more and she would use them.

She had taken an instant dislike to his mother but nevertheless took good care to talk to her because she could tell that it pleased him. She soon discovered that she needed to say very little because the woman never stopped talking about the family's hotel business. All she needed was an audience. Irritating though she was, Anna thought, there were advantages – her constant babble meant the old man was largely ignored, there were no tricky questions about him, plus she gave Anna the opportunity to look kind and considerate in front of Joe. She was a distraction, which lessened the pressure, for Anna was nervous; it was a make or break meeting; she would not get another shot.

So she laughed in all the right places, was impressed by all the right things and always, every blessed second, she was aware of

Joe's eyes upon her, and it was paradise. Now, at last, she had his attention. She wanted to savour it, glory in it, live in it forever. But time was ticking by and she knew it couldn't be long before the old man's nurse returned. Casually, she glanced around and looked for her.

Helen Greene had begun a rambling tale about some politicians who'd been hotel guests during a Labour Party conference in Brighton. She kept going off at tangents from the main story to give her listeners the benefit of her very definite views about politics and politicians. Anna thought, with growing alarm, that this could last all day.

Hard as it was to part from Joe, it had to be done. She looked at her watch, exclaimed, and interrupted his mother's monologue. She was so sorry but she had to go. She stood up and as she did so, saw the nurse arrive at the place where the old man should be; her hand was slanted against her forehead screening out the sun, scanning the grounds for him.

Anna Pelham grabbed hold of the wheelchair and Joe stood up beside her.

'I'll walk back with you. Make sure you don't have any more collisions with that chair,' he teased her. 'All right with you, Mum? I shan't be long.'

Her mind raced. He was planning to ask to see her again, she guessed, but if he walked back with her he would find out about the old man and the affair would end before it had begun.

'No, dear, please,' his mother complained, 'I'm getting cold here, there's rather a wind, can you take me over there,' she pointed with an imperious finger in the opposite direction.

Anna Pelham could have hugged the old bag.

'Lovely to have met you both,' she said, and then, because she knew he would like her for it, bent down and kissed Helen Greene on the cheek.

She set off at speed with the old man and at once heard Joe running up behind. She had known he would chase and it filled her with joy and triumph. She was glad of her sunglasses; he would not see it in her eyes. He caught up with her, put his hand on top of one of hers to slow down the wheelchair and her heart jolted as if she'd touched a live wire. He asked to meet her again and she agreed. He blew her a kiss as he walked back to his mother.

The nurse was huffy but, luckily, had not got round to raising an alarm. Anna turned on the charm, said she'd thought the old boy would appreciate a trip round the gardens, apologized if she'd done the wrong thing, reminded the nurse that she had an elderly father and could be a potential customer.

'I do think he really enjoyed it,' she gave the nurse a broad smile. The old man looked on, fearful as ever.

CHAPTER THIRTY-SEVEN

Joe had been her lover for eight months now and Anna was more besotted with him than ever. But the happier he made her, the more she feared losing him. It was like an addiction. She needed him body and soul. Forever. She wanted to see, stretching before her, thousands of wonderful days like this one; days full of commonplace detail and closeness which would carry the two of them, high on happiness, into a shared and enchanted old age. Was that too much to ask?

Although he had told her countless times that he loved her, she could not totally believe it, and even if it was true, she could not believe it would stay that way. It was that little bit of loser still left in her, she thought, that strand of weakness, lack of faith in herself, which she had been unable to root out. She knew she was beautiful and desirable but could not let herself rely on it. Men changed, grew cooler. She needed certainty, complete control.

That was why she had chosen Laura Maxwell to represent her; it was a way to bring her closer to those things, a kind of insurance policy. Once her affair with Joe had begun she had to leave Harry Pelham, she would go mad otherwise. What better way to get shot of him, what better way to get the best deal for herself, and what better way to keep an eye on her rival. It had been a bold idea and she had grabbed on to it at once.

On Easter Day she manufactured a furious row with her husband during which she walked out, taking Martha with her. Two days later she instructed Laura Maxwell to act in her divorce.

It had been a performance that far outshone any acting ability her lover might have had. Oscar winning. She had played the abused wife to a tee.

Up close, Ms Maxwell was nothing special, nothing special at all. Superficially attractive, maybe, but oh so dull. From the word go, she had lectured Anna about the modern approach to divorce – no blame, no points scoring, let's be reasonable, let's all sit round a table and sort it out with a civilized little chat. Screw that. She was having nothing to do with that. She was going to hang Harry out to dry. Condescending cow.

Poor Joe, she thought, how dreary the sex must be. It was a dangerous thought, a thought that rocked her and brought bile to her mouth; it spoiled the pleasure she had been getting from thinking that she was sleeping with the lawyer's husband.

It had been hard, very hard indeed, to suppress her feelings. But she had done so and she was pleased with herself; she had passed this crucial test, she had mastered her emotions. But there was one final twist of the knife to come. The first interview was over. She stood up to go, the rictus grin still firmly plastered on her face.

Laura came with her to the door, handed her a business card. Anna forced herself to take it, forced herself to beat back the wave of nausea that filled her throat. She hardly saw the card; all she could focus on was the wedding ring, cool and solid on the other woman's hand.

The memory was like poison. And now, all this time later, Joe was still living with Laura Maxwell, the ring was still on her finger. To make it worse, he had told her he was 'concerned' about his wife. Laura had fallen off her horse, Laura was upset, Laura was highly stressed, Laura needed help. Anna wanted to put her fingers in her ears and scream. She wanted to yell at him, to ask him why the hell he cared one little jot; he'd made it quite clear he wanted to be rid of her.

She lay beside him in bed, watching his chest rise and fall. There was a patch of scarring beneath the black, curly hair. Soon after their affair began, she had asked him about it and he had recounted how, aged three, he had reached up for the handle of a teapot and it had fallen, spilling its boiling contents on his chest. He had needed a skin graft.

As he told the story, she had smiled secretly to herself because she already knew all about the scar and what had caused it. She had known for twenty years, ever since the days when she raided the dustbins outside his home, gathering information. The teapot accident had been referred to in a discarded letter from his aunt. She had the letter still; it was part of the collection.

How useful that information had been and still was – because of it, she could show interest in the things he liked before he ever told her that he liked them, she could give opinions she knew he would share, make remarks to make him love her. Occasionally she wondered if she had gone too far, had shown an almost incredible ability to hit the right spot, but why should he be surprised, wasn't compatibility an important part of love? She had been right when she'd told him they were soulmates.

It was that dangerous time just after sex when lovers talk about risky subjects, things like commitment and love and the future. Anna wanted to talk about all of them though she was smart enough to avoid using the actual words.

'You must be under a lot of strain, honey, what with having to worry about Laura,' she began.

'It's weird. I've never known her like this before. She's always been able to handle stuff herself.'

'I don't mean to sound hard, Joe, but the thing is not to get distracted by her problems,' She smiled and eased her breasts against him.

'No chance of that sweetheart. You're the only one who distracts me,' he kissed her neck.

'I've been thinking,' she said, 'maybe it's time. Maybe we should just get on with it. Why don't you leave her?'

193

He made no reply, kissed the top of her breasts.

'Let's not wait any longer, Joe, just leave. Now.'

She regretted the words as soon as she said them. They were too pushy, just a whisper away from clinginess and desperation. She knew that with any couple there was always an imbalance, separating the one who loves from the one who is loved. She worried that the imbalance was all against her, that she was the one who loved too much.

He leaned on one elbow looking into her green eyes and stroking her hair.

'Don't you think I want to, Anna. There's nothing I'd like more. But it would be stupid to do it now.'

She was relieved that he didn't seem put off by her eagerness, perhaps he hadn't noticed. But, almost at once, relief was replaced by frustration. He wasn't leaving Laura Maxwell. Not yet, anyway.

He always said he was terrified of divorce. Laura would take him to the cleaners, of course she would; she did it at work, she was bound to do it at home. He was now a partner in the Greene hotel business and he had a lot to lose. Things would be bad enough without Laura knowing that he had found someone else and that the someone else was Anna Pelham.

So they had agreed to wait. They would wait until Anna's divorce was through, until Laura Maxwell had secured for her as much of Harry Pelham's wealth as she possibly could.

For Anna, it had been the most delicious payback. Every time she brought Laura more details of her husband's hidden assets, playing the victim and begging Laura to investigate them thoroughly and claw them back, she got a tremendous thrill. It was wicked, really it was. To have your lover's wife working her socks off to make you rich, well, that was hard to beat, wasn't it? On two occasions, she had bought Laura a present just, as she told her, to say a small 'thank you'.

But there had been a downside. When she told Joe his wife was handling her divorce, he had been horrified. She'd had to struggle hard to get him to accept it, explaining to him that it had happened by accident; friends had told her Morrison Kemp was the best firm to use and she had not realized his wife worked there, nor had she known his wife's maiden name, which she used for work. By the time she'd found out, it was too late to change. At least, Anna persuaded, she would know if Laura's attitude to her ever changed and if she suspected anything.

Joe had lived with it but it made him ultra-cautious about their affair. He had absolutely insisted, despite Anna's best efforts to convince him otherwise, that her divorce must be finished before he could leave Laura. To begin with Anna had agreed, grateful he had been placated, but now she didn't want to wait, she couldn't wait, anymore. The longer the delay, she believed, the less chance she had of getting him. There was a crucial window and it was passing.

She tried again. 'You know it's just that I love you so much, Joe,' she moved on top of him, her legs straddling him. 'I dream of the day when we can be together all the time.'

'Me too, honey. It won't be long now, I promise.'

'You know one of the things I love best about you? One of the million things. You always make me feel like there's going to be a happy ending.'

He pulled her to him and kissed her forehead.

'Of course there's a happy ending. The thing to hang on to is that when this is over we'll have the rest of our lives together. We just have to be patient a bit longer. Trust me.'

It was not what she wanted to hear.

It was as she hung there above him, his lips on her breast, that she saw it: his mobile, sitting on the bedside table.

It was not what she wanted to see.

Panic engulfed her. He never used to bring his mobile when they were together, but he'd had it with him recently and now here it was again, up close and personal, right next to the bed. There could be only one reason it was there, so he could keep in touch with his wife.

When he'd gone to the bathroom, she reached for the phone to read his texts, but it was gone. With a sinking heart she realized he had taken it with him and she felt sure she knew why. She leapt from the bed, ran to the bathroom door, and listened. Nothing. Of course not. He would not be so crass as to actually call Laura from his lover's house. He would be messaging her, that was it; messages of love and concern.

CHAPTER THIRTY-EIGHT

When Joe had gone she gave herself up to the black mix of rage and frustration that filled her. She felt the weight of it beginning to crush her from the inside out. She must not let it unhinge her, she could not afford any mistakes, she must keep her mind clear, perfectly focused, sharp with hate.

Anna Pelham stared out of the bedroom window at the long narrow garden and the wooded hill beyond. A black cat was scratching in a patch of soft earth behind the old compost heap, roughly at the spot where the briefcase containing Joe's collection was buried. She couldn't recall if a black cat was a sign of good or bad luck and she didn't care. She would make her own destiny; she did not need luck to help her.

She went into the garden, dug up the case, and unlocked it. There were two collections inside, and with a pulse of loathing, she took hold of the second one. The Laura Maxwell collection. So much smaller than Joe's but oh so toxic. Just a few things she had gathered in a hurry after she'd found out about Joe and Laura, twenty years ago, before she'd been taken into the psychiatric hospital. Lately it had grown with notes she'd made about Laura's habits while stalking her, with pages of information printed off the Internet, with a scarf stolen when she visited Laura's office in case it might come in handy sometime.

She looked at Laura's collection with a heart full of hate, and the pain of all those years ago was back with her, as sharp as ever.

When she had first instructed Laura to act in her divorce, Anna had wondered if she might remember her name from school. She'd had to hand over her marriage certificate showing her maiden name: Annabel Roberts. There had been no sign of recognition. Why should there be? They had been in different years, had never spoken – the adult Anna Pelham could not have been more unlike the shy, fat, ugly schoolgirl.

But one thing had not changed; one thing in common remained. They both wanted Laura dead. Annabel Roberts had prayed for it, Anna Pelham would make it happen.

She tried to remember what Joe had said about his wife. At the time, listening to it had driven her insane and she had tried to blot it out. But she needed to know it now, because the information could be useful, as it had been before. Like the time he'd told her about Laura's problem with Sarah Cole and Mary Hakimi.

Afterwards, she had googled Clive Walters and found out from his LinkedIn profile that he was a personal trainer at a Brighton gym. She had called him and told him she was a friend of Sarah Cole, the lawyer who worked – correction, had worked – for Morrison Kemp solicitors. Sarah had confided in her, she said, told her the whole sorry story. Sarah had been very upset about what had happened to his sister. It hadn't been her fault, she wanted him to know that, but still she had been fired for it. She also wanted him to know that there never had been any letter from the solicitors telling his sister that she needed to remind them to renew the court order. Laura Maxwell had wanted to forge one, but Sarah had refused to take any part in it. That was why she'd lost her job.

Clive Walters had lapped it all up. He'd never asked her name, probably assumed it was really Sarah herself who was calling him. Later that day he'd rung back, leaving a message saying he wanted 'to check a few details' with her, and telling her he was putting in an official complaint, on behalf of his sister. The whole thing was a disgrace and he wasn't going to let it go. Anna heard the greed in his voice; he was onto a good thing and he was going to make the most of it.

She hadn't called him back. He was making a complaint, there would be an investigation; she had no further need of Clive Walters. It would cause Laura Maxwell a lot of grief and that was the object of the exercise. She put the mobile in her bag, took a walk on the cliff path, and threw it into the sea.

This time, Joe had told her that Laura was highly suspicious, thought that someone was trying to kill her. Joe said he thought that was ridiculous; she was overstressed; there was no evidence. That was good. Laura had gone to the police with her fears. That was bad. What was their attitude? It was important that the police, too, were sceptical, that Laura was undermined on all sides. Anna concentrated, but couldn't recall Joe saying anything about the reaction of the police.

She thought it was unlikely they'd make much of an effort. There was nothing concrete to prove that Laura had been deliberately targeted, nothing that couldn't have been accidental. Investigating would involve considerable work that might well turn out to be wasted time. She felt confident until she remembered that Laura was a lawyer and would know how to deal with the police; she might be able to pull strings to make sure they took an interest.

A beautiful idea occurred to her and she laughed out loud. She thought it over, looking for flaws but she couldn't find any; without a doubt she could get away with it. She could see no way it could backfire and be traced to her, and if it worked, it would damage, maybe destroy, Laura's credibility with the police. Better still, it would damage Laura, would seriously frighten her.

She went to a drawer full of underwear and fished out another pay-as-you-go phone stashed at the back, a spare one, in case of emergencies. She lay down on the bed, and for a few happy moments, smelled Joe's scent on the bedclothes. She buried her head in them, breathing in greedily.

Very soon now, she and Joe would truly be together, all the impediments to their love would be cleared away. The end of twenty years of wasted life. Twenty years that were like dust and ashes to her. A wasteland.

She entered Laura's mobile number into the phone. She didn't even need to think about the message; it seemed to have been screaming in her head forever.

Next time I'll get you, you fucking bitch.

Pressed send. Felt pleasure. Hot and thrilling.

The texts came thick and fast, her fingers itching to tap out the words, words that would sow terror and dismay. Keep cool, she told herself. Think about it. Think what's going to scare the shit out of her.

After the sixth one she forced herself to stop, dropped the phone on the bed as if it was red hot, clasped her hands together behind her back so she would not touch it again. Now, she thought, let the bitch wait, let her suffer.

It felt so good imagining Laura suffering, imagining her staring at the phone, horrified by what she was seeing, dreading the arrival of the next message. The possibility that Laura was not actually reading the texts, was doing something else entirely, never entered her mind.

She breathed deeply; lay back on the bed, and thought of Joe, of love instead of hate, of life instead of death. After a while, she felt cool enough to pick up the mobile again and send another text.

Anna looked at the message she had just tapped out and fury rose in her, starting in her gut and reaching her throat, almost blocking it. It wasn't until her jaw began to ache that she stopped clenching it. If Laura were suffering now it would be just a tiny amount of the suffering that she had inflicted on *her*; a pinprick compared to what *she* had gone through.

She heard, as if it were yesterday, the voice of the self-important psychiatrist in the hospital where she'd been taken twenty years before. In her darkest hours, she talked to him of the schoolboy Joe, the saviour, of how she loved him, how she was sure he returned that love.

The doctor had said she was 'obsessive' and she recognized that was true. How could it be otherwise when she knew, beyond any doubt, that she and Joe were made to be together and that she must fight, tooth and claw, against all the difficulties fate threw in the way? It was a match made in heaven and nothing and no one would threaten it.

The shrink had been full of grand theories and enjoyed explaining them.

'You can be obsessed about so many things, Annabel,' he said, 'but the real obsessions are centred on abstract ideas like love, hate, revenge, life or death. It starts at ten miles an hour, speeds up to sixty, then to ninety and you just can't stop or slow down. In the end, you lose control and you crash and burn.'

Well he was wrong about that. She wasn't going to crash and burn. She knew the dangers, knew how to deal with them; she knew all about self-control. She had ditched that old, pathetic schoolgirl self, and the hated name of Annabel that reminded her of it, totally and forever. It was a pity she could not let rip the vengeance inside her, but that time was coming. Very soon. For now she needed to follow the plan, to point the finger of suspicion firmly elsewhere.

Quickly, while the calculating part of her brain was still in charge, she tapped out one more text and then gave herself up to the memories because she couldn't stop them, however much she tried.

CHAPTER THIRTY-NINE

Christmas 1997

For one crazy moment Annabel Roberts thought he wanted to dance with her. The boy from the beach: Joe Greene. Dancing with her. Was it possible? She felt a rush of exquisite pleasure.

Then she realized. He was taking photos. That was all. The three beloved cameras were round his neck and he was snapping away at the dancers.

Her legs had gone weak with shock and she was desperate to sit down or lean against the wall. She stopped dancing, suddenly self-conscious again, her bravery gone. From the side of the room she watched as a dozen girls surrounded him, posed for him. They were laughing and shouting and pulling him in to the dance. The old feelings of isolation, of not fitting in, swept over her.

And then it happened.

A girl walked up behind him, put her arms around him and he turned and lifted her off her feet. He pressed her close to him and together they began a slow, sensual dance.

Annabel's brain refused to take it in. She couldn't, wouldn't believe what her eyes were seeing. They stared. Stared at a girl with shining, black, shoulder-length hair. A pretty, petite girl with a creamy, spotless complexion and pale pink lips parted now in a wide smile. And a stab of pure hate, visceral and primeval, went through her like a gunshot.

Joe kissed the girl long and hard, the girl whose name was Laura Maxwell. Annabel knew it was a picture she would never ever be able to wipe from her mind. It was imprinted on her eyes for all time; she would see it as clearly on her dying day as she did now. The sounds of the crowd faded in her ears and she thought she might faint; she was going down in flames.

She had to get away, from the two of them, from the hellish party. She stumbled out into the hall, and then Michelle Cullen and Jennifer Fleming were at her side. She couldn't speak to them, couldn't speak to anyone, she was desperate to find a quiet place, somewhere a million miles away.

She headed towards the front door but the hallway was more crowded than ever and the two girls were crushed up against her. They smiled, they giggled, they whispered secrets to her, told her what a great dancer she was. Then they offered her some pills. They said the pills would make her happy, very happy, so happy she would dance all night. They said they were going to take some themselves, but they never did.

Annabel hardly hesitated. She put two of the little white pills into her mouth and swallowed them with a gulp of wine. She would have swallowed anything then, even poison, especially poison, to get away from what she was feeling.

Half an hour later she had her escape, but it turned out to be no escape at all for it led to a place of darkness and despair.

Little rushes of happiness started to run through her, loosening the tension and the rage. In the next hour, the highs got bigger and longer and the nausea and disorientation she'd felt at first, disappeared. She was happy, euphoric, and the fact that she never usually felt this way, made it all the more potent.

She saw no more of Joe or Laura Maxwell, and the thought of them became less painful. Her world became a wonderful, benign place as it had never been before. The people around her were her friends, her very close, very dear friends. She looked at them and was filled with a warm glow. She wanted to hug them tight.

Jennifer Fleming touched her arm. It felt great, sensual, her flesh tingled with heightened sensation. She drew the girl towards her, embraced her, rubbed her face against her cheek and kissed it. Pleasure rippled along her skin. Standing behind, watching, she saw Maria Burns, smiling. Maria, who had not spoken a word to her for eight months, seemed to be looking at her now as if she was her best friend. Annabel was enchanted. To be friends again with Maria. Her heart swelled with the thought of it.

They were dancing. All of them together as she'd always wanted. Anna and her friends. She loved them. The music pounded deep in her soul and she loved it. It sounded so good, clearer, more vibrant than she'd ever known it, as if she was dancing on the notes themselves. And she had discovered she had a talent. She could dance. Now that she knew it, she was never going to stop.

She felt so up there, as if she was in heaven and so she failed to notice Maria Burns slip away from the dancers and head over to a group of older boys, failed to notice her giggling with them and pointing at her.

Soon afterwards Whitney Houston's 'I will always love you' came on. The bitter-sweet words rang loud in her ears and when the boy appeared in front of her and put his arms around her, she reached out to him and held him tight.

She pressed herself against him, revelling in the intensity of touch that the drug brought with it. If she had known she had taken Ecstasy, she would have thoroughly approved of its name. When the song ended and he took her by the hand, she went with him. He was going to a club, he told her as he led her out of the house, going dancing, and he wanted her to come with him. How about a drink first? There was some in the car.

There were two other boys in the car. They started kissing her, groping her breasts then pulling off the tight, Lycra top. To begin with they didn't need to use much force because, by that time, the drug was working at full strength and Annabel's inhibitions were long gone. She felt a bond with these boys – men, really, as they were all eighteen-year-olds – and she didn't put up much resistance when they started to touch her. By the time her drugged brain realized something was going badly wrong and she tried to fight them off, it was way too late. They held her down, forced her legs apart, and they all had sex with her.

They dumped her back at the party, on the front doorstep, confused and stunned. Violated. It was freezing cold but she didn't want to go inside. The Ecstasy high was gone, abruptly chased away by what had happened to her. No gradual comedown, just a hard landing. She leaned against the wall of the house, sank to the ground, and began to sob, head in her hands.

It was there, about ten minutes later, that Michelle Cullen's mother found her when she came to pick up her daughter. She tried to talk to the traumatized girl, tried to get her up off the ground, but Annabel just yelled at her to fuck off and leave her alone.

Annabel's father got the same result. He had arrived shortly before and was waiting inside the house wondering where his daughter had got to. He stood in front of her, flanked by the Cullens and a growing number of interested onlookers, as his daughter screamed at him to go away. He looked at her; she was fast becoming a public spectacle and his concern mixed with embarrassment and, try as he might to suppress it, disgust. His eyes took in the low, too-tight top, now badly disarranged, the heavy smeared make-up, the hysterical behaviour. He grabbed hold of her left arm and pulled her sharply towards him. To his surprise there was no resistance. She stood up quickly, throwing her arms around him and almost overbalancing him. As fast as he could, he hustled her out to his car.

She cried all the way home, refusing to answer when he asked what was wrong, shouting at him to let her be. He was used to her moods and he was used to ignoring them, but this was different.

Usually she was sulky or gloomy, giving him monosyllabic replies and shutting herself up in her room. He had never known her cry and scream like this. He felt his nerves wearing thin. It was hard enough to deal with his wife's depression; he could not cope with a crazy daughter as well. He had to fight down the urge to stop the car, slap her face and tell her to pull herself together, and just for once in her life, behave normally.

In the days that followed, Annabel lived in a pit of despair. She was tired beyond belief, depressed beyond belief. She wouldn't get out of bed because she didn't want to take any more part in life. She simply wanted it to end. She never spoke about what had happened to her, even though she knew it would not have been hard to track down her attackers. But they would deny it or say she'd wanted it and she couldn't bear the humiliation. The horror of the sex they'd forced on her was inextricably bound up in her mind with the horror of witnessing Joe, her Joe, kissing Laura Maxwell.

She lay rigid in her bed, weeping. Sometimes it was noiseless and then, as the cruelty of life began to burn in her, the sobbing increased in intensity until she was choking with tears, her head throbbing and her chest aching. She felt as if some part of her had died and that she dragged it with her, a cold heavy weight, draining away all her strength.

Her mother forgot her own problems for once and resolved to help her; now her daughter was having a breakdown, she felt drawn to her – a kindred spirit in the same kind of agony as herself. She tried her best, but her determination wavered as Annabel refused to speak to her or engage with her in any way, except for furious outbursts of hostility. She couldn't cope with aggression and before very long retreated into her sad shell and handed over her child to the doctors.

The GP suspected drug abuse but not sexual abuse, and since his patient would not talk to him or let him fully examine her, he prescribed sedatives and said he'd arrange for her to see a psychiatrist. The day after his visit, three days before Christmas, Annabel swallowed the whole lot, plus some of her mother's lorazepam tablets, and hoped to die.

She didn't even come close. Her father found her lying on her bed, comatose, and the hospital pumped out her stomach. She did better with the second attempt, a few weeks later. She was back at school and Maria Burns and Jennifer Fleming and Michelle Cullen were sniggering big time. Someone had scrawled 'Slag' across her school books. These things contributed to her suicidal state of mind, but none of them was the decisive factor. That came on a Friday afternoon when she saw Joe standing at the school gates. He was chatting to some girls; one of them was Laura Maxwell.

Annabel had gone straight to the chemist to buy some razor blades before returning to the near empty school and that all too familiar girls' cloakroom. She locked herself in a cubicle and slashed her wrists. It was the weekend, she thought, no one would find her this time.

She watched the blood running down her fingers and on to the floor. It did not flow as freely or as powerfully as she'd expected but eventually, surely, her life must drain away. In a detached way, she wondered if the urge for self-preservation would suddenly cut in, but there was no sign of it yet. All she felt was a tremendous tiredness and relief – relief that this attempt was going to work.

A short time later she started to feel sick and confused and couldn't remember where she was. She opened the cubicle door and fell to her knees, began crawling across the floor towards the washbasins. It was there, underneath one of the basins, that she collapsed and lost consciousness. It was there that a conscientious caretaker, checking the cloakroom an hour later, flashed his torch beam. Pools of congealed black blood gleamed in the light.

CHAPTER FORTY

Harry had always known his wife had a lover but he'd never come close to finding out who it was. The hidden cameras, the bugs, the spying – the man had eluded them all. He'd even employed a private detective who had cost thousands of pounds and come up with a big fat zero. After six weeks, Harry had fired him, convinced the detective was lazy or stupid or both. Because Harry knew, knew without a shadow of a doubt, that his wife was cheating on him. She'd just been too clever to get caught.

He'd given up the chase a few weeks after Anna had left him. He told himself it was because he didn't care anymore, but the real reason was fear. Fear that if he carried on snooping or followed her or staked out her new home, she would find out and tell Laura Maxwell and they would use it against him. It would give them ammunition to prove that he was a crazy obsessive, a danger to his wife and daughter.

Now, at last, Harry thought he might have a clue. The name Martha had mentioned: 'Joe'. He considered it. He knew two 'Joes', business acquaintances who his wife had met on a few occasions, but neither man could he ever imagine as Anna's lover.

On Tuesday afternoon, as soon as it was dark, he drove once more to the lane where his wife lived and took up position behind the hedge. There were lights on downstairs in what he thought was the main living room, but he couldn't see anything as the curtains were drawn. He had never been invited into the house; whenever he collected Martha, he had waited for her outside in his car.

There was a flower bed in the middle of the front garden with large, straggly shrubs in need of pruning, He slipped from the hedge and edged his way in among them. To his left was the driveway leading to a detached brick and timber garage.

Harry Pelham waited, waited for the man called Joe to arrive. It wasn't a great plan, but it was the best he had for now; if he stuck at it he might get lucky. His teeth chattered and his feet froze and he didn't dare stamp them up and down for fear of disturbing the shrubs.

He'd been there two hours when he heard a car coming up the lane. His wife's black Peugeot pulled into the drive. An external lamp flashed on, bathing the garden in light. Harry shrank back among the plants. Doors slammed, women's voices. Anna with Martha and a woman he didn't know.

'Thanks a lot for offering, Claire. I totally forgot it was tonight. I won't be long,' he heard his wife say before the three of them disappeared into the house.

It sounded as if his wife was going out, and excitement stirred in him. Carefully, he extricated himself from the flower bed and took off back to his car. He turned on the ignition, got the heater blasting hot air on his feet, then slid down in the driver's seat.

Headlights on the windscreen. He sat up slightly, peered into the night, trying to be sure. Yes it had to be. It was his wife's car. He glimpsed her behind the wheel as it passed by. He started up the engine and followed.

The clock on the dashboard read 20.34. She had left the woman babysitting, he thought, while she went off somewhere. The boyfriend. She was going to meet the boyfriend. He blew air out through his teeth. Gotcha.

Fifteen minutes later his excitement had become uncertainty. Twenty minutes later it was confusion and suspicion.

The black Peugeot was parked at the end of a wide avenue called Chapel Road. It was under a tree, away from any street light, and Harry, who had been keeping a safe distance behind his wife, almost missed it as he turned into the street. He drove on by, teeth gritted, seriously upset. He knew this road, knew it very well indeed. He had been here only yesterday. It was where he lived.

CHAPTER FORTY-ONE

Anna Pelham got out of the car and pulled the hood of her dark green Parka tight around her face. She didn't want to be seen. She reached a gloved hand into the back seat, pulled out a plastic bag and zipped it inside the coat. It was bulky and it made the Parka bulge, but she didn't care. She had put in as much as she could, every last bit she could get away with; the idea of being rid of it in this way was hugely cathartic.

She set off quickly towards the other end of the road, straining her eyes for signs of the police or one of her former neighbours; she had a cover story ready but she didn't want to have to use it. She wasn't worried about running into Harry, she thought he would steer well clear in case the police nabbed him.

The houses here were Edwardian, large and detached, set well back from the road, and no one was going to look out of their window and spot her. The risk would be from a car – if one of the neighbours happened to be going in or out as she went by. She had done this kind of thing before, several times. So far she'd been lucky but she worried about the law of averages.

No problem. Without incident she reached the long drive that led to her old home. Her feet crunched on the gravel and a security light came on, but she was now out of sight, the house screened from view by a tall evergreen hedge. There were two lights on downstairs but she knew they were the ones Harry had on timers.

Confidently, she strode to the front door. She took the key from her coat pocket. He had changed the locks when she'd left but he'd given a new key to Martha. Typical of him, she thought. Martha didn't need it, she wasn't likely to be coming or going on her own, but to Harry it was a symbol, a symbol that his daughter was still firmly part of his life. Martha had proudly told her how Daddy had solemnly presented it to her. It was a grown-up thing and Martha had been pleased. Anna had warned her not to carry it round with her in case she lost it. So she left it in her bedroom; the same day, her mother had it copied.

Anna didn't have much time. She'd told Claire some cock and bull story about forgetting that a friend of hers was having birthday drinks for her husband and that she'd promised to drop in. It was a chance. If Claire offered to babysit for a while she would put her plan into action; if not, so what, she would find another way.

The plan had come to her that afternoon. She had gone through the Laura Maxwell collection, sorting it carefully, with the kind of meticulous attention to detail that hate can give. She put to one side the things Harry would have been unlikely to come by – the things from school, some of the Maxwell family details. The rest, including the scarf she'd stolen from Laura's office, she put in a Sainsbury's plastic bag.

At the same time, she had added one new item to Joe's collection. She held it up, examined it, then laid it gently on the top. She had collected it only that morning after she'd had sex with him. It was a used condom.

Now she planned to leave the Sainsbury's bag in Harry's wardrobe, together with a knife, which she took from his kitchen and used to score through Laura's face in several of the photographs before adding it to the bag.

She darted down the hall, glancing into the big living room with its cream and pale blue furnishings, then went into Harry's office where a light was on. She smiled, remembering how Harry had changed his passwords as well as his locks, how she'd found his new ones written on a Post-it note stuck to his computer when she'd first revisited the house. With pleasure, she noted the signs of the police search and that the computer was gone. She would soon be sending the police another anonymous tip suggesting they search the house again. By now, they should have found the child pornography on his computer and would be happy to oblige. They would find no more porn, but they would find the collection and they would know that Harry had killed Laura Maxwell.

Anna Pelham didn't have much time, but she didn't need it. She headed up the staircase and into the bedroom she'd shared with Harry, opened his wardrobe and shoved the plastic bag underneath a pile of his old sweaters, leaving it half hidden. Her previous visits to the house had been much more time-consuming – she'd had to send death threats to herself from the Paul Giles email address, access child pornography sites, and input Harry's credit card details, and she hadn't known for sure where he was or when he might come back and find her.

She was back home at the cottage little more than an hour after she'd left it.

'How was your birthday friend?' Martha asked in a flat tone of voice she used a lot lately. The dark brown eyes regarded her mother coolly. She doesn't believe me, Anna thought, not for the first time.

CHAPTER FORTY-TWO

Harry drove slowly along the road, anger rising inside him. What the hell was she up to? Nothing good, that was for sure. If she was coming to visit him, which he thought most unlikely, why park her car so far away, as if she was trying to hide it?

Ahead, he saw a figure hurrying along the pavement huddled into a coat with the hood pulled up tight against the weather. For a second it didn't connect, and then he realized it must be his wife. A furious urge to confront her took hold of him; to grab her, shake her, slap her until she told him what she was doing – what she had been doing and who she had been doing it with.

He beat it down and was surprised at how easily he did so. He felt a new emotion stirring for his wife, one he'd never have dreamt he would feel. Fear.

She was not the person he had thought she was, not a bit as he had thought. Loving, caring, honest – once he would have listed all of these, but not any more. He was more than a little scared of her, he thought bleakly; she had him off balance. He would almost certainly lose a confrontation with her; instead, he needed to be as cunning as she was.

He pulled over, waited for her to walk on, then turned his car around. He parked in another wide avenue, which led off Chapel Road. He wasn't taking any chances that she might spot his car.

He set off fast towards his house then told himself to slow down. The last thing he wanted was to run straight into her.

He reached the house without seeing her again and edged cautiously into the shadow of the large hedge which formed the front boundary. Hiding in bushes, he thought sourly, was getting to be a habit with him.

None of the security lights were on, which meant she wasn't standing at the front door or anywhere near the outside of the building. He started to think she'd gone somewhere else, maybe to visit a neighbour, though, so far as he knew, she hadn't been friendly with any of them. Could one of the neighbours be Joe? He was struggling with this idea when a light went on in his bedroom.

'Jesus Christ,' he whispered.

Almost at once the light went out again, and shortly afterwards, Anna came out of the front door. He drew back into the darkness, watched his wife walk quickly down the drive, the hood of her coat drawn close around her face. Again came the urge to confront her but he pictured her calling the police afterwards, concocting some damning story about him forcing her to come to the house. He stayed put until she was safely on her way back up the road, then went inside.

He stood in the hall and sniffed her perfume in the air. Dior's Pure Poison. How often had he bought it for her, how appropriate it had turned out to be. He wondered how many times she had done this before, how many times she had been here without his knowledge.

He went up the stairs, along the landing, and into his bedroom, and smelled her perfume again. Memories, unsettling. He stood looking round carefully for some clue as to what she had been doing there but he could find nothing, no sign that anything had been disturbed. He checked all the upstairs rooms, his daughter's bedroom especially, in case Anna had some dark purpose there. Nothing. Whatever her purpose, he could not pin it down.

He walked back down the stairs and picked up the post lying on the hall floor. With a sinking heart he realized that she could have taken it, realized that, in the past, she almost certainly had taken it. It might explain why Laura Maxwell was so well informed about his financial affairs. It might explain quite a lot. He glanced at the letter on top of the pile. It was his Visa bill and he opened it almost without thinking, his mind still occupied with what his wife might have done.

Suddenly, the bill got all his attention, his eyes locked on it, specifically on four transactions. Four payments on two separate dates to companies he'd never heard of but about which he had a very bad feeling. One in Moscow and one in Bangkok. He guessed what the payments were for and his stomach knotted. Child pornography. Seeing them in black and white, listed on his credit card bill, left him petrified. The vile stuff was on his computer, then, and the police would find it.

As he stood staring at the bill, a few things started to add up. He turned towards his office; the door was open but he couldn't remember if it had been when he'd left the house to go to the police station. Everything had been disturbed in the search, and he would have found it impossible to tell if Anna had been inside if it hadn't been for that tell-tale scent lingering in the air.

The computer was gone, taken away by the police but, he thought, she wasn't to know that. How disappointed she would have been to find she could not log on, download more pornography, and pay for it with his credit card. Maybe that explained why she hadn't stayed long.

Harry no longer understood his wife, knew that she was a different woman to the one he'd believed her to be. But what sort of awful creature was she, he wondered, to do this to him?

He crumpled the bill and stuffed it in his coat pocket. He was out of options. All he could think of was to go to see Ronnie and try to persuade him. There was no hard evidence that his wife had set him up he realized that only too well. He would have to call on years of friendship, would have to beg Ronnie to hear him out and to take his word on trust.

CHAPTER FORTY-THREE

Anna gave her daughter a hug and told her how much she'd enjoyed the birthday drinks. Martha pulled away from her and Anna felt, as she so often felt, a pang of disappointment that Martha should be so like Harry, so obviously his child. She not only had his looks but his character too. Lately, it had been obvious that Martha doubted her and it would not be long, Anna guessed, before she openly challenged her. How different to have a child of Joe's. What bliss that would be.

'Thanks for hanging on here, Claire,' Anna turned towards the woman, 'I really appreciate it.'

'Oh, don't thank me. I've been on my own. I know what it's like. I'm just glad to help out.'

'You've certainly done that,' Anna laughed. 'Lending me the car's been a real lifesaver. I hope you didn't miss it too much.'

Anna had scraped the side of her Peugeot in a multi-storey car park in town. It had needed repairs, and while it was in the garage, Claire had offered to lend her the car. It was a bit old and battered because it was used on the family farm, but if Anna wanted it for a couple of days, she was more than welcome.

'Not a problem, we don't use it much,' Claire said. She stood up, ready to collect the car and get going. Martha sat still, glaring at her mother.

'Come on, aren't you coming to say goodbye?' Anna called as they went out to the front door. Reluctantly, Martha followed. Anna headed for the garage and the other two waited while she fiddled with a bunch of keys, unlocking the doors.

Inside was a black Nissan Pathfinder 4x4. It had dark tinted windows.

Anna started up the engine, reversed fast up the drive and stopped out in the lane. She had no intention of letting Claire see the Nissan in the lighted driveway. There were new scratches on it and a new dent in the side panel. They hadn't been there when she'd borrowed it.

'See you cleaned it up for me,' Claire remarked. She wasn't laughing.

'Sorry, I did mean to, but what with half-term and all.'

'Doesn't matter, it was pretty dirty before but', she eyed the vehicle, 'it looks like it's been through a swamp!'

Even in the dark it was obviously filthy. The tyres and chassis were thick with mud and the bodywork was badly spattered. Anna had thought about washing off the worst but decided against it. The dirt helped to hide the damage. The vehicle had been messy and scratched when she'd got it and she was hoping no one would bother to clean it up for a while. Too bad if they did, she thought. Once it was off the premises it would be nothing to do with her.

She laughed, kissed Claire on the cheek, and hustled her into the driver's seat. The monster moved off, its powerful headlights raking the lane ahead. Martha ran indoors, up to her room and slammed the door. Her mother shrugged, unconcerned. She was remembering the chase.

It had been a spur of the moment thing, because she happened to come across Laura Maxwell, because she happened to have the 4x4, because … Anna thought about it, because it was the answer to all her problems. An answer that had been sitting in her brain for a long time. Suddenly, there was a chance and she had grabbed it.

That day, the day of the chase, she had woken at 3 a.m., panicky, desperate to see Joe, tormented by doubts about the future. It was happening a lot lately and this particular nightmare was becoming more frequent. She was going to lose him, she knew it; he was slipping through her fingers. Her chest filled with a hot choking sensation and she could hardly breathe.

She phoned him as soon as she could. She had to talk to him, needed to hear his voice, the same way she needed air or water. It calmed her but not enough. She had to see him, to touch him, to know that he was hers.

Joe had a lot on, business meetings with his brother that he couldn't skip. There was no time to come out to the cottage, so she met him at the Greene House Hotel in Hove. Room number '21'. Erotic memories. It was where they used to meet, before the cottage, before Anna had left her husband. Their meetings had been all about sex, the excitement heightened by their restricted access to one another and the slight, but ever present, danger of discovery. It was a room that was let only in emergencies when the hotel was full and needed the space. It was too small to be comfortable, with a cramped bathroom and a view of a brick wall. But it had a double bed and Joe had the key and so it was perfect. For Anna, to be back there felt like a homecoming.

They were still in bed, Joe dozing by her side, when his wife rang her. Her mobile was switched to silent but she was sending a text about Martha's sleepover that night when she saw Laura's number come up. She knew it was stupid to answer, but something inside her couldn't resist. She dashed into the bathroom with it.

She wanted to howl down the phone with laughter. How hilarious was this? To be phoned by Laura Maxwell while she was actually shagging her husband in his hotel. She sat on the edge of the bath with her hand in her mouth to stop herself giggling, told Laura the line was bad and she'd have to call her back.

After the hotel, Joe walked with her along the sea front. He'd been worried then, said that what they'd done was a stupid risk because they had to be careful until her divorce was through. He'd enjoyed it at the time, though, she knew. And she wasn't so sure any more that she wanted to be careful. Why shouldn't the bitch know? Wouldn't it be better that way? Part of her, a growing part of her, longed for discovery. Bring it on, she thought. It would shake things up a little. There'd be some kind of action and she was sick of waiting.

She thought a lot about arranging for Laura to 'accidentally' find out, fantasized about it, but the truth was she didn't dare. She was scared that, if it happened, Joe would be frightened off. Same old problem, same old nightmare; when the chips were down, she didn't trust him to choose her.

Anna was free for the rest of the day, and with Martha spending the night away, she wanted Joe to come to the cottage that evening. It was a rare opportunity. She would cook dinner for him, watch a film with him, they could be like a normal couple. Maybe he would even stay the night, and even if he didn't, she could go to sleep with his smell fresh on her sheets.

He couldn't make it. He really wanted to, he said, but he couldn't. He didn't have a choice – he had to work late, an evening meeting with clients. Anna heard the regret in his voice, saw it on his handsome face as they lay in the hotel bedroom, but as soon as he was gone from her she began to doubt.

The doubt grew as the afternoon went on and by half-past six it was full blown suspicion. Most likely he'd never wanted to come. Of course not. He'd enjoyed the lunchtime sex but that was enough of her for one day. He'd rather go home to Laura Maxwell.

Paranoia. Maybe, but if it was, she couldn't stop it. She went to a drawer, pulled out a cropped brunette wig picked up in a charity shop, and put it on, cramming her own hair inside it. She looked in the bedroom mirror; she appeared older, tougher, and with her height, more mannish, her long face and strong chin no longer softened by shoulder-length blonde hair.

It was windy and raining heavily outside. She wrapped herself in her Parka and drove back to the Greene House Hotel. Was he still there working or was he lying? She would check if his car was in its allotted space. She left the Nissan in a nearby street; she didn't want to drive it into the hotel car park, it felt too big and conspicuous. She was pleased that she had it, though, and wasn't driving her own car because it lessened the chance of him spotting her.

The weather buffeted her as she walked up the road and she was pleased by that too. Nobody paid attention to anyone else in this kind of weather – heads were down, minds concentrated on getting back indoors.

His car was there, just where it should be and she felt some of the tension drain away. But it was not enough. She needed more. She crept from the car park into the hotel grounds towards the bay window of a room on the ground floor. It was where he would be, she guessed, if he was with clients. It was the conference room.

She peered through half closed curtains into the lighted room. Seven people inside, one of them Joe. He was sitting at the table, looking gorgeous, next to his very ordinary brother. She laughed softly to herself. There was no cause for worry, she could see that now, and she could see the funny side. Standing there in the pouring rain, spying on him, wearing a crazy wig. What was she thinking of?

A face stared back at her. A youngish woman she didn't recognize, seated two chairs away from Joe. Her mouth was open, she was pointing at the window. Anna stopped laughing. She turned and fled.

Safely back in the Nissan and on a high because Joe had not deceived her, she drove off towards Brighton, pressed play on the CD; someone else's choice that had come with the car, a heavy pulsing beat, drum and bass. She liked it, wound up the volume.

It was about ten minutes later, nearly nine o'clock, when she spotted the white Audi TT on the other side of the road. She recognized it at once and the sight of it abruptly ended her good mood. Hatred filled her brain like a flash fire. She turned the 4x4 around, pulled the hood of her coat over her head.

The Audi stopped at traffic lights and she drew up beside it. Close, very close, crowding it. She looked straight at Laura. She didn't worry about being recognized; the windows were tinted, no one could see in, certainly not on this dark and rain-filled night. Even if they could, she thought, they would hardly identify the tall, hooded figure behind the wheel as Anna Pelham.

'Wouldn't it be great if she crashed,' a voice in Anna's head, a lovely picture in her mind – the sports car in a crumpled heap and Laura Maxwell dead, smashed to bits inside. Elation rushed through her and she forced herself to calm down. From what seemed like far off came the hoot of a car's horn. She waited.

The Audi shot away. The Nissan moved off more slowly. She had no immediate need to chase, she knew where Laura was heading and the route she would take.

Anna followed along the main road, continuing for a mile past the lane that Laura had taken, then turned off herself. Almost at once she was in the forest, thick woods either side of the road, the air full of autumn leaves swirling in the wind. She came to a visitor car park on the left-hand side, turned into it, and from the far end, set off on a track though the woods. It was used by forest rangers in their Land Rovers and it was no problem for the Nissan, muddy and rutted but Anna hardly noticed. Her foot was hard down on the accelerator.

It would be touch and go: she had followed Laura Maxwell before and knew how she enjoyed the Audi's speed. She took a chance, wrenched the wheel, swerved off the track and into the woods. It was a shortcut to the lane that Laura would be on, but the view through the thrashing windscreen wipers made her yelp with fright. Trees loomed everywhere, hemmed her in, came at her out of nowhere.

The Nissan pitched and rolled, roared over a bank and hit the lane hard. She fought with the steering wheel to bring the car straight. Then she laughed out loud because she saw the Audi powering towards her. There was a car in front of it and Laura Maxwell was pulling out to overtake.

Anna didn't think, didn't care, about the danger. Her brain filled with bloodlust. She stamped on the accelerator, switched the headlights to full beam, and slammed down her hand on the horn.

Too late. Seconds too late. The Audi squeezed by on a wing and a prayer. Shit.

She wasted no time on disappointment because she was not a loser, not anymore. She swung the 4x4 to the right, across the road, careering up the bank and disappearing into the woods. She nosed her way carefully through the rain and the trees until she came to one of the forest tracks. Laura had escaped, she would have sped off home and there was no chance of catching her now.

Anna stopped and got out to inspect the Nissan. She checked the plates, old mud from the farm covered with new mud from tonight, unreadable. She set off again, following the track as it looped round and back towards the lane.

On first sight she wasn't sure. It was only visible for a second as the Nissan went over a rise. A car parked off the road at the end of the track. Next time she saw it there was no doubt. The Audi. Waiting, vulnerable. Anna Pelham caught her breath.

The driver's door hung open. Was the bitch inside? Anna couldn't see her. The Nissan charged onwards and then, with a stab of excitement, Anna saw Laura Maxwell picked out like prey in her headlights. She couldn't believe her luck; she was getting another chance.

There was a flimsy barrier ahead but she didn't give it a second thought. The Nissan raced up the hill towards it, smashed it like a matchstick. Suddenly, the Audi screeched into action.

Anna's bloodstream filled with the thrill of the chase, the music pounded in her skull. It had got away but not for long. She would catch it, run it off the road, force it to self-destruct.

She revved the engine, closed in for the kill, pulled out and drew level with the driver's window. She wanted to see her victim. See the fear. She looked out from the side of her coat hood, strained to make out Laura's face. Yes! There it was turned towards her, wide terrified eyes staring out. Or was it? Was it her imagination, hot-wired, seeing what it wanted to see? Beautiful images filled her head; the Audi, ploughing headlong into a tree, its driver crushed to a pulp.

Collision. But not the one she'd expected. The Audi swung to the left, its back smacking into the Nissan's side before it vanished down a side road. Anna swore in fury then got herself under control and started calculating. Half a mile further on, she turned off again into the woods.

She pulled up by the side of the road, the road the Audi should take as it headed home. She was tucked in the trees just after a bend, ready to pounce as soon as she saw it pass by. It didn't come. Fifteen minutes later she shrugged and gave it up.

No worries, she thought. There would be a next time.

She pulled down the hood of her coat, snatched off the wig and shook out her hair with a shout of delight.

It had been a blast.

CHAPTER FORTY-FOUR

It was close to midnight when Harry arrived at his solicitor's house on the outskirts of the village of Ditchling. He hadn't phoned first, afraid that Ronnie would tip off the police that he was on the way.

With relief, Harry saw the first floor lights were on – that meant Ronnie probably hadn't gone to bed yet. The house was built with the bedrooms downstairs and the living space upstairs to take advantage of stunning views across the countryside to the north. Eventually, after three rings on the doorbell, he saw Ronnie's tall figure coming down the stairs. The front door opened.

He hadn't expected a warm welcome so he wasn't disappointed. Ronnie, not pleased to be disturbed so late, was less pleased still to see who his visitor was. He gave a brief, graphic opinion about Harry and his recent behaviour, then turned away and walked back up the stairs, leaving him to follow.

They crossed the galleried landing and into the vast sitting room. They stood opposite each other, huge windows on three sides, the bright and starry night all around them. Unwanted thoughts came into Harry's mind of times he had been here with Anna, of how she had loved this room on nights like this. She had called it 'magical', said it felt 'like sitting in heaven'. He shook his head; how deluded he had been about her.

225

'The police have rung me,' Ronnie said immediately, 'They've found sixty-two indecent images of children on the computer taken from your house.'

'It's nothing to do with me, I promise you, Ronnie. I can explain,' he said. It sounded pathetic, he thought, the age-old cry of the guilty man.

'They were downloaded from two websites on two different occasions. They were paid for with your credit card,' the lawyer continued, disgust clear in his voice.

I revolt him, Harry thought. He despises me because what he thinks I've done is something no decent person could ever excuse. There was a phone on the table between them and Ronnie moved towards it.

'I have to let the police know you're here. They want to charge you.'

Charge him. For some reason, probably self-preservation, Harry had never fully contemplated being charged. Now, in a clear, terrifying picture, he saw all the appalling consequences. He was a successful local businessman and the Brighton papers would love it. Maybe the nationals would love it too. He would be a figure of public hatred. Even if, eventually, he could prove it was all a lie, the damage would be done. Some of the mud would stick. He thought the unthinkable. What would it do to Martha?

Before Ronnie could pick up the phone, Harry was on it, snatching it away.

'For God's sake, I didn't do this,' he roared. 'It's Anna. She's set me up.'

The lawyer said nothing, his eyes sliding away.

It made Harry madder still. He ripped the phone from its socket, pushed Ronnie down on a sofa.

'Now you're going to listen,' he spat, his face taut with anger. The rage helped. It stopped him trying to consider what to say, what would have the best effect on Ronnie. Instead, the words just poured out, straight from the heart and they gave his story a raw, authentic feel.

The solicitor's harsh expression softened a little as Harry told how he had followed Anna to his house, how she had gone inside, how she had, without doubt, done it before, how he believed she had downloaded the porn onto his computer to frame him.

Ronnie looked sharply into Harry's face. 'Why would she want you accused of that?' he asked.

'To destroy me, destroy my reputation, to weaken me and strengthen her hand in the divorce. Who knows what's going through her mind? But if I'm fighting to clear my name, I won't find it so easy to fight the divorce.'

'If what you say is true, she's taking a hell of a risk. She could have been caught out at any time. It's hard to believe she'd go so far. It's very extreme.'

'She is extreme and she hates my guts.'

'The police tell me they also found the death threats to Anna on your computer,' Ronnie said thoughtfully.

'Of course they did. She'll have sent them to herself when she was logged onto it.'

Harry had been standing over Ronnie as he talked, but sensing that his attitude might be changing, he sat down beside him on the sofa.

'Come on mate, you don't still think it was me, do you?'

'I was surprised when you were accused of it, I must say. It didn't seem likely, but then, you never know. People are not always what you think they are even when you've known them for years.'

'Amen to that. Do you believe me now?' Harry pressed.

'Maybe. People do all kinds of awful things during a divorce. I really don't want to think you did it.'

'There's something else you should know,' Harry said, and he told Ronnie about his visit from Ben Morgan. At the end of it, he had the impression that Ronnie had shifted a little further in his favour.

'We need to talk to the police and you need to make a statement to them in the same way you've made it to me.' Ronnie suffered a rare moment of embarrassment. 'It was, er, very powerful. I think, perhaps, I should have given you rather more of the benefit of the doubt.'

It wasn't exactly an apology but it meant a lot to Harry. It meant that his old friend had not deserted him. It was a shame, then, that he was going to have to fall out with him again.

'I'm not waiting around for the police,' he stated flatly. Harry expected an argument but Ronnie simply shrugged and raised the palms of his hands in the air. 'I can't let them charge me. You understand; it's Martha.'

'I sympathize, but what's the good of hiding. You're going to have to face them sometime, better to tell them what you told me and let them investigate.'

'No chance. They've got the computer and they've got the evidence that the filth on it was paid for with my credit card. They'll charge me, and even if I can clear my name later, people will think it was true. No smoke without fire.'

Ronnie didn't argue and he still didn't argue very much when Harry told him he intended to 'disappear' again and try to get evidence to prove he was innocent.

'I'd prefer that you didn't, but I can't stop you,' was all he said.

He agreed to give Harry a week – after that he would expect him to contact the police or he would do it himself. If, in the meantime, the police asked him if Harry had been in contact, he would have to tell the truth.

Ronnie's lack of any real protest surprised and pleased Harry, but it worried him too because it showed how serious his position was.

'I'm grateful,' he shook Ronnie's hand with both his own. 'One thing. I'll need some cash. I don't want to risk using a card.'

Ronnie nodded, went to a desk and unlocked a drawer.

'You know,' he said, handing Harry a bundle of twenty pound notes, 'we need to pin down the dates and times when the porn was downloaded onto your computer.'

Harry pulled out his Visa statement. The dates were there but not the times. A Tuesday and Friday of the same week.

'Do you know where you were then, what you were doing?'

'I'd need to look it up. Sally at the office will have my diary. Can you check with her?'

'The dates alone aren't enough. We need precise times.'

'What difference does it make?' Harry asked, but even as he said it, he realized what Ronnie was getting at. His credit card details had been entered into his home computer at certain times on certain dates. Maybe he could prove he'd been somewhere else at the time, maybe he could prove he couldn't have done it.

He felt a tiny spark of hope.

CHAPTER FORTY-FIVE

Joe Greene scowled when he saw the text.

Where are u? x Missing u. Axx

Delete. It was the fifth one in forty minutes and they were irritating him. Didn't she realize he had to do some work sometimes, had a business to run? He'd told her about today, told her it was important he got it right. Very important, given Saturday's debacle when he'd missed the meeting with the Americans. Brother Peter had been sour with him ever since.

A Slough software company was looking for a place to hold a few days' conference in mid-December, hoping the pre-Christmas spirit would help staff bond and come up with bright ideas. Two of the directors were checking out venues and it was Joe's job to sell them Greene's. Peter was away on a half-term break with his young family so it was all down to Joe. It would be good business to get, and if things went well, it could lead to recommendations and more of the same, but competition was tough – the south coast was stuffed full of attractive hotels and the directors were spending the day looking round several of them.

Joe very much wanted to strike the deal. He wanted to show he could be a success, wanted to show his brother, wanted, he realized with surprise, to show his wife. He needed it, too, for his own self-esteem because he never could quite shake a feeling of failure.

He'd made a big effort this time, followed all the tips in the manual about how to pitch to prospective clients. He'd read up on the software company and the men he was meeting, thought of questions to ask them to show off his knowledge of their business, worked out examples of value-added services his hotel would provide, which they might not get elsewhere. He'd carefully positioned chairs for them in the conference room to give them the best view, made sure the walls weren't scuffed and the paintings were hung straight. So now he was nervous because, if he failed, it would be despite his best efforts.

He looked at his watch. 10.25 a.m. The software men were late, most likely their train had been delayed. He'd sent a taxi to collect them from the station and he was waiting impatiently for a text to say they were on their way. His iPhone pinged again.

Room 21 – lunchtime?! Axoxo

He wished she would shut the fuck up and leave him alone.

'Too busy,' he tapped out.

The phone rang, Anna's number, and he dismissed the call, exasperated. She was getting clingy and it was getting on his nerves. He hoped she wasn't going to keep nagging him about leaving Laura as she had the other day. The time wasn't right, he'd told her that, and she needed to accept it and chill out. He wasn't so sure now that the time ever would be right. She was a glamorous, fascinating woman and he loved her, but … did he really want to throw his whole life into turmoil, risk his home and his business, become a stepfather to Martha? How much better, really, would his life be with her than it was with Laura? She was very high-maintenance.

There was the sex, of course, that still sizzled. His actor friends would say that no one could leave someone they have good sex

231

with. You can try, but you always go back. Well, he wasn't planning on leaving just yet but he should cool things down a little, see less of her.

The text alert pinged and this time it was to tell him that the taxi was on its way. Then the mobile started ringing again. He cursed as he saw who it was, and switched the phone to silent.

Joe looked at himself in the large mirror in his office and smiled at his reflection. It always boosted his confidence. Tall, square jawed, a natural for the part of thrusting, successful entrepreneur. He brushed the shoulders of his suit jacket and realized his palms were sweating. He'd have to be careful with the handshakes.

From his office window he could see the car park and he watched the taxi drive in and park. Two people got out. One of the men he'd been expecting – he recognized him from the company website – and a woman he didn't recognize. As she left the taxi, he noticed her long, shapely, legs. He waited a few minutes, no point in appearing too eager, then set off to the lobby to meet them. When he got there he found Ellie the receptionist, as instructed, doing her best to welcome the visitors and make them feel special.

The woman introduced herself as Amy Walker. Her colleague, who'd been due to come, had taken some last minute leave so she'd replaced him. She was glad of a day out of the office, she smiled.

Joe looked at her and flashed back a smile. She was young and blonde and wearing a blue dress. He thought it fitted her very nicely. He'd imagined these guys would be a couple of geeks: the man, George, some kind of software development boffin, had more than a trace of geekiness. But Amy who, it turned out, worked in HR, was totally free of it and perfectly charming. The day was looking up; he always felt at an advantage with women.

Two hours later his hopes were higher still. It had all been going very well indeed so he asked them if they'd like to stay for lunch. George hesitated, said there were other places they needed to see and they'd already got behind, but Amy gently intervened saying they had to have lunch somewhere so it might as well be here.

She seemed in no hurry to move on and George, having made his one effort to keep to the schedule, made no further protest. He had a few glasses of wine and began to enjoy himself, explaining the details of his company's new pet project, developing video conferencing.

'Ground-breaking stuff. World class. Gonna change the way business is done.' he said proudly, waving his wine glass in their faces.

Joe politely nodded agreement and refilled George's glass.

'This technology is top secret. You understand, yeah?' George hissed in a loud whisper.

'Your secret is safe here,' he grinned across at Amy and wondered if he should risk a conspiratorial wink. She grinned back at him.

'We should go, I guess,' she said at last, reluctantly, standing up and smoothing out her skirt over her long legs. It was almost 3 p.m.

George took his time getting to his feet. His mobile was beeping and he was having trouble locating it. He sat down again heavily, flummoxed.

'Come on, George.' She began to leave the dining room and Joe followed, rolling his shoulders as he walked, filled with new confidence.

'I've really enjoyed it,' she said, stopping in the corridor by the door leading out to the car park. Rain was spattering on the glass and she started to put on her coat.

He helped her into it. 'Me too. I hope we'll be seeing you again.'

'I'd like that.' Joe noticed that she'd ignored the corporate 'we'. She touched his arm as she spoke, moving closer to him. Her lips were inches away and getting closer all the time. She kissed him and he kissed her back.

The glass door shuddered as two tremendous blows hit it accompanied by a scream of fury. They sprang apart. There, staring in at them, face contorted, yelling abuse, was a crazy woman. In his surprise, it took Joe a few seconds to register that the woman was Anna.

She was yelling at Amy, yelling at her to leave him alone, calling her a slut and a fucking whore. She was coming out with every cliché in the book and if it hadn't been so shocking, Joe might have found it funny. But it wasn't funny, not funny at all. Amy's face was white. Another blow hit the glass and she jumped a foot backwards.

Joe mumbled an apology, opened the door and took hold of Anna, pinning her arms to her sides. He couldn't stop her yelling though, and as he wrestled her away from the door and over towards her car, he caught a glimpse behind him of Amy's pale, stunned face, joined now by George's, gawping in amazement. This sure beat video conferencing.

'Anna, please, calm down,' he said, desperate.

'No!' she screamed at him. 'No! No!' Then she started sobbing.

He managed to get her into her car and to get her to promise to stay there. He went back to the others and guided them out to the hotel taxi which was waiting, fortunately, some distance away on the other side of the car park. He couldn't quite meet Amy's eye and there was nothing he could think of to say to her. She shot into the back of the cab, looking grateful for the escape, and, without another word, slammed the door.

'Well,' George stood by the other door, swaying slightly, trying to find some words.

'It's been awesome,' he said, finally. 'Really has,' and he shook Joe's hand before stumbling into the car.

As the taxi drove off Joe knew it was the last he'd ever see of either of them and their software company.

He walked back towards Anna. As he approached, she opened the car door and looked up at him with a tentative smile, no trace of the tempest she had so recently unleashed.

'What the hell do you think you're doing?' he demanded, furious, banging his fist in frustration on the car roof.

'Joe, you were kissing her. I … I couldn't help it.' she stuttered, nervously. He'd never been angry with her before and she didn't like it.

'She came on to me. She's an important business client. I'm not going to push her away, am I?'

234

Anna marshalled every bit of self-control to stop herself from screaming at him, screaming that he was hers, that no one else was having any piece of him and if any stupid tart tried sticking her tongue down his throat then she, Anna, would put a very definite stop to it.

'I'm sorry,' she said in a small voice, getting out of the car, taking his hand and pulling him towards her.

He shook her off in annoyance. 'That's not fucking good enough, Anna. Your mad bitch from hell act has lost me that job and probably quite a few others.'

She took hold of his hand again. 'I really am sorry. Forgive me?'

He looked into the sharp green eyes. There was something a little weird in them, he thought.

'How about we go to Room 21 and forget all about it,' she whispered.

He wanted to ask if she was crazy but he was pretty sure he already knew the answer to that question. He turned on his heel and went back to work.

CHAPTER FORTY-SIX

Harry struggled to understand what it was he had just witnessed. It had been an astonishing drama and he knew it was crucial in helping him discover what was going on.

He was sitting in his silver Volvo estate in the Greene House Hotel car park. The taxi had been parked close by and he had slid low in the driver's seat while the man who had been fighting with Anna came over to it with the two passengers. Harry had opened his window a fraction but hadn't managed to catch any of the conversation. He didn't think there'd been much. The woman had looked icy, like she couldn't wait to get away.

He could see Anna sitting in her car, slumped across the steering wheel with her head lying dejectedly on her arms. He had spent the day following her. No doubt Laura Maxwell would call it 'stalking'. It was risky, very risky, but he couldn't fuss about that. Things were bad enough already and he'd have to take risks if he was going to save himself.

Martha had been collected early that morning by the family who were taking her to London. Anna stayed put at home and he assumed that, with her daughter away, she had nowhere particular to go. He remembered she didn't have a lot of girlfriends, but he kept hoping she might visit the boyfriend or he would visit her. It had been looking like a cold and dull waste of time and he was thinking of getting something to eat, when she came out, got in her car and drove to the hotel.

He had been to Greene's a couple of times for business lunches but had always come by taxi and had no idea of the size of the car park. He took a gamble following his wife's car into the enclosed space, fingers crossed that she wouldn't spot him. Until then, he'd been careful to keep his distance and he was relieved to find the car park was large and he could slot into an empty place well away from where his wife parked.

She sat in her car for almost an hour. It was too far away for him to see her clearly, and although he had binoculars with him, he didn't dare use them. He saw her get out of the car, walk to the door of the hotel as if she was going in, then hesitate and go round the side of the building, stopping to peer in windows as she went. It was bizarre. Who was the stalker now? he wondered grimly. He thought she was heading for the front entrance, but not long after, he saw her coming back through the grounds still looking in windows on the way.

Suddenly, she stopped dead in her tracks, staring hard. Moments later all hell kicked off and she was running towards the car park door, beating on it and screaming. He had no idea why, but he heard her yelling, though he couldn't make out the words.

He didn't recognize the man who came out and tried to calm her down, nor the couple with him, but he could see the man was very angry with Anna. It was obvious, too, that they knew each other pretty well.

It was a puzzle, but now he would have to stop thinking about it because Anna's car was on the move and he had to decide whether to follow her or go into the hotel and track down the man.

He chose the hotel, waited until his wife had left, then walked round to the main entrance and into the lobby. The receptionist was busy with some guests so he sauntered casually past and into the hotel proper. He turned left down the corridor sign-posted to the dining room, found it empty, the last of the lunchtime

237

stragglers had gone. He carried on and stood by the door to the car park, returned and investigated another corridor with an office and a conference suite.

He was about to knock on the office door when he heard someone coming along the corridor behind him.

'Good afternoon, sir. Can I help you?' It was the receptionist. He read the name 'Ellie' on the badge she was wearing.

'I'm interested in what conference facilities you have,' Harry gestured towards the suite.

'I can give you our brochure and maybe you'd like to talk to one of our organizers about exactly what you're looking for?' she said, heading back towards reception.

He followed her and waited at the desk while she got him the brochure, telling her he was the managing director of a local housebuilding company.

'Pelvale Homes. You might know it, Ellie?' Harry said.

'Yes, of course, I've seen it all over the place,' she smiled at him. Joe had told her to always flatter a potential customer.

She picked up the phone, dialled Joe's extension, explained there was a client who might want to hire the conference suite. He sounded delighted. She knew his earlier meeting had ended badly though she didn't know why. Strange, because it had seemed to be going well. She liked Joe a lot. He had brought some fun and a little bit of glamour to life at Greene's hotel and she wanted him to succeed. She kept smiling at the pushy man in front of her.

'Can I just take your name, sir?'

Joe, still on the other end of the phone, heard the reply and the smile left his face. Anna's husband, here in the hotel only a short time after she had left.

'Sorry, Ellie, I can't see him just now. Can you ask Simon,' he put down the receiver fast.

Joe didn't believe in coincidence. This was not good news, he felt sure.

Ellie dialled again. The man was leaning towards her, a little too much in her face. Simon, the hotel manager, answered her call, said, yes, he'd be round at once to talk to Harry.

Harry waited, flicking through the brochure.

'Business good?' he asked, conversationally.

Ellie said it was.

'I used to know a guy who worked here,' Harry smacked his hand on his forehead. 'Can't get his name. Tall guy, black hair. Maybe you know him?'

'I can't really say, sir, there's a few fit that description,' she said.

The manager arrived and he certainly wasn't the man in the car park. Harry strung it all out as long as possible, asked to see round the conference area, asked to see round the hotel. He sat in the bar for an hour or so, slowly sipping at a beer, positioned where he could see passers-by, but there was no sign of the man he was looking for. At 6 o'clock he reluctantly decided to give it up.

Ellie was at reception when he was leaving and he waved to her.

'Have you found what you want?' she asked.

'I've certainly come pretty close,' he gave a rather twisted smile.

'Great. Just give me a call if you decide to book or, if I'm not here, talk to Joe Greene. He runs the conferences.'

If there was business in this, Ellie wanted Joe to have it. It was a shame he'd been too busy to see the man; she was sure he was a lot more charming than Simon.

Harry turned round on his way to the door and stared at her.

'Joe Greene, you say.' He emphasized the 'Joe'

'Yes, he's one of the owners.'

'Is he here now?'

'You've just missed him. He left about ten minutes ago.'

CHAPTER FORTY-SEVEN

The vet had left a message to call, and when Laura rang back, she found him increasingly agitated by Valentine's condition. Two of Valentine's 'four more days' were gone; after that, in all conscience, she could not let the horse suffer any more. Laura sat with her head in her hands asking herself the dreadful question, should she even wait that long?

The shrill ring of the phone on her desk startled her and she picked it up cautiously as if it might explode in her face. Her fear-ridden mind felt slow and clumsy. It trailed round and round on the same track, like a hamster on a wheel, unable to come up with any new thought about what was happening to her or what she could do about it. She would have to get a grip, she knew; pull out of this passive state of terror.

She heard a foreign voice with a heavy accent and her mind was so preoccupied with her own problems that she couldn't immediately place it.

'Laura, you cannot have forgotten me so soon.' he said, laughing.

She remembered then. It was Karim Chehoudi, the lawyer from Tunis.

'I'm sorry, Karim, there's been a lot happening here' she pulled herself together, 'But it's always lovely to hear from you.'

'You are flattering me, I think. But you will be pleased to hear my news, I'm sure of that.'

He'd had a tip off. The boy, Ahmed, and his father were booked on a flight to Istanbul in three days' time. They were spending a week with relatives before returning to Tunis. He waited for the information to sink in, waited for her to understand, was disappointed when she didn't pick up on it at once. She was usually such a smart lady. 'Laura, this is Turkey we are talking about. Turkey has signed the Convention.'

She came to life then, concentrating on what he was saying. Fear retreated a step from her immediate thoughts. Of course, he was right. It was that small chance she had been hoping for, that the boy would set foot in a country that had signed the child abduction treaty. If she could get a court order issued urgently, get it served by immigration officials when the pair arrived in Istanbul, the boy could soon be back in England. For the first time in a long time she sniffed success, felt the rush she always felt when she won a case against the odds.

'Thank you, Karim, I'll get onto it at once. I owe you.'

'Dinner will be good,' he said. 'I am in London in two weeks' time.'

Two weeks. It seemed like another century. Would she be alive then? She told him how much she hoped to see him and meant every word.

Morrison was in her office almost before she realized it. He'd given his usual perfunctory knock and marched in just as she was putting down the phone to Karim Chehoudi. Her brief diversion into another life, a life she used to have where she worked as a solicitor and no one tried to kill her, even though they might have wanted to, was over. It seemed that Monica had spread the word and Morrison had been listening.

'I'm hearing things, Laura, worrying things. What's going on?'

'Not sure I'm with you, Marcus?' Make him spit it out.

'The police,' he hissed. 'Monica has been telling me.'

She knew his tricks and she wasn't falling for that one. He wanted her to tell him the story, so he could check her version against the one he'd got from Monica.

241

Laura felt stronger, buoyed up by the call from Tunis and the chance of getting Mary Hakimi her son back. She would follow Morrison's own golden rule – never apologize, never explain.

'Monica?' she said, puzzled. 'Has something happened? Afraid I've been so busy today with developments on the Hakimi case, I haven't had time for much else.'

That got his attention as she'd known it would.

'Developments? Progress, I hope.'

She hadn't intended to tell him, not yet, not until the boy was back home and safely reunited with his mother, because there were still an awful lot of things that could go wrong. She would have much rather waited for that happy ending, then dropped in to his office and mentioned, casually, that the whole business was resolved, as if there had never been any doubt that it would be. But she wanted to divert him from Monica's tittle-tattle and so she told him.

Morrison tried hard not to show how pleased he was that her unpromising scheme might actually deliver a result.

'We need that court order asap. Get the barrister onto it now,' he ordered, as if it was all his own idea and she hadn't just said she would be doing exactly that. He was already preparing to take the credit, but, given the nightmare her life had become, she wasn't in any mood to fight over it.

'As I said,' she dredged up a smile, 'I was about to ring him when you came in.'

There was silence for a moment. She guessed he was considering whether to raise the police visit again. In the end, he contented himself with reminding her about that night's Law Society dinner, then got up to go.

'Well, let's hope there's an end to this appalling mess.'

'Yes, with luck we may be close to sorting it out.'

He paused in the doorway, couldn't resist a parting shot.

'Don't celebrate too soon, Laura. Close doesn't get the cigar, eh?'

CHAPTER FORTY-EIGHT

Anna sat on the bed and swallowed hard but the lump in her throat wouldn't go away. Joe had been angry with her, walked away from her, dismissed her as if she disgusted him. She felt she would go mad, the terror of being abandoned by him growing in her brain like a huge, ugly tumour.

She took his photo from under her pillow and kissed it, examined every inch of his handsome face, gazed into the laughing blue eyes, softly stroked the cleft in his chin and ached to put her arms around him.

She loved him. Always had and always would. Nobody could ever love him the way she did. He was her saviour and he belonged to her. But other women would take him from her if they could. Laura Maxwell had taken him, the blonde at the hotel had wanted him. Men were led by their dicks. It was not his fault.

Her breath came in uneven gasps; there was a screeching in her ears from the mayhem in her head. There had been too much love and not enough hate. Too much time already wasted. Joe still lived with Laura Maxwell, slept in her bed. Who's laughing now? Not you Anna, she thought, certainly not you.

She looked at her watch. 4.30 p.m. Tenderly, she replaced the photograph and went downstairs, brought back a kitchen knife from the rack and sat down again on the bed, running her fingers up and down the blade, testing it. This time she would make sure; the car chase had been a chance grabbed in the heat of the moment, a chance to frighten Laura and hurt her, though she hadn't cared if she killed her. It had shown her the way and as the idea of badly hurting Laura, maybe killing her, grew large in her mind she had planned a second attack: she had strung the wire between the trees to bring down Laura's horse.

But the bitch was still alive and Joe was no closer to being hers, in fact he seemed further away than ever. Anna shook her head in murderous fury. There would be no more half measures; she wasn't stopping now until Laura was dead.

She gripped the knife's handle, held it high above her head, thrust it down with all her strength into the mattress. Laura Maxwell before her eyes. Stab, stab, stab and stab again. Slash and stab. Face, heart, neck, chest. This is how it would be. She could hear the screams; smell the blood.

Anna had read somewhere the story of a survivor who'd been stabbed nineteen times: 'You don't feel the stabs when they're happening,' he said. 'You think you would but you don't. And you don't feel pain either, because pain is a distraction while you're fighting for your life. I felt nothing at all, except the fear and the adrenaline that it gave me.'

But Laura Maxwell would know pain because Anna would make certain of it. It would be the pain of a knife twisted in her heart, the pain Anna had endured for so many years.

'This is how it feels,' she shrieked, stabbed again, then again. 'See how it feels.'

Anna Pelham's face in the bedroom mirror was smiling and triumphant. Her breathing grew more regular and the noise in her head died away. She felt calm again. She would do it tonight.

With Laura dead, she would get her happy ending. Joe would live with her, wake up next to her every morning and go to sleep next to her every night; she would be happy at last, free from the crippling fear of losing him, of seeing his love grow cold. She would watch over him and never again would any other woman take him from her.

Laura would be alone tonight. Anna knew this because it was the beginning of the 'special' time that she had planned to enjoy with Joe. The first evening of Martha's absence and she'd hoped Joe would spend it with her, had fantasized that he would spend the night with her. She had been badly disappointed – again. He couldn't make it; he was taking his mother to see a musical at the Theatre Royal in Brighton. He had no choice, he told her.

Laura alone in the house. Would she be just a little bit scared?

You'll be dead by the end of the week.

It was only Wednesday. There were a few days left.

Want to know how you're going to die?

No thank you. Please, will you leave me alone.

Painfully. Very painfully.

Anna laughed. Had the police found it yet, she wondered.

It had been so very easy because Laura Maxwell had been out when she'd arrived at Morrison Kemp. Her plan had been to see Laura on the excuse of giving her more of Harry's financial correspondence. She had ready, in her bag, a letter stolen from his house. It was nothing much and Laura might think her over-anxious for wanting to hand deliver it. But so what? It would get her into Laura's office, which was where she needed to be.

The mobile was also ready in her bag, the one she'd used to send the texts. She intended to drop it somewhere in the office, somewhere out of sight where it could later be traced by the police, and the lawyer discredited and humiliated. It would be tricky, she knew, dropping it in the right place; a place where it wouldn't be spotted too soon, before the police arrived.

She needn't have worried. It had worked out a treat. That nosy cow of a receptionist had been there, of course, had tried to get her to come back later when the bitch was in, but Anna knew exactly how to deal with people like her. They were leeches, thriving on other people's problems; hadn't she met enough of them in her life? So she told Monica all about Harry, the pervert, watched her suck in the salacious details and digest them. Hinted at things too gross to relate.

'Monica, it is Monica isn't it? I just can't tell you … I really can't,' she had gasped in distress.

Best friend. Confidante. Pour it all into Monica's eager ear.

'You poor thing, come in and wait, Laura won't be long I'm sure, would you like a cup of tea?'

She'd been shown to a room, and finally, left alone there. It took a couple of minutes to dash up the stairs and plant the phone behind the books in Laura Maxwell's office. Fingers crossed for a result.

Anna Pelham really didn't care anymore. Result or not. Whatever. She was ready. It was just past 5 o'clock. Time to go. Carefully, she wrapped the knife in tissue paper and placed it at the bottom of her bag.

She put on the Parka, pulled up the hood.

CHAPTER FORTY-NINE

Harry checked carefully before approaching his house just in case the police were there. Just in case his wife was there, he thought bitterly. He didn't plan on staying long, no longer than it took to pack a suitcase and rig a spy camera in the hallway, trained on the front door, to record her next visit. He hoped she would come back soon.

He hadn't checked carefully enough. As he put his key in the front door, he heard footsteps on the gravel behind him. He fought the urge to run; it would be stupid. He couldn't escape and trying to would only make him look like a guilty man. He blew out his cheeks in frustration and turned around to face the police.

Ben Morgan was walking hesitantly up the drive. He appeared more the worse for wear than ever, his gaunt face and shabby clothes thrown into sharp relief by the light from the security lamp. He must have been standing in the cover of the hedge waiting for Harry to return. He looked like he'd slept under it.

Ben stopped a short distance away. He was wary: Harry was violent and unpredictable.

'Can we talk?' he asked nervously.

Harry wanted to get away, but he also wanted information out of Morgan.

'Come inside,' he said.

'I've come to tell you all I know but I'm not coming in unless you promise not to hurt me. OK?'

'OK, I promise. But last time you hit me, remember.'

Ben followed him cautiously down the hall and into the kitchen, making straight for a chair by the radiator. His teeth were chattering. Harry put on the heating and made some coffee. Morgan's mood was neither high nor low, and once he was sure there would be no immediate hostilities, he relaxed a bit. The heat from the radiator entered his coat, then his body, and a sour smell filled the air. Harry sniffed it.

'When did you last have a wash, mate?'

Ben ignored the remark and launched into the reason for his visit. He was going back to Reading. He'd had enough, he could do no good by staying longer, the police were after him. They'd come asking at his guest house and he'd only avoided them because the landlady felt sorry for him and she'd stalled them, giving him a chance to get away. That had been yesterday evening; he'd spent the night at a hostel for the homeless.

He gulped the coffee, stretched out gratefully in the chair. Harry wondered if he was after a bed for the night.

'I'm not living here right now, Ben. You can clean up but you can't stay.'

'You're not getting it, are you? I don't want to stay. It's the last place I want to be. I'm going, going now – tonight – just as soon as I've told you. Now do you want to know or not?'

'Of course I want to know,' Harry said mildly, trying to put Morgan at his ease.

Ben reached into the pocket of his smelly coat and pulled out a tatty, dog-eared letter. 'Your girlfriend wrote me this. It's why I'm here. She asked me not to tell you and I've kept quiet but now I think you should see it. Tell her I'm sorry.'

'What fucking girlfriend?' Harry said, outraged, unable to keep his voice from rising, snatching the letter from Ben's hand and starting to read it.

Dear Ben,

Excuse me contacting you like this and not giving my name. I don't feel I want to at the minute, but I hope we can meet and talk things through and maybe become friends.

Your story made me cry so much. I read it on your website and also in the newspapers and it was all so cruel and unfair. They didn't understand how you were driven to violence, made out it was all because you were bipolar and weren't behaving normally. Well I know that's not true. I know you lost your little girl because of that lawyer, Laura Maxwell. It was not your fault, it was hers.

You're not a violent man. Anyone who had to go through what you did would have done the same. That woman was out to get you and you couldn't win however hard you tried. She stacked everything against you and you had to do what your heart told you. You showed real courage and love for your little girl.

The reason I am writing to you is because I'm going through the same thing. It's all happening to me, well to my partner, just like it happened to you. He's bipolar too and he's terrified of losing his daughter and his wife has got Laura Maxwell working for her. She is so toxic, I can't tell you. Well, I don't need to tell you. How you must hate her. Harry, that's my partner, he is terribly depressed. He goes up and down, of course, but I've never seen him like this. If he loses Martha I don't know what he'll do. Suicide probably.

Harry looked up for a moment, appalled by what he was reading, and glared at Ben Morgan. Then his eyes went back to the letter, eating up the lines.

I'm desperate. I don't suppose there's anything you can do but I want to ask if you'll meet me. Just to talk to someone who understands would be such a relief. Laura Maxwell is

*making Harry out to be a bad, mad dad just like she did
with you. She's working in Brighton now at Morrison Kemp
solicitors. Our lawyer, he hasn't a clue how to deal with
someone as poisonous as her.*

*Martha is heartbroken. She wants to be with her dad, she
misses him so much, she says he's her best friend. She cries
herself to sleep and talks to him through her favourite
teddy bear.*

*Harry has Bipolar 2, the mildest form. He's never had a
manic episode, he's not psychotic and he doesn't have
substance abuse problems. He's been in hospital twice for
depression but they were both voluntary admissions. He's
been on medication for three years and his condition is fully
stable with no relapses. He loves Martha very much and
would never do anything to hurt her. He's a good dad but
he's so worried that everything is being twisted and he'll end
up losing her.*

*Laura Maxwell doesn't care about any of that. She's only
interested in winning and she plays on ignorance and
misunderstanding about bipolar. There's so much prejudice.
I know some people have it so bad they find parenting hard
but it's not like that with you and Harry. You love your kids,
they mean everything to you.*

*Please, please, please don't mention this letter to anyone. I
think it would be the end for Harry if he found out I'd
written it but, like I said, I'm desperate.*

The letter ended with details of where and when Ben could meet
her. She would be in Kim's Café, near the West Pier, between 1
p.m. and 3 p.m. The date she gave was four days ago.

'You met this woman?' Harry asked in a low, tense voice.

'I tried to. I went to the right place at the right time but she
wasn't there.'

'I bet she wasn't.'

'The thing is,' Ben said gloomily, 'I hope nothing's happened. I thought maybe she'd had enough, I mean, that you two had broken up. It's difficult for people, I know, dealing with someone who's bipolar – the mood swings and stuff … ' he tailed off as he saw the expression on Harry's face.

'There are a few things you need to know,' Harry stood, leaning over him, 'One, I have no girlfriend; two, I'm not bipolar; three, someone has been playing mind games with you.'

Ben Morgan looked up at him apprehensively. Harry was a big guy and he didn't want any more physical contact with him.

'Stay cool,' Ben got out of his chair and backed away. 'I understand. I really do. It's hard to accept, sometimes, that we have this illness and we lose people we love because of it.'

'For the last time, I do not have any fucking illness.'

'Please calm down,' Ben said, circling round Harry to get to the door. 'There's another thing you should know,' he stopped in the doorway, 'something's going on with Laura Maxwell. She's been seeing the police.'

'The police,' Harry grunted, 'I guess that wouldn't be so unusual for a lawyer.'

'Don't treat me like I'm an idiot,' Ben was suddenly touchy. 'She has some sort of serious personal crisis going on is what I'm saying.'

He related how he'd gone along to Morrison Kemp, intending to speak to Laura's boss about Harry's case, but he'd come across her the moment he walked through the door, and hadn't been able to handle it. He'd turned straight round and left. He'd waited outside, trying to get up the courage for another attempt, but before he could do so, she'd come out herself.

She was acting strangely, gasping for air and clutching her stomach so that, at first, he thought she might be having some kind of attack. She stood in the street, staring up and down, before walking off. He had followed. He'd had to be careful because she kept stopping, looking behind her, waiting in doorways. As though she was being hunted, paranoid, and he gave a weak smile, he should know.

He tracked her to the police station and waited outside for forty-five minutes until she came out and got into a police car. It was clear she'd been crying, a fact that had shaken him. He had thought her incapable of tears.

Harry waited impatiently for more. But there was no more.

'That's all?' Harry snapped, exasperated, and Ben flinched. 'It's, well, it's interesting I suppose, but what to make of it?'

Ben shrugged, 'Dunno. I'm just telling you, that's all. It's got to be something really serious to get her in that kind of state.'

'What I'm interested in is this letter,' Harry waved it at him.

Abruptly, Ben turned away, moving fast towards the front door.

'Hey, come back, you can't just leave like that,' Harry shouted.

'Good luck, Harry,' Ben said, running off down the drive.

CHAPTER FIFTY

Anna Pelham crept close to the farmhouse cradling the knife in her pocket. Laura should be home alone by now, she thought joyfully. She rounded the corner of the house, passing recycling bins and a pile of sawn logs. Never before had she dared come so near to Joe's home. Just standing there, looking at the everyday things that were his, sent a thrill of delight through her.

She stayed in the shadow of the back wall, well away from the light spilling out of the kitchen window and across the garden. She could partly see into the kitchen: cream painted wood cabinets and an Aga. Slowly, she craned her neck out as far as she dared, impatient, itching for a sight of her prey, then pulled back as if she'd been stung by a hornet. She had seen Laura, sitting at the kitchen table.

Take your time, she told herself. There's no rush, no need to take risks. Stay calm and pick your moment.

No sign of the moon tonight, luckily, the sky was full of cloud. She flitted across the lawn towards the double garage, stopping in an area of deep shadow beside it. She planned to wait for the kitchen light to go out then try the door, and if it was unlocked, go into the house and take Laura Maxwell by surprise. If not, she would revert to her original scheme. She would ring the doorbell, and when Laura answered, she would tell her that Harry was after her, had been to her house and threatened her. She would rush into the house, scared and upset, throw her arms around the lawyer and bury the knife in her back.

The light stayed on and Anna stayed put. Her right hand strayed to the pocket of her Parka, feeling for the knife inside, curling her fingers round the handle. Comforting.

After fifteen minutes she could wait no longer. There was now a light on in what she guessed was the main bedroom, the bedroom shared by Joe and Laura. Her body fizzed with outrage at the disgusting thought. Her heart was pumping, her senses razor-sharp. She moved out from the shadow, and at the same moment, the bedroom window opened and Laura stood framed in it. Instinctively, Anna swung back towards the cover of the garage, tripping the security light as she did so. She dived into the darkness, lay on the ground, her face pressed into the cold, damp grass.

The window shut with a thud, and after a minute or so, when she turned her head to look, the bedroom light was out. Quickly, she got to her feet and headed back to the front of the house, taking a wide loop down and across the garden, using the flower beds to screen her from sight. No more pussyfooting around, she thought, time to go straight in through the front door. She heard car tyres crunch on the gravel drive.

When she got in sight of the door, there was a minicab parked in the drive. Laura must be going out. She swore under her breath and the muscles in her jaw clenched tight with anger. This was not in the script.

She couldn't see the front door, it was hidden under the tiled porch, but she heard the bell ring. She waited, heard the bell ring some more, watched as a man returned to the car. Then she heard Laura's voice shouting out for the cab to hang on. The engine started up. Anna smiled – it seemed that Laura had missed the lifeboat.

CHAPTER FIFTY-ONE

Laura left work early because of the Law Society dinner and decided to take the following morning off. She let Monica know she wouldn't be in until Thursday afternoon. The receptionist pursed her lips, disgusted that Marcus had invited Laura to the dinner; it was a privilege usually reserved for the firm's partners, or potential partners. She hoped, fervently, that her boss had not gone off his head.

Laura visited Valentine on her way home. He was in the same pitiful state, but a rather surprised Jeff Ingham told her that, in the last two hours, he had started eating more. It was too early to say if that would last, the vet cautioned.

She got home soon after four. Joe wouldn't be back until late; he was going straight from work to the nursing home to collect his mother and take her to the theatre. Laura rang him to ask how his day had gone and whether he'd clinched the business deal he'd been so keen to get. He was curt and uncommunicative, then accused her of checking up on him because she didn't have any faith in him. She guessed the meeting had not been a success.

It was one more thing to worry about and she fished out a bottle of brandy from the kitchen cupboard. She drank two glasses of it, fast, and felt it calm her jagged nerves. But then fear dropped over her again like a black sack and she realized, sick inside, that she didn't feel safe anywhere, not even at home. Exhausted with it, she laid her head down on the kitchen table. She drifted off to sleep, woke, then drifted some more; broken thoughts and half dreams chased through her head.

When she woke again the time was 6.23 p.m. Laura groaned, the taxi that Monica had ordered for her was due in less than an hour. It was a shame it was coming, otherwise she would just stay where she was and to hell with the tedious dinner. She struggled to her feet, crawled up the stairs to shower and change.

Pain ran through the whole left side of her body; her left hip and back were stiff because she'd been trying to avoid putting any pressure on them, and her shoulders ached from hunching over to protect her rib. Bruises flared vividly against her white skin, swollen skin, the stitched cut on her leg was red and angry. In the bathroom mirror, her eyes looked tired and haunted.

She chose a knee-length black dress and a red jacket, which would cover up all the damage, put on some pearl earrings and a lot more make-up than usual. Then she sat on the edge of the bed, feeling shattered. The shower and the alcohol had relaxed her and she badly wanted to lie down and sleep. She opened the bedroom window, breathing in the cold air to wake herself up. A cloudy, black night stretched across the lawn and the fields beyond, broken suddenly by a stab of light as the lamp on the side of the double garage snapped on.

It was then that she saw it, or thought she did. A movement by the side of the garage, just for a moment, then nothing, only shadows. Someone was out there. She felt her skin contract with fear.

Laura shut the window, turned off the bedroom light and stood in the dark looking out, looking for movement, a figure creeping towards the house. Nothing. Just the hairs on the back of her neck standing at full attention and her scalp prickling.

The doorbell rang and she nearly shot through the roof. Relief. The cab had arrived and now she was delighted to be going to the dinner, because she would be with other people. She would be safe.

She snatched up her bag from the bed and headed for the front door, then stopped on the landing, paralysed by a new, awful thought. How could she be sure? Maybe it wasn't the cab at all, maybe it was something else entirely. What if she opened the door and there, waiting for her, was the killer.

The bell rang again, twice this time, insistent. She stood, frozen, for a few more seconds, then took off her shoes and ran into the front bedroom where she could see the driveway from the window. The minicab was there. She sobbed with relief. But then the driver came into view, got into the cab. Dear God, he was leaving! She banged on the window, opened it, shouted for him to hang on. The engine started.

Laura flew down the stairs, clutching her shoes, out into the night, sharp gravel spiking her feet. Just in time, she wrenched open the door of the cab and collapsed onto the back seat.

The cab drove off and Laura's heart slowed down a little. So glad to be gone; so glad to escape from her own home. It had come to this.

CHAPTER FIFTY-TWO

The waitress refilled her glass with the sweet, sickly dessert wine. It tasted foul and was giving her a headache and she wondered who had chosen it, then remembered the Society had a wine committee and its chairman was Marcus Morrison.

He was sitting across the table from her, holding forth. Earlier, he had been keen to introduce her to his cronies and remind them of her notable career. He explained that he was building on that and giving her new opportunities to develop her talents. He talked about her in the third person as if she was a clever monkey and he was conducting an interesting experiment.

Not that his behaviour mattered; she knew that at the same time as she resented it. How could it matter when someone was out there waiting to kill her; had vowed to kill her by the end of the week? She was surprised she had the emotional space left to feel annoyed by him.

Time had slowed down now that every moment was precious. It seemed like the man on her left had been talking at her non-stop for hours, days – who knew how long? His monologue, about government plans to cut legal aid, didn't leave room for any input from her and she was grateful for that because she couldn't focus on what he was saying. She sat, fiddling with an earring, not listening, her mind filled instead with dark and fearful things.

Had there been someone prowling round the house? She couldn't be sure; she could have imagined it, her nerves were shot to bits. Maybe it was a fox or a cat that had set off the light. Sudden hot rage flooded her. Her fists clenched hard and her fingernails dug into the flesh of her palms. She tilted her head back, opened her mouth ready to let out a scream of frustration and grief.

The drone from the legal aid man stopped; from the corner of her eye she saw him look at her oddly. Morrison had also stopped talking and was staring at her: some achievement to silence them both. The urge to scream subsided, now she wanted to laugh insanely instead. With an effort she closed her mouth, forced a smile at Morrison. Sitting at the table behind him, Laura saw another man watching her. Ronnie Seymour, the rather smooth, rather out of his depth lawyer who was representing Harry Pelham.

No-one had brought her any of that horrid wine for some time and it looked like the dinner was over. The legal aid man got up from the table without another word and went off to find a new victim. Morrison waved at her to join him, and with a sigh, she eased herself carefully out of her chair. She had sat too long and her battered body didn't like it.

'Are you all right?'

Ronnie Seymour was beside her, a look of concern on his face. She told him she was fine. He hovered, asking if she was enjoying the dinner, asking if she liked living in Sussex and if she missed her London firm; was life at Morrison Kemp a bit dull in comparison? I wish, Laura thought.

'Not at all dull, no,' she told him.

'You're happy then. Happy you made the switch?'

'Very much so.'

He hesitated, 'It's a shame the Pelham case has become so nasty. My client is anxious to calm things down.'

'Do you know where he is then?' she asked sharply.

For a second he was thrown off balance. She was shrewd, but then he knew that from tangling with her over the divorce.

'I'm hoping it won't be too long before the police can talk to him,' Ronnie said. 'I wonder if we could have a proper chat about what's happening? Tomorrow, maybe, if you have time? I can come to your office.'

Before she could reply Morrison appeared with three other men. He put his arm proprietorially round her shoulders.

'As Ronnie has already found out, Laura is a worthy opponent.'

Ronnie managed a grin and Morrison waved his free arm around the dining room in a sweeping gesture.

'Excellent dinner. Big improvement on last year, eh? Good move, I think, to insist on having our own wine, courtesy of our own wine committee, chosen, I have to say, by yours truly.' He tried to look modest.

'In my opinion, Marcus,' said one of his sidekicks, swaying on his feet, 'the waitresses were a lot better looking last year … and a lot more friendly.'

There was a burst of lewd laughter. 'No comment,' said Morrison holding up his hand for silence. 'Laura, you must pass on our compliments to your husband. Great dinner, great hotel.'

Some 'hear, hears' from the others.

'Your husband?' Ronnie queried.

'Yes,' she said, and for some reason her voice dried up. She coughed to clear her throat. 'He's Joe Greene. This is his hotel.'

CHAPTER FIFTY-THREE

She had been close, so very close to a kill. Anna woke up next morning full of purpose, convinced that today was the day she would deal with the Maxwell bitch once and for all. She'd slept badly, plagued by the dream from her childhood, more bloody than she could ever remember it. At four in the morning, it had left her clutching at her mouth in panic.

It always began with a loose front tooth; her tongue would touch it and feel it move. She knew she must leave it alone, but however hard she tried not to, she would put her fingers in her mouth and move the tooth back and forth to test it. It would come out in her hand with a tearing, sucking sound and a jet of bright red blood. Other teeth would follow and she would try, frantically, to push them back in. Blood gushed from her lips, her remaining teeth split with loud cracking sounds, crumbling until all of them were gone, leaving her mouth a mess of gore and tissue.

The psychiatrist had told her the dream was all about her hatred of being fat. He had leaned back in his chair, half-moon glasses perched on the end of his nose, and explained it to her at length.

'Teeth', he said, 'are closely linked to feelings of attractiveness.' He smiled at her, showing all his own sharp little teeth. He looked like a rat. 'How many times, Annabel, have you heard somebody say, "Oh she has really nice teeth" or "she's got a great smile"?'

She hadn't replied.

'If you lose your teeth, you lose your smile, and with it, your attractiveness. So we can see that this kind of dream is reflecting your own fear, in fact your own subconscious belief that you are an unattractive person. You are experiencing feelings of inferiority and low self-confidence and that makes you very unhappy'.

You moron, she thought, of course I'm unhappy. I've just tried to kill myself.

Anna banished the dream from her mind. She had a job to do. Today she would kill Laura Maxwell. Shortly after nine o'clock, she rang Morrison Kemp to fix an appointment to see Laura. Monica answered her call, and within seconds, had supplied crucial information.

'She's not in till later so it will have to be this afternoon. That OK for you?'

'Aah,' Anna tried to sound disappointed, 'I was hoping for earlier. It's just I really need to talk to her, urgently, about Harry, you know … ' Anna paused to let Monica remember all the bad things she did know about Harry, then asked, 'where is she? Any idea exactly when she'll be in?'

'She went to a dinner with the boss last night and she's taken this morning off. I can call her at home if you like and get a time,' Monica offered.

At home. Laura was at home. Anna Pelham could hardly believe her luck.

'Thanks Monica but don't worry. This afternoon will do. Say three o'clock?'

It was an appointment she would never have to keep, for by then, Laura Maxwell would be dead.

She had Joe's collection open on the bed and now she took the used condom out of it and put it in her coat pocket. She picked up a large envelope from her dressing table, and then she picked up the knife and set off again for Laura's house.

CHAPTER FIFTY-FOUR

He had laid it all out on the table in his hotel room. The life and times of Laura Maxwell, up to and including her marriage to Joe Greene. Harry had discovered it as he sorted hurriedly through his wardrobe, throwing a few clothes into a suitcase. He had been in a rush to get away from the house because he had stayed there too long and the police might come calling.

He was pulling out a couple of sweaters from a pile when he spotted the Sainsbury's bag. He almost ignored it, assumed it contained some old piece of clothing stashed away and forgotten, but he knew he hadn't put it there. He frowned. That meant Anna must have done it, and anything his wife had ever done he now considered suspect.

He took hold of the bag, opened it, and with growing confusion, flicked through the contents. Inside, was the Laura Maxwell collection. What the hell was it and what the hell was it doing in his wardrobe? There was no time to study it. He threw it into the suitcase to look at later.

Now, after most of the evening and half the night spent puzzling over it, he had reached not very many conclusions. Just that his wife had placed it in his wardrobe, that she had done so deliberately and that, possibly, it had been the purpose of her latest visit to his house. Why she had done it, as so many of her actions,

God alone knew. All that was certain was that somehow, in some way, it was bad news for him. He thought it was also bad news for Laura Maxwell.

For the hundredth time, he read the letter Ben Morgan had given him. There was no doubt in his mind about who had written it, not a shadow of doubt. His wife. For sure. The million dollar question was why and to that he had no answer.

The letter was clever and calculating, it preyed on all Ben's miseries and weak points, it was designed to mislead and manipulate him in the cruellest way. It forced him to relive the worst days of his life. It was downright evil.

He knew Anna had written it, but her motive was a mystery. The letter was sympathetic to Harry, vicious about Laura Maxwell, the opposite of everything he'd expect her to say. What possible reason could she have for sending it? He couldn't work it out, but he knew there was one – a devious, scheming, monstrous one.

Harry had thought Laura Maxwell directed every move his wife made but now he changed his mind. The Maxwell woman could hardly be responsible for this; Anna had done it all by herself. He picked up a print-off of Laura's Facebook page and read again that her husband was the man called Joe Greene. But this little bombshell just added to his confusion. He had been so sure that Joe Greene was his wife's lover, but if that was true, why then would she choose Laura, of all people, to handle her divorce?

He went to sleep with no answers and a whole lot of questions and he woke, just a few hours later, with suspicion humming in his bones. He had an idea now why she might choose Laura. The idea started small, but it grew fast until he was sure of it. It fitted her sick mind perfectly. She would get a real kick out of it – hiring her lover's wife to screw her husband in the divorce settlement.

He fought down the rage rising inside him. He needed to talk to Laura Maxwell and he needed to do it fast; he had a hunch that there wasn't much time. Harry didn't trust hunches but this one wouldn't be ignored, it was growing all the time, warning him to hurry as if there was some oncoming doom.

He checked his watch, just gone a quarter-to-ten. He looked up the number for Morrison Kemp and dialled it from the hotel phone. He would talk to Laura Maxwell, the lawyer he had learned to hate, and tell her what he suspected. She might think he was crazy, or driven by spite, but he had to try. If she called the police, so be it. It was no longer the police that scared him.

His mouth twisted into a bitter smile. If Laura Maxwell really was the cold-hearted, pitiless woman he imagined her to be, then she had surely met her match in his wife.

Monica answered the phone and Harry gave his name and asked to be put through.

'Ms Maxwell is acting for your wife in her divorce isn't she?' Monica's voice oozed disapproval.

'That's right. That's why I'm calling. I need to speak to her about it.'

'I'm not sure that will be possible, Mr Pelham. It sounds like there might very well be a conflict of interest.'

'There's a conflict of interest all right,' he growled, 'but it's not the one you think it is.'

Monica bristled and her lips pursed. She didn't like being told she was wrong.

'What I think is that Ms Maxwell represents Mrs Pelham and she won't be able to discuss her client's business with you, of all people.'

'Look, I don't give a toss what you think, sweetheart. Just do your job and find out if she'll talk to me.'

It was just as Anna had said; the man was a pig.

'I'm afraid I can't do that because she's not in the office at the moment,' she paused, enjoying her small triumph. 'I'll pass on your request. If you leave a number, I'm sure she'll get back to you, if it's appropriate.'

Harry didn't want to leave a number. He didn't trust her.

'When will she be in? I'll call back.'

Grudgingly, Monica told him he could try again later, but not until after 4 p.m. She wanted to make sure that Anna got in first. With a satisfied smile she put down the phone.

'Shit!' Harry kicked the table in front of him hard. It banged against the wall, papers scattering on the floor. He collected them up and sorted through them until he found the details of Laura's address in Rooks Green. He wasn't waiting a second longer.

CHAPTER FIFTY-FIVE

Laura didn't wake until late, after half-past ten, when the front doorbell rang. She'd been exhausted when she went to bed but her mind refused to close down and she'd had to take a sleeping tablet. She was trying not to take them because they made her groggy the next day, but they were the only way she could get some rest.

Joe was home when she'd got back from the dinner, thank God. She'd texted him from the taxi, her heart hammering as it neared the house, and then he'd replied saying he was back. Relief washed over her. She climbed out of the cab on wobbly legs.

He was still in a bad mood, and before she could say anything, he told her he didn't want to talk about the awful day he'd had and was going to bed. Laura let him be; there was no point in telling him her worries about a prowler, not tonight anyway. She had not forgotten the look on his face when he'd heard where Barnes had found the phone. She hadn't told him Barnes's reaction or given any hint that the police thought she'd sent the texts to herself, but she suspected Joe had come to the same conclusion. He'd said he believed her, but he hadn't looked that way. He hadn't mentioned the texts since.

He was asleep, or pretending to be, when she went to bed herself a short time later. Even if he did doubt her, it was good to have him next to her, to know she was not alone in the house.

Laura wasn't sure what had disturbed her until the door-bell rang again. She couldn't be bothered answering it, turned over to go back to sleep, but a stab from her rib woke her up properly. There was a note on the pillow beside her – from Joe, to say he'd gone to work and hadn't wanted to disturb her peaceful sleep.

She got up, put on her dressing gown, and went downstairs to make some coffee. Sun was streaming in through the kitchen window and when she looked out at the garden and the fields, she found her fear of the night before had receded. The world looked different in daylight.

She ate some toast and jam and wondered what Ronnie Seymour wanted to say to her. Before she'd left the dinner, he'd asked her again about a meeting and fixed to come in and see her at 2 o'clock. He'd said that Harry Pelham was anxious to calm things down; did that mean he was planning to offer some kind of deal? He wasn't in much of a position to bargain.

The letter box banged and she went to the door. There was one large white envelope lying on the mat addressed to 'Ms Laura Maxwell'. That was unusual, the post she got at home was usually in her married name of Greene. She slit open the envelope with her thumb, and suddenly, the white envelope was turning red and drops of blood spattered on the oak floor.

Laura watched in shock as blood poured down her right thumb. Inside the envelope were three glossy funeral brochures; stuck to the top of each of their front pages was a row of razor blades. The doorbell rang.

Laura dropped the envelope and the brochures spilled out on the hall floor. She stared at them; stared at the front door.

'Who is it?' she called, her voice croaking. Silence.

'Hello, who's there?' her voice, louder this time though she could hardly hear it over the noise of her heart thudding in her ears.

'Hi Laura, it's me Anna. Anna Pelham. I'm really sorry to bother you at home but I just had to see you.'

Blessed relief flowed through her, it was so good to hear a friendly voice.

'Thank God it's you, Anna. Just a moment.'

Laura kicked the brochures away from the door and opened it half way, tentative, in case it wasn't Anna after all but some crazed impersonator. But there she was, shy and nervous with an apologetic look on her face. Laura swung the door wide and hugged her.

The hug caught Anna off-guard, and before she could make any move, she found herself being pulled into the house.

'I'm so glad to see you, you won't believe what some madman has just done.' Laura held up her hand for Anna to see. 'Razor blades in a letter, for fuck's sake.'

Anna put on her most concerned face. 'Oh my God, Laura. Do you know who did it?'

'I'll tell you in a minute, I just need to stop it bleeding.'

Laura rushed into the kitchen and turned on the tap, running cold water over her cut thumb.

'Are you OK, Anna?' she shouted over her shoulder. 'What's happened?'

Anna didn't reply. She was too busy drinking in the place where Joe lived; the sofa he sat on, the TV he watched, the inglenook fireplace with the log burning stove that he filled with wood. She couldn't help smiling, her senses overloaded, she could feel him now in her arms, smell him; for a moment, she thought she might faint with excitement. Then her eyes locked onto the shelf above the fireplace, a thick black beam above the stove, and the smile was wiped from her face.

It was crammed full of photos. The sight of them killed her. There were happy, smiling photos of Laura Maxwell, taken no doubt, Anna thought furiously, by ace photographer husband Joe. There were photos of Joe and Laura together, the loving couple on various holidays and at work dos. Everywhere he was, so was she. She had even managed to intrude herself into a picture of Joe with some of the cast of *Holby City*. He stood among them with his arm around Laura's shoulders.

'Do you want a coffee or anything?' Laura called, getting a plaster from the kitchen drawer.

What was it the bitch was saying? Anna Pelham hardly knew. The rage pounding in her head was like a deafening white noise, drowning out everything else. She couldn't bear the photo fest a moment longer. With a vicious swipe she sent the whole lot cascading to the floor. She began stamping savagely on the photographs, grinding the heel of her boot into Laura's face.

Laura heard the racket and ran into the room, stopping in amazement when she saw what Anna was doing.

'What the hell's going on?' Laura shouted.

Anna put her hands on the oak beam, leaned her head forward and breathed in deeply to calm herself, to try and get control.

'You bitch. It's about Joe. My lover,' she shot Laura a look of pure hatred as she spat out the words, 'your husband.'

Laura swallowed hard unable to take in what Anna had just said.

'That's right. You heard me. That's what I said. Joe and I are lovers. Have you got that?'

Laura stared at the other woman, unbelieving. Surely she was deranged. She certainly looked it.

'You're crazy. What are you talking about?' Laura gave a snort of disbelief.

The noise infuriated Anna.

'Joe loves me and I love Joe. Get it? I've always loved him, always, do you hear, and you,' she was spraying spittle, 'you have always been in the way.'

Laura gasped as if she'd been punched hard in the stomach. Shock, not just at the words, but because the face in front of her, the face of her grateful and friendly client, was now twisted with hate, teeth bared like a beast of prey.

'I don't believe you. You're insane,' she said, desperately.

Anna put her hand in her coat pocket, drew back her arm and hurled something at Laura. It hit her on the side of the face before splattering onto the dark wood floor. Some of its contents

270

sprayed over the large antique rug in the centre of the room. It was the used condom.

'Jesus Christ, Anna, what are you doing?' Laura cried out, stunned.

'That's a little souvenir I've been keeping for you. Joe and I have been together for eight months now and I want you to know that the sex is great.'

Laura put a hand on the back of a chair and sat down heavily. She closed her eyes for a moment. Anna was behaving like a madwoman but her very passion testified to the likely truth of what she said. Her heart sank as she realized it might explain some of the things that had been bothering her about Joe.

'Why have you come here?' Laura asked in a whisper. She wanted to stand up, to face Anna, but she couldn't trust her legs.

Anna Pelham was cooler now and calculating. Much as she longed to tell Laura that she was going to die, that she and Joe were finally to be rid of her hated presence, it would not do to put her on her guard.

'Because I wanted you to know. It was time you found out.'

Laura tried to think if it had ever even crossed her mind that Joe might be having an affair. She didn't think so. How total her faith in him had been.

Quickly, Anna moved away from the fireplace and came towards her, stood right in front of her.

'Take a look,' she said, shoving her mobile in front of Laura's face. It was the photo, the one she had taken when he was sleeping; herself and Joe in bed together. 'Go ahead and look. He's hot in bed isn't he? But maybe you don't remember.'

Anger erupted in Laura then, pushing through the shock and she stood up, with no problem at all, knocking the mobile from Anna's hand onto the floor.

'How dare you!' she yelled in Anna's face. 'How dare you do this to me!'

Anna Pelham battled for self-control. 'You ask me that?' she spat. 'After taking him from me, after ruining my life. I've waited twenty years for this moment.'

Laura looked into green eyes full of hate. 'Get out,' she shouted, 'Get out of here now.'

'Oh no, you're not getting rid of me. Haven't you noticed', Anna Pelham hissed, 'that we've been trying to get rid of you?'

'I don't know what the hell you're talking about,' Laura said, and then her breath choked in her throat as the ghastly thought struck her that perhaps she did. The pieces of the puzzle flew together in her head, faster and faster, slotting into place until the picture was whole. A chilling, monstrous picture. Laura reeled under it, heard her world crack apart.

Suddenly there was a knife in Anna Pelham's hand.

The jolt of adrenaline through Laura's body came long after the moment of understanding. Too late. She felt the knife strike her flesh.

CHAPTER FIFTY-SIX

Laura heard herself cry out in terror as she was knocked over by the blow and fell on the rug. At the last moment, instinctively, as Anna Pelham lunged at her, she moved to the side and the blade missed her chest. Instead, it ripped through the sleeve of her dressing gown and slashed her upper arm. She felt a sharp burning sensation but no pain. Her adrenaline was pumping too hard for that, nor was there any shriek from her cracked rib – it too had been silenced by the need to survive.

Vaguely, she registered that blood was bubbling up through the gash in her sleeve and then she was rolling away, trying desperately to get out of the awkward dressing gown, as Anna Pelham came after her and the knife skimmed through the air again. It caught her face, slicing her left cheek, as she tried to twist away. Blood ran down her chin.

Her hands grasped the edge of the rug, and as she rolled off it on to bare floorboards, she yanked at it hard. Anna staggered backwards as the rug moved under her feet, almost lost it. Just for a second. Then she was up and running again. Laura saw her face as she came towards her. It shocked her, even at that moment when there was no time to be shocked anymore, only time to stay alive.

Gleeful. That was the word for it. The look on Anna Pelham's face was gleeful.

Laura crouched on the floor, breathing hard, looking round frantically for something she could use to defend herself. Nothing. There were two small tables near the fireplace that might have done, but they were too far away. No time left now anyway. Her attacker stood over her, the knife raised high in a killing arc.

It was the moment Anna Pelham had waited for, had dreamed of for oh so long. Laura Maxwell was going to die now, in this room, among the debris of her shattered photographs. She waited a beat, savouring the moment, looking down at her victim. Saw the blood trickling down the smooth, creamy skin, saw terror in the large hazel eyes. A smile of absolute contentment lit up her face.

'You will feel the pain,' she said, politely. 'You will know how it feels to have a knife in your heart.'

Laura stared up at her. Anna was tall and athletic, maybe five-foot-eleven, a good six inches taller than she was. She would have a long reach with the knife.

'You don't remember me, do you? From when we were at school. When I loved him and you took him from me,' Anna's voice rose.

'Get off me! Get off me!' Laura screamed, struggling to get free.

'Remember me now,' Anna said, screeching out the words, 'because I'll be the last thing you ever remember.'

She brought down the blade in a furious, hard thrust.

Laura's right arm was still in the sleeve of the dressing gown and she swung it backwards and hurled the garment towards the knife hand, enough to deflect the blow from her heart, but not enough to completely avoid it catching her left arm again, this time hitting exposed flesh just below the elbow. She hardly registered the injury, thought, in passing, that it would just add to the mess that was the left side of her body.

The dressing gown had wrapped itself around Anna and it took her a few seconds to pull it off. Seconds for Laura to use, to get away from another stabbing. She ran towards the tables, grabbed one of them and held it in front of her. Broken glass dug into the soft soles of her slippers.

Anna stared at her. She tried to laugh because she could see the damage done, see the blood from Laura's bare left arm starting to soak her nightclothes. But the laughter wouldn't come. It stuck in her throat, because all she could really see were the clothes – the cute little pink camisole and silk shorts. This was what |Laura wore in bed with Joe and it was undeniably attractive; disgusting, hateful images of the two of them together crowded into Anna's mind.

They were so vivid that she shook her head violently to try to clear them, but they would not go away. Bubbles of anger fizzed in her brain, more and more of them, like a tablet dissolving in water. She struggled with the rage; she struggled but she lost.

Anna Pelham started screaming. Screaming that Laura must die, that she deserved to die, that she would not escape again. She flew at her, like a cat pouncing on its prey. Laura tried to block her, to force the table legs into her face and upper body and knock her off balance, but Anna hardly faltered. She jumped nimbly to one side, grabbed one of the legs and began wrestling the table from Laura's grasp. With her left arm injured, it took all Laura's strength to hang on, and as she clung to the table with both hands, Anna lashed out again with the knife, slashing the cute pink camisole and cutting deep into the flesh beneath. Laura lost her grip on the table, stumbled to her knees, her right hand clutching at the bloody new wound.

Anna Pelham's eyes burned with hatred and triumph. This was it then. *Finis.* She went in for the kill.

'Die now, you fucking bitch.'

Anna sprang at her again, hitting her full on and knocking her to the ground. The speed and power of the assault sent both women sliding together, struggling, across the polished floor. Their progress was stopped by the fireplace and then, despite all Laura's efforts, Anna was sitting astride her and she was staring into the glittering green eyes of the woman who was to be her executioner. The gleeful face was back; Anna Pelham looked very pleased with herself, very pleased indeed.

Time stood still for Laura. She was at the frontier of existence, facing extinction. There was terror in her mind but there was also determination not to go without a fight. Fight like a tiger, not just lie there, cringing, waiting to be butchered. She watched as Anna's head turned on its slender neck and the eyes searched for the blade that had dropped from her hand in the struggle. It had not gone far. Just a few inches away among the sea of smashed glass and photo frames. Anna reached for it easily and her long, slim fingers once more curled lovingly around its handle.

Laura lay back, apparently in submission, her arms stretched out behind her head as if she had given up herself to her fate.

Anna smiled.

'You understand now, don't you,' she asked, soothingly, 'why you have to die?'

Laura's right hand grasped something smooth and sharp in the mess on the floor. She gripped hold of it hard though it cut her fingers. It was a glass shard and it felt horribly small. Too small, surely, to do much damage, but it was all she had. The knife had begun to move, begun its strike down towards her chest and if she didn't stop it she was done for and the last thing she would see in her life would be the red fingernails and triumphant face of Anna Pelham.

Her hand came up off the floor, moved fast towards Anna's throat. The jagged piece of glass, which not long ago had framed a photo of her and Joe, was clutched between her fingers. She shoved it, with all her remaining strength, into the soft white skin.

A look of surprise came on to Anna's joyful face as the glass entered her flesh and pierced the artery in her neck.

'No!' she screamed, 'No! No!'

A massive wall of warm, bright red blood spurted into Laura's eyes and blinded her. Anna's screams stopped, drowned by the blood spraying and bubbling in her throat. Laura felt hope begin, knowing she'd hit something big. Thick jets of arterial blood were coming at her and a weight was falling on her, pinning her down.

Then a searing, terrible pain ripped through her chest as the knife punctured her left lung.

After that, Laura lost track of things. Hazy, light-headed, she could hardly breathe. There was a period when all hell seemed to break loose again, though it was a different kind of hell, full of noise and people and general confusion. She really couldn't say because she was so tired. Incredibly tired, as she had never been before in her whole life. And she wanted so much to go to sleep, absolutely had to go to sleep, but some man with a moustache kept shouting at her and telling her to stay awake, to stay alive.

She knew who this man was and he was no friend of hers. She was sure of that. Now he was yelling at her again. And she wanted to yell back at him to shut the fuck up and just let her go to sleep where she was. But she didn't have the breath to do it. In fact she didn't have any breath left at all because a huge hand was squeezing her chest, squeezing the life out of her. Suffocating her.

Resurfacing. Excruciating pain. Cold. So cold. Sleep. Death coming to meet her. More noise and more men and the first one, the one who was definitely not her friend, was shouting again – he never seemed to stop – and then, thank God, he wasn't there anymore.

It was such a huge relief. Laura went to sleep at last.

CHAPTER FIFTY-SEVEN

There was an appalling amount of blood. A dark, viscous pool of it spread across the floor and as Harry ran towards the two women, his shoes slid in it and he almost fell. He stared at the scene, forcing down the urge to be sick.

His wife was lying collapsed on top of Laura Maxwell, her right hand still grasping the knife she had buried in the other woman's chest. Her head lay twisted on Laura's shoulder, blood oozing from her throat though it no longer pulsed. The big green eyes were open though they no longer sparkled. He winced, remembered how they used to look at him, sincere and loving, the way she always did before she told a lie. Remembered how they had fascinated him, how everything about her had fascinated him.

Now he could hardly bear to touch the flesh that once he had loved. Quickly he bent down, checked for a sign of life, and when there was none, felt his chest heave with emotion, with a terrific sadness for what he had lost even if it had existed only in his imagination. Once upon a time, she had made him feel so good, so special. He thought, wretchedly, of Martha. Not just to have lost her mother, but to have had such a mother. His heart ached for his daughter.

All he could see of Laura Maxwell was a bloody mess. Her head and upper body were covered in the stuff, her hair matted with it. She'd been stabbed and slashed and he assumed that she too was dead. So it came as a shock to him, if anything else at that moment could shock him, to see bloody air bubbles coming from the wound in her chest. They frothed around the hilt of the knife.

Harry shoved aside his wife's body, pulled off his jacket and began wiping the blood from Laura's eyes and nose, shouting at her to wake up. He didn't dare shake her or slap her, just yelled in her ear, and after what seemed a very long time, her eyes flickered open. She tried to speak but no words came out, just a soft gurgle as if she was under water. A trickle of blood fell from the corner of her mouth and he was terrified that he had come too late and she was going to die in front of him.

Drowning. Suddenly he was certain she would drown in the blood in her throat. Keep her alive, dial 999. He hadn't got a mobile and he looked round frantically for a phone. Can't see one. Jesus Christ. Blood in her mouth. Lips turning blue. Please God, surely not. He was bellowing, as if yelling at her to survive would make it happen. Think, block out the panic getting in the way. Dial 999 was all his brain would say. No go. No time left. Drowning. Up to you, mate. No-one else to help.

Clear the airway, crucial, do it now, the answer shot into his mind. He knelt beside her, put one hand on her forehead and the other behind her neck, tilted her head back and lifted her chin. Heard another gurgling, struggling, breath. Her eyes opened and she coughed up a mass of blood, then fell back exhausted. He had to roll her, had to turn her on to her side so the blood could drain out of her mouth instead of clogging her windpipe and choking her. Harry hesitated.

It was dangerous to move her. Dangerous, because he didn't know where the blade had lodged and moving her might kill her. Maybe he should wait, find a phone, call for help. But she isn't dead yet, he thought, so it must have missed her heart, and if you don't do it, she's going to stop breathing and die. And that's not going to happen sometime in the future, it's going to happen now because the blood is blocking her throat and her skin is going blue. Roll her then, onto her left side, so there's no pressure on the good right lung. For God's sake be careful. Don't disturb the knife. Do it gently.

He turned her slowly, very slowly, watching more blood spill down from her slashed right side, but there was nothing he could do about that. The shredded pink camisole was soaked again in red.

Eyes open. Pain in them. He didn't want to see it, but then they closed and he wanted that even less. Slipping away.

'Wake up!'

He saw it then on the floor, half hidden by the edge of the rug. A mobile. He ran for it, shaky hands pressing the screen into life. The picture of his wife and Joe Greene in bed together stared up at him. Harry howled, then punched in the numbers, wiping it from his sight.

'Ambulance. Emergency. Get here quick or she'll die.'

He squatted beside Laura, shouting at her to stay awake, shouting answers to the questions from the woman dispatching the ambulance. His mouth was dry as a husk, but despite all his shouting, Laura would not stay conscious. Blood leaked from her mouth, flowed steadily from the knife in her chest and he was filled with dread that he had done the wrong thing by moving her, the wrong thing entirely.

'Don't touch the knife,' said the emergency call handler. 'It's very important you leave it where it is.'

He told her what he'd done. 'You're sure she's still breathing?' she asked.

He listened for the gurgle. He liked the sound now because it was the sound of life. But he couldn't hear it. Nothing.

'I don't know!'

Panic. He threw down the mobile, bent closer to her, heard her breathe. Thank Christ. The pulse in her neck was weak and rapid. He touched skin like ice and he was suddenly aware how cold the room was, how a bitter wind was blowing through it from the large sash window he'd smashed to get into the house. He covered her with his jacket, wiped his face on its sleeve. The room might be freezing, but he was sweating.

'Jesus, Laura, wake up!'

'Are you there? If you're still there please pick up the phone.'

The mobile squawked at him and he grabbed it.

'I'm here. She's breathing, but her lips are blue'

'Please stay on the line, sir, so that I can tell you what to do until the ambulance arrives.'

'Yes, sorry.'

He followed her instructions. Took off his shirt, wrapped it around the chest wound, carefully avoiding the knife. She told him to press gently on the shirt to try to stop the bleeding and to seal the wound so that no more air was sucked in to the chest, warned him to watch closely in case too much air became trapped between the chest wall and the lung – if that happened he would need to loosen the seal at once to let the air escape.

He bawled at Laura again, and for a moment she opened her eyes. Just for a moment before the lids came back down. Goose bumps on his arms and not from the cold. Sirens were outside now, and then the ambulance crew was beside him, praising him, putting a blanket round him, reassuring him that, without him, Laura Maxwell would surely be dead already.

'I'm coming with her,' he told them. He squeezed her cold hand.

The arrival of the police put an end to that idea. They gave him something else to think about. There were four of them and they approached him with mouths set in thin, unfriendly lines.

'Harry Pelham?' said the sergeant in charge.

'Yes.'

'We've been looking for you.'

'I know,' Harry raised his palms in the air, placating. 'I can answer all your questions now.'

'You're under arrest.' Two of the officers grabbed his arms, pinned them behind him, handcuffed his wrists.

'What the hell are you doing. There's no need for that.'

The sergeant stepped up close to Harry's face. He was young and excited and his eyes were hostile.

'In my opinion, sir, there's every need.'

Harry felt rage flood him. 'Look, you moron,' he jerked his head towards the stretcher being carried from the room. 'My wife has very nearly killed that woman, probably has killed her. I need to go with her. To the hospital.'

'You're not going anywhere except the police station,' the sergeant wagged a finger in his face. 'And you'd better pray she doesn't die because if she does you're looking at a charge of double murder.'

CHAPTER FIFTY-EIGHT

It was three days before they could be sure she would live and another two before she woke, clear-headed at last, in a hospital bed in a room on her own. There was a drain in her chest and a sharp pain every time she breathed. There were stitches and bandages all over the place and it took her a while to work out where all her injuries were. She remembered the stabbings all too clearly but she had no memory of arriving at hospital and very little of the days following. The doctors told her that her chances of survival had been put at less than thirty per cent. She heard, too, that Harry Pelham had saved her life.

Physically, then, she was a bit of a wreck, but the physical fallout she could deal with, it was the mental fallout that was the problem.

Joe was waiting to see her, had been waiting for days, and she could not put it off any longer. He walked in looking dishevelled and worried; he hadn't shaved and his usually smart clothes were rumpled, as if he'd slept in them. She had always thought he looked rather cute when he was a mess but now it did nothing for her.

'Laura, sweetheart, I've been going out of my mind.' He moved towards her as if to kiss her, but either the extent of her injuries or the look on her face made him pull back. He dropped into the chair at her bedside. 'How are you feeling?'

'I'm OK,' she said, not looking at him.

'That's great. It's so good to have you back.'

She felt her mouth tremble and said nothing; she could not trust herself to speak.

He fidgeted in the chair, then said, 'I love you so much.'

'Why did you do it?'

'What? What do you mean?' he said, as if he hadn't the least idea what she was talking about.

'Did you love her?' Laura ignored his pretended ignorance.

'You mean Anna Pelham? God no, Laura. Why would you say that? I don't know what she told you but she was insane, a grade A psycho.'

'Are you saying you weren't having an affair with her?' Laura stared straight at him.

'I was stupid,' he looked away, as though he was embarrassed, then back at her. 'It was just a kiss one time, and yeah, I know it should never have happened ... after that she got obsessed, wouldn't leave me alone.'

'Oh Joe, please stop, I don't want to hear your lies. She showed me a photo on her phone, of the two of you in bed together.'

He put his hands over his face then, and Laura saw his broad shoulders shaking. At last, he looked at her again; his eyes full of tears, his handsome features distorted with misery. He wiped his eyes and his face on the sleeve of his Armani shirt, ran his hands through his hair in a gesture of despair. Not a bad performance for a failed actor, she thought bitterly.

'I am so, so sorry for what I did,' he began, but she interrupted him.

'I really don't want to hear any more.'

He seemed to panic then, and possibly it was genuine, because the drama was gone and he told her in a small, serious voice how much she meant to him, how he couldn't live without her, how he messed up everything in his life and he would never forgive himself for what he'd done and what she'd gone through.

Afterwards he waited as if he was hoping for some kind of acceptance of his words, and when none came he said, 'Laura,

284

you're the only person I've ever loved, ever will love. Give me another chance. Please. I'm on my knees. I know how awful this is, but don't let it break us up. She's won then.' He reached out to take Laura's hand but she snatched it away.

'Did you want me dead, Joe?'

He looked as though she'd punched him very hard in the face. His bright blue eyes were wide with surprise and hurt. 'Jesus, Laura, that's crazy. Of course not. How can you say it?

She wanted very much to believe him, but Anna Pelham's words were in her head: *Joe loves me and I love Joe. You have always been in the way,*

'She told me so,' she said, her voice arctic.

'She was deranged. You know that.'

'She wasn't deranged when she told me you were lovers.'

'You have to believe me, Laura, you just have to. I never knew; never ever had any idea what she was doing.'

She wanted to believe him, wanted to think that all he was guilty of was extreme selfishness; didn't want to have to live the rest of her life thinking that he had hated her so much he'd wanted her dead.

'Why should I believe a word you say?'

'I don't know. You've got every reason not to. All I can say is it's true. I would never hurt you. I love you, Laura. I always will, and if you let me, I'll spend the rest of my life proving it to you.'

Suddenly she felt exhausted. 'I'm tired, Joe. I'd like you to go now.'

'OK, sure' he said, uncertainly. 'Of course, you've got to rest. I'll come back this afternoon and we can talk some more, find a way through this.'

She lay back on the pillows, closed her eyes and waited for him to leave. It took a while.

'See you later then,' he said at last. 'I love you.'

She heard his chair scrape on the floor as he stood up. When, finally, he was gone she knew she never wanted to see him again. Tears flooded through her closed eyelids and poured down her cheeks.

CHAPTER FIFTY-NINE

It was surely too cold for snow, but even as she thought it, a few flakes fell from the grey sky. Laura stood looking up at the Downs, breathing in deeply, holding the crisp sea air in her lungs. Despite all that had happened, despite the Exocet that had hit her life, her heart lifted. It felt so good to be here, out of hospital and out of danger. She held the breath for at least ten seconds as the doctors advised, to get her lungs working normally again. Breathe out. Do it again. In through the nose, out through the mouth. Deep breaths, four or five at a time, avoid hyperventilation.

The third one set her off coughing and that brought the pain. She never could tell just where the pain was coming from: lung, ribs, stitched flesh wounds, it seemed as though all of her was one big aching mess. Coughing was good, the doctors said, because it cleared mucus from the lungs and cut down the risk of chest infection. She hoped they were right because it sure was agony. She stopped to recover, then walked on across the field; a longer walk than she'd tried so far, heading for a bench where she sat down carefully, and gratefully, and watched the snow settle on the grass at her feet.

It was more than four weeks now since Anna Pelham had very nearly succeeded in killing her. She tried not to think about it, but she couldn't stop the pictures replaying in her mind in the middle of the night when her guard was down.

286

She had been allowed home from hospital three days ago. Joe had moved out before she returned; she'd asked him to go and he'd finally agreed to, after much pleading and arguing and stating it was only temporary to give them time to sort things out. She was hugely relieved to see the back of him.

Emma had stayed with her for the first two days and they'd talked it all through. The police believed Joe had not shared Anna's murderous intentions; all the evidence was against it. Anna had been obsessed with him since her schooldays and Laura had just been terribly unlucky to get in her way. Maybe Joe, too, had been unlucky – by crossing her path in the first place – but that bad luck had been compounded by his own weakness.

'It's so weird,' Laura said, 'because that woman said she'd hated me for years, since we were at school, but I don't even remember her, and God knows, I've been trying. What about you, Em? Do you remember anyone called Annabel Roberts?'

Emma shook her head. 'There was Annabel Georgiou, you know, in our class and Bella Cameron – her name was Annabel – and I think there were a couple of other Annabels in our year, but I'm pretty sure they weren't called Roberts.'

'She wasn't in our year. That's what the police say anyway. She was younger than us, in the year below.'

Laura shivered, remembering how she'd been taken in by Anna Pelham.

'I can't believe how she fooled me.'

'The main thing is you've survived and you're safe now. Hold on to that.'

Laura smiled, 'I'll try to, Mrs Brightside.'

Harry Pelham had visited her several times in hospital. On the last occasion he had been very happy – he'd been allowed to have Martha back home living with him again. He had been able to prove to the police that he couldn't have been the one who downloaded the child pornography to his home computer on one of the dates listed. Visa had supplied the times for his credit card transactions. On the Friday, when two of the pornography payments had been made – at 2.18 p.m. and 2.27 p.m. – there was a third payment – at 2.24 p.m. – to a restaurant in Horsham. His company had a housing development there and he'd been taking a business partner to lunch. Someone else had been in his home using his computer and his wife was the only suspect.

Morrison had visited too, and to Laura's surprise, offered her a partnership. He made his usual song and dance about it, telling her how he'd pushed the other partners to agree, what a great honour it was, how pleased and awed she should be, the level of commitment expected in return. She told him she'd think about it and hugely enjoyed the look of astonishment on his face that anyone would need to think twice.

He told her that ten-year-old Ahmed Hakimi had been detained with his father, at the airport in Istanbul.

'Excellent result. I gather there was a dinner date dependent on it. I've told Mr Chehoudi it will have to be postponed.'

The snow was getting thicker and an icy wind blew her hair across her face. She got to her feet, began to retrace her steps back to the stables about two hundred yards away. This might take me a while, she thought.

She was almost there when Jeff Ingham appeared, hurrying towards her, hair flopping over his forehead.

'You OK?' he said, looking worried.

'I walked a bit further today,' she smiled at him. 'It's getting easier.'

'I was wondering where you'd got to. I'm not really sure you're safe to be let out on your own.'

He held open the stable door for her and together they went inside. She had spent a lot of the last three days here, but it still gave her a thrill to see him: Valentine. The great survivor.

He stood grazing from a haynet, and as she came in, he brought up his head and whinnied.

It was all down to Jeff Ingham. She had been lying in a hospital bed while he had spent hours with the horse, soothing him, persuading him to eat, trying to get him to accept the life of confinement he would have to put up with for some time yet. Jeff had done an astonishing job and it looked like Valentine just might make it.

She glanced at the vet, caught him staring at her and looked away, embarrassed.

'Do you think Valentine is pleased to see me or pissed off at me because he's stuck in this stable?' she asked.

'Difficult one. I guess a bit of both,' he said, teasing her.

'Yes,' Laura said. They were grinning at each other like idiots. 'I guess you're right.'

Acknowledgements

For all their help and advice, my thanks to: the members of the family law group, Resolution, who supplied legal details; Robert James Sayer for sharing his knowledge of all things equestrian; Hilary Long, Elizabeth Madge and Rose Phillips for their feedback and constructive suggestions; and my husband, Robert, for his patience in reading and rereading the drafts.

Many thanks as well to Kate Stephenson and the team at HarperCollins for all their encouragement and support and last, but by no means least, to my agent and friend, Mary Greenham.